Golden
Oldies
Guesthouse

BOOKS BY DEE MACDONALD

The Golden Oldies Guesthouse

Dee MacDonald

Bookouture

Published by Bookouture in 2019

An imprint of StoryFire Ltd.

Carmelite House
50 Victoria Embankment
London EC4Y 0DZ

www.bookouture.com

ISBN: 978-1-78681-730-3
eBook ISBN: 978-1-78681-729-7

For Rosemary Brown

PART ONE

CHAPTER 1

FALLING IN LOVE AGAIN

'It's so beautiful here I could stay forever!' said Simon, stretching his legs out on the sun lounger. 'Life could be one long blissful holiday!'

'And what exactly would you be using for money?' asked Tess.

It had been Simon's bright idea to come down to Cornwall for their belated honeymoon, eighteen months after their whirlwind wedding. Simon Sparrow was sixty-two and Tess was sixty-three, blissfully happy to have found each other after ill-fated first marriages.

Simon cherished childhood memories of wielding his bucket and spade on this dramatic coast; he'd started learning to surf round here, he'd got a tiny part in the first *Poldark* series, and he'd quaffed his first pint of bitter with his dad in The Portmerryn Arms. Simon was, as are many actors, an incurable romantic. Which is one of the many reasons Tess had fallen in love with him.

At times she did wonder why on earth he'd fallen in love with *her*. Tess MacKenzie from Strathcoy in Scotland, who'd come to London, married and later divorced Gerry Templar (after his ridiculous affair), had his two children, and found a lover some years later who'd unfortunately died and left her heartbroken. Tess would describe herself as being 'quite pleasant looking', with her green eyes and rapidly greying hair, now an interesting mix of highlights and lo-lights, thanks to A Cut Above back in Milbury, where she'd been living. But she had managed to shed two stone in order to look good at her daughter's wedding, which was where she met Simon. He'd whisked her off her feet and married her three months later, and she still had to pinch herself that this had really happened. After all the disasters with an Internet dating site it seemed like a miracle.

'We must explore the area,' he said as he padded through the tiny kitchen of their (belated) honeymoon retreat, en route to the equally tiny bathroom, both of which had been tacked onto the back of the 'genuine fisherman's cottage' which they'd rented for the week. The genuine fisherman had probably bought a nice semi somewhere, with an en suite and central heating. As had apparently all the other fishermen who once inhabited Fishermen's Row, where the cottages were now rented out to tourists at exorbitant rates. But having to trundle down the narrow stairs several times a night for a pee had rapidly ceased to be a novelty for Simon.

'It was your idea to rent an authentic little cottage,' Tess reminded him. 'We could have gone to a nice hotel somewhere and you'd only have had to totter a few feet to the loo three times a night.'

'Hotels are so soulless,' Simon said. 'When you've had to stay in them as often as I have you're happy to forego the convenience of an en suite, a hospitality tray and a fridge full of overpriced booze.'

Tess would have been extremely happy with an en suite, a hospitality tray and a fridge full of booze, whatever the price. But at least she didn't have to go to the loo several times a night. Yet. And it was bliss to lie in bed and listen to the thundering of the surf and the crying of the gulls. She was bowled over by the competing shades of turquoise of the sea, the glorious beach and the sheer grandeur of the cliffs. She watched in awe as the surfers rode the waves, and she couldn't help but admire the big brawny lifeguards with their wetsuits and tousled hair, and dreamed of being young again – and wished it were *now*. How did they manage to race across the shingle barefoot? Not that she wasn't madly in love with Simon, of course, but some of these hunks… wow!

Then it had rained non-stop for three days and their ideas of further exploring the area in Simon's open-topped Triumph Stag had dissolved into the grey gloom. They squelched along the beach in waterproofs and wellingtons, and got to know The Portmerryn Arms very well indeed.

The Portmerryn Arms was reputed to be an old smugglers' inn, complete with black beams and nicotine-stained walls, and a huge inglenook in which an open fire was burning even though it was July. Horse brasses and copper warming pans were hung around the fireplace, and there were some interesting corners, one of which accommodated the domino players. There were, Tess was delighted to see, no fruit machines.

But on the fourth day the rain stopped and there were even a few tiny breaks in the cloud here and there where the sun struggled to get through. So, off they set in the yellow Stag, which was Simon's pride and joy. And with the roof down as they wound along the country lanes – which in itself normally tempted fate – the sun finally emerged, the sea sparkled again and their spirits soared.

They'd only driven the short distance along the coast road towards the pub when, for the first time, Simon noticed a narrow turning up the hill opposite.

'Seagull Hill!' he exclaimed, stamping on the brakes and making a violent turn up the steep, potholed lane.

That was the thing with Simon: he could never resist lanes, streets, avenues or roads with birds' names. When Tess first met him he was living in the townhouse in West London which was now their home, bought purely because it was situated on Goldcrest Road, and never mind that it didn't have a garage or even a parking space. It was close to the Tube station, though, and had a large back garden which wasn't overlooked, both big plus points in London.

Now, as they bounced their way up over the potholes, Tess muttered, 'Not much up here!' And it was then, at that exact moment, that they saw the 'For Sale' sign at the entrance to a rhododendron-lined drive, although no house was visible through the trees. 'Shall we have a quick peek?' he said.

And that was how they found Over and Above. It stood there, in splendid isolation, a large Edwardian heap in an overgrown garden, blinds down, empty and forlorn. It had a steeply pitched roof, some impressive chimneys sited halfway down the slope, a multi-paned front door and sash windows through which they could see little. When Tess peeled a loose layer of paint off one of the front windows with her fingernail, a chunk of wood fell off as well.

'Just for a start the windows are rotten,' she remarked.

Simon, as if in a trance, seemed not to hear her. 'Let's walk round and see what it's like at the back.'

They navigated their way with difficulty, past overhanging rampant blackberries and knee-high nettles, until they came to the rear with its rotting French doors and damp façade.

But neither of them noticed any of that because they were completely seduced by the vision of blue sea and Atlantic surf which took their breath away. And probably their common sense with it.

'Wow!' said Tess, as they both stood mesmerised by the view.

'Imagine waking up to *that* every morning!' sighed Simon.

When they eventually turned round to look at the house again Tess said, 'Just *look* at that wisteria! This must be its second flowering!'

Covering most of the damp around and above the French doors was an enormous and very prolific wisteria, cascading tassels of misty mauve still trailing from its gnarled boughs. It was three times the size of Simon's at Goldcrest Road.

'Yeah, that's pretty impressive,' he agreed, before turning back to admire the view of the Atlantic. 'And this has to be one of the best views in North Cornwall!'

So, on that day in July, two mature romantics fell in love with a dodgy house with a very spectacular view.

CHAPTER 2

GREAT POTENTIAL

The estate agency, Michael Millhouse Properties, was situated miles away, near Bodmin. As the yellow Stag sped along the country lanes in search of the A30, Simon said, 'It won't do any harm just to get the particulars to see what it looks like inside.'

Tess had her doubts. 'I suppose not.'

'And I'd love to know how much they want for it,' Simon said. '*Not* that we'd be interested, of course.' He gave her a sideways glance.

'Of course not,' Tess agreed. 'Anyway, who'd want to live away down here for more than a couple of weeks a year?'

'Exactly,' said Simon,

The agent, chubby and balding, said, 'Call me Mike.' He shook their hands heartily. 'Ah yes, Over and Above, with that wonderful view! Needs a teeny bit of work, of course.'

'Of course,' echoed Simon.

'Been looking for properties long?'

'We weren't looking—' Tess began.

'Not long,' Simon interrupted.

'You won't find another house with character like this anywhere,' enthused Mike, 'or with a better view. Now, let me have a butcher's at the diary. I'm tied up today but I could do tomorrow afternoon about four o'clock to show you around, if that suits you.'

'Well—' began Tess.

'Perfect!' said Simon.

'We are most definitely *not* going to be buying that house,' Tess said as they sped off in the Stag.

'Of course not,' Simon soothed. 'But no harm in having a look.'

According to the brochure there were four large airy reception rooms downstairs, plus six bedrooms and one bathroom (ouch!) upstairs. The grainy photographs were mainly of the outside, with only a couple depicting the interior: one showing what looked like a bedroom with a fireplace, and the other an enormous room with French windows overlooking the sea. Both rooms were empty.

All evening, back in their fisherman's cottage, Tess thought about Over and Above and that view, and the wisteria. She knew one of them had to be practical here, and it wasn't likely to be Simon. The 'needs some updating' and 'a teeny bit of work' worried her; you bet it does, she thought.

They were sitting in the cottage's tiny back garden, which was wedged between the added-on bathroom and the beach, sipping some chilled rosé wine, when Simon said, 'There was just *something* about that house, Tess, wasn't there? And I like the price.'

Tess sighed. 'We're in Cornwall, darling. Of course property is going to be cheaper than in London!'

'But if we got a good price for our house in London we'd probably be around a hundred thousand in pocket.'

'We're *not* going to be selling Goldcrest Road,' Tess said, thinking of the thousands they'd lavished on the kitchen in their London home this year alone.

'Of course not! Just *saying*.'

'Anyway, what would two sixty-somethings like us want with a great big house like that?'

'It would be perfect for our retirement years. We'd have plenty of room for friends and family to stay!'

'Are you kidding? And what exactly would *you* be doing? I can't imagine there's much call for sixty-two-year-old actors round here.'

'There's not much call for sixty-two-year-old actors anywhere,' Simon said sadly. 'I'm Simon Sparrow, not Simon Callow.'

Over the past year since they'd married there'd been just a couple of voice-overs and one bit part, which had necessitated him growing a beard and which he now refused to shave off. If, perchance, they were relying on Simon's financial input, they'd have been on the breadline months ago. And that was in spite of his many sidelines while 'resting' which, over the years, had included trying to farm culinary snails, painting plant pots and being a children's entertainer, to name but a few. It was Tess's income which mainly supported them. She was an established dressmaker with a boutique in Surrey, which she ran with her friend, Orla. They made flattering outfits for outsized ladies and, with Tess's expertise in cutting and sewing, and Orla's ability to sell anything to anyone, they'd set up a very successful business. 'But we're getting too old for all this palaver,' Orla groaned every morning as they opened up the doors to a line of large women waiting to be measured and fitted. And Tess was beginning to agree, particularly as she now had the beginnings of arthritis in her fingers and her wrists.

'But we could always rent out a room or two if we really needed to – and we'd have that nice lump sum from the difference in house prices, don't forget.'

'This road's not designed for sports cars,' Tess remarked as they rattled their way up Seagull Hill again the following day.

'It'll be OK when I work out where the worst holes are,' Simon said. 'But really you'd need an off-road vehicle if you lived around here.'

'Hmmm,' said Tess. 'I hope you're not getting ideas about Land Rovers and Labradors?'

'Don't be ridiculous!' Simon retorted.

Mike had got there ahead of them and was sitting, rooting through some papers, in a brand-new Range Rover.

'He must be doing *something* right,' Simon muttered as they parked alongside in the old Stag.

'Probably selling overpriced heaps to idiots like us,' Tess replied.

'Hi, folks!' Mike emerged from the Range Rover. 'Great cars, these old Stags!' He ran his hand over the car's dusty yellow bodywork. 'Not so practical round here, though!'

'But great on a day like this,' Simon said, squinting at the sun.

'Hope the hood's in good nick,' Mike said cheerfully, ''cos it rains a lot in these parts.'

They followed him up to the front door where he fumbled around for a few minutes with an enormous bunch of keys. 'Must be here somewhere,' he muttered as he inserted one after another into the lock. Finally, he succeeded and the door creaked open. They followed him into a large hallway with a ceramic black-and-white tiled floor and an impressive wooden central staircase.

'Who does this house belong to?' Tess asked, looking around and, in spite of her reservations, impressed.

'Well,' said Mike, 'a young couple own it now but they haven't been near it for ages 'cos he got a job in Dubai or somewhere. They'd all sorts of plans for it but lost interest when he got this posting.'

'They certainly don't seem to have done much updating,' Tess murmured, looking around.

'Think they might have bitten off more than they could chew,' said Mike. 'But they fell in love with the rooms at the back, and the views, which I'll show you shortly.'

'Love the floor,' said Simon.

'How long has it been empty?' Tess asked, sniffing the damp.

Mike took a noisy breath through his teeth. 'Ooh now, let me see; must be a couple of years.'

'And it's been up for sale for *all* that time?' Tess sounded incredulous.

'Yeah, pretty much.'

'So how come nobody's bought it?'

Mike shrugged. 'Just needs the right people to come along and realise the potential.'

Waiting for idiots like us to come along, Tess thought, but oh, it could be so wonderful. Really lovely.

She could frame the view with beautiful fabrics; wicker sofas on the terrace piled high with sumptuous cushions. She could imagine herself sitting out here with a gin and tonic. OK, time to get back to earth. 'Perhaps the price is too high?' she suggested.

'Not at all!' Mike pushed open the door on the right. 'You get a lot of house for the money. Lovely big kitchen, though it needs a *teeny* bit of doing-up of course.'

A *teeny* bit! Tess looked round in dismay at the yellowed walls, the 1940s cabinet, the ancient electric cooker. At least there was a butler's sink, even if the wooden draining board had almost rotted through.

'There's a nice little scullery, too,' Mike said, opening a door at the far end.

'Boot room,' said Simon, peering in the door.

'Since when did you wear boots?' Tess saw a metal sink and some dusty shelves. '*Utility* room.'

They crossed the hallway into another large room at the front.

'Dining room,' announced Mike, consulting his particulars. 'Lovely big room. You could seat a dozen or more people in here. Think of Christmas! Fire blazing!' He indicated a hole in the wall, from which a fireplace had obviously been removed at some point. 'You'd get a nice big log-burner in there. Great potential!'

'Potential' was the only honest word you could use in this house, Tess thought.

He wanted them to see the six bedrooms next. They clattered their way up the wooden stairs, their footsteps echoing eerily. Four of the six bedrooms all had their original fireplaces and all had wooden floors. Two of them also had large damp patches on the ceilings and upper walls.

'Needs a bit of an airing,' said Mike cheerfully. 'And just look at these floors! Just need to sand them down and polish them up a bit!'

Tess could see the potential up here, particularly when he led them into the two large rear bedrooms with their breathtaking views of the ocean which was crashing against the rocks below the house. She then groaned when she saw the antiquated bathroom but could see that the roll-top bath could be painted and there was plenty of space for a shower. She'd already worked out that they could sacrifice the two smaller bedrooms to perhaps make en suites for the other four.

Mike had them clip-clop their way downstairs again and led them with a flourish to the rear where the two large rooms with their French doors overlooked the patio, small lawn and the drop to the ocean. The panoramic views were just visible through the cobweb-festooned doors.

'We could put bi-fold doors right the way along that wall,' Simon said dreamily.

'I told you it had great potential,' said Mike.

Tess gazed for a long time through the dust and the cobwebs at the sea which sparkled and smiled in the late afternoon sunshine. Damn it, she thought, this place has got to me, and I'm supposed to be the practical one! My common sense has gone through the roof, or escaped out of this window into the ocean! It was at that moment when she just *knew* they were going to be buying this house.

CHAPTER 3

THE MOVE

'We can't possibly offer the full asking price,' Tess said as they ate supper in The Portmerryn Arms, 'because it's going to cost an arm and a leg to get that place the way we want it.'

'We can do a lot of it ourselves,' said Simon.

'Are you kidding? Look, we're talking about replacing windows, fixing the roof, putting in a kitchen and bathrooms, central heating, wood-burners. A hundred thousand will go *nowhere*! And we haven't even got Goldcrest Road on the market yet! Not only that, we should have a survey done on the place.'

'What's the point, darling? Just lining some surveyor's pocket to tell us what we know already?'

'It's what most people do, Simon. I mean, how many kinds of rot could be lurking in the walls or somewhere? There's dry rot, wet rot—'

'We're not *most* people,' he interrupted airily.

That much is true, Tess thought. She'd fallen in love with Simon because he was *different*: romantic, optimistic, cheerful, imaginative, amusing… but at times like this she would like it if he could just adopt some down-to-earth common sense.

Simon covered her hand with his. 'You do want it, too, don't you?'

'Yes, damn it, I *do*!'

'Well, then. It'll make money for us. We can rent out the rooms, make it an upmarket boutique bed and breakfast hotel, guesthouse, whatever you want to call it, adults only, charge ridiculous prices...'

'I'd like the grandchildren to be able to come sometimes, too.' Tess thought fondly of six-year-old Ellie and Joshua, her eighteen-month-old brother. And that was something else; what would Amber and Matt think about their mother and stepfather moving miles away? How would her best friend Orla react and what would happen to the shop they ran together? Curvaceous it was called, because of the large ladies. They'd spotted a gap in the market and, with Tess's expertise as a dressmaker, and Orla's as a saleslady, they'd hatched a very successful business.

The few acting parts Simon was offered were normally in London. In any case, Simon didn't have the same family considerations as she did; he only had the one son: Damien. Damien, the so-called guitarist, touring around with The Shambles, the aptly named group destined to play their outdated punk music in scruffy clubs and pubs. He'd appear on their doorstep every so often, begging a bed for the night, and then take himself into the spare room to strum chords on his guitar and smoke pot.

'He'll grow out of it,' Simon had assured her.

At thirty-six years of age Tess doubted he had a lot of growing up still to do. Well, at least he wasn't likely to be landing on their doorstep down here very often.

At least her own children had homes and jobs, thank goodness. Tess adored her two grandchildren, of course and, although she didn't mind occasionally babysitting, it had become a regular occurrence as time went on. Looking back, she realised that was why she'd joined the online dating site – to find a different life.

Dating! At her age! What had she been thinking of? It had been Orla's idea, of course. Orla was her best friend, business partner and mentor, and it was she who'd come up with the idea of joining MMM, 'Meetings for the More Mature'. And, just when she'd given up the will to live and love, along came Simon! He was a guest at her daughter's wedding and she'd fallen in love with his voice first, when he'd read out a poem at the reception. Then she'd rapidly fallen in love with the rest of him. But she'd known from the first that she was going to have to be the sensible, practical one of the partnership, with Simon doing the charming and the soothing of the way.

The following day they put in an offer of £30,000 below the asking price and subject to survey, which Tess had finally persuaded Simon to have done. There was some grunting and sighing from Mike before he finally agreed to put the offer to the vendors in Dubai.

'You must understand,' he said, 'if someone should come along with a similar, or better, offer, and they've already *sold* their place, I'm going to have to take it.'

'Well,' Simon said, 'if it's been sitting here for a couple of years without a single offer, it would seem highly unlikely that someone else might suddenly show up now.'

'Stranger things happen,' said Mike, tapping his nose.

'I don't want anyone else to make an offer on that house,' Tess murmured as they drove away. In spite of her initial misgivings she now felt excited at the prospect of what they were going to do, despite the work that needed to be done.

'Nobody else will put in an offer,' Simon said. 'That's just estate agent's patter to get us moving.'

As a result of this conversation Simon suggested they should head back to London the very next day to sell their property. A desirable three-bed townhouse in West London should sell quickly, of that Tess was certain.

When they got back she gazed at the beautiful open-plan living area, at the luxury kitchen, at the desirable bi-fold doors leading to the patio. What are we *doing*? she wondered, as she ran her fingers along the pristine surface of the granite worktops. Then again it was Simon's house, and she felt no nostalgia, not like when she sold her little cottage in Temple Terrace in Milbury when they got married.

'Are you absolutely mad?' asked Amber, sinking into her enormous white settee in her enormous white minimalist lounge. 'Is this Simon's doing? You never used to have harebrained schemes like this, Mum!'

'No,' Tess agreed. 'I've become more adventurous, I suppose.' She sipped her coffee carefully, intent on not spilling a drop.

'And what will Orla say? How can you just leave her with the shop?'

Tess was worried about Orla, and their little boutique on Penny Lane. How was *she* likely to react?

She found Orla chatting on the phone, the shop empty of customers.

'Orla,' Tess said, coming straight to the point, 'I don't quite know how to tell you this, but Simon and I are looking to buy a property in Cornwall.'

'So you're going to be moving? Just so long as you don't expect me to go down there and open up a Cornish Curvaceous with you!'

'Of course not! But it means you'd be on your own here.'

Orla sighed. 'Do you know, I was wondering how to tell you I'd had enough? Lauren is dead keen to take it over now that the kids are almost grown up.' Lauren was one of Orla's daughters-in-law who'd stepped in on several occasions to run the shop. 'But, of course, I'll expect free holidays in Cornwall forever and a day!'

'Oh, that's such a relief, Orla,' Tess said with feeling.

'How about some lunch together? Boulter's, perhaps? Then you can tell me all about it.'

Later she called on Matt, Lisa and the two grandchildren.

'Oh, Nana, is Cornwall *very* far away?' Ellie's lip trembled, and it was the only time Tess nearly gave up on the whole mad idea.

'No, darling, not these days. You can be down there in just a few hours. You can even come on an aeroplane to Newquay, which is quite near. Think of all the lovely things you can do: building sandcastles, swimming, learn to surf… *much* more exciting than just going to the park in the summer.'

That was a condition. She'd agree to the move if the family could come down any time they wanted. Even Damien. And there was plenty of garden space at Over and Above. Perhaps that could be used to provide some sort of accommodation for them – a caravan, maybe – until the house was habitable. Then there would always be plenty of space for visiting friends and family.

'Yes, yes, of course!' Simon enthused. Not that he'd have much idea how to make the house habitable. 'Don't forget we can live far more cheaply down there: go fishing, grow our own vegetables and all that!' he added.

Tess couldn't see how they'd ever have time to go fishing or grow vegetables – supposing either of them had the first clue how to go about it – when there was this huge house to bring into the twenty-first century. However, at the far side of the house there was a sizeable patch of level ground, full of assorted weeds, nettles and stones which, with work, could indeed produce a supply of vegetables at the very least, and still not interfere with the appearance of either the front or rear of the house.

But now was not the time to suggest it. There was plenty more to think of first.

Their house on Goldcrest Road sold within ten days at the full asking price. Their celebrations were short-lived because, soon afterwards, there was a message from their London conveyancer to say that 'apparently the agent down there has received another offer for Over and Above, so would you be prepared to up *your* offer?'

'I don't believe this for one moment,' Tess said. 'He's trying it on! He wants to get the full asking price. And we can't afford to up our offer because of all the work that needs to be done. And we only have *his* word for this so-called other offer. I'm willing to bet he's chancing his arm. Tell him we're not offering a penny more.'

Simon, of course, would have paid it. He sulked for several days, and neither of them slept a wink for the next few nights as they awaited some sort of response. On the third day their conveyancer telephoned to say that the vendors of Over and Above had accepted their offer because, according to Michael Millhouse Properties, the other prospective buyers had decided to pull out.

Tess was torn between gloating over the fact that there hadn't *been* any other buyers, and wondering if, in fact, there *had* been, but they'd decided to pull out because they had more sense than to take on all the work that needed doing. They were never to know.

Over and Above was vacant, the purchasers of Goldcrest Road were renting, and keen to move in, and so all transactions were completed in a matter of weeks. Including the survey which, much to their relief, did not indicate any variety of rot, but only some rotten windows, the leaking roof, the damp and dodgy electrics which should be checked as soon as possible.

And so, on one drizzly day in mid-September, Tess and Simon Sparrow found themselves heading down the A303 in the yellow Stag, hard-top firmly in place, along with Tess's meowing cat, Dylan, in a basket behind, and just ahead of two Pickfords vans containing all their worldly goods. As they hit heavy traffic where the road narrowed at Stonehenge Tess thought again about what they were about to take on. Most people of our age, she thought, are *downsizing*. And here we are, *upsizing*! We'll have to buy more furniture! We are mad, quite mad.

Four hours later, having collected the keys from Mike, they lurched their way again up Seagull Hill. 'SOLD' pronounced the sign at the end of the drive. And Over and Above, in all its peeling glory, glowered at them amidst the trees through the low-lying mist.

Here was a challenge, thought Tess, looking sideways at Simon. She could visualise how this house was going to look in a few months' time, with the sun shining and the birds singing. Yes, it was going to be hard work but she'd longed for a change of direction and somebody lovely to share her life with. Well, she certainly seemed to have scooped the jackpot!

Tess's first priority was Dylan, her old cat, who'd been cooped up in a basket for four hours. She knew that cats should be kept inside for ten days or something when moving house – but she couldn't work out how they could do that with Dylan. Did they keep him in the kitchen, or the bedroom or where? At least she'd remembered to get a tray and cat litter so she'd be able to shut him in somewhere. The kitchen did not appear to be a good bet since they were in and out all the time and he was bound to escape. She decided it had to be their new bedroom.

Simon then insisted their enormous bed was placed in a bedroom with a sea view, and had to be positioned against the wall that faced the view even though it had no electric points.

'What are we supposed to do for bedside lights?' Tess asked.

'No idea!' said Simon, who rarely read in bed. 'We'll have to use the extension leads.'

'And where might they be?'

'Good question,' he replied, surveying the mountain of storage boxes which filled the hallway.

Tess looked round the kitchen in despair. Everything would have to remain boxed until they found some storage units and she doubted that they'd ever be able to afford lovely granite worktops again. Maybe, in the meantime, perhaps they could just paint up some old cupboards or something to place round the walls? Then she heard a tapping sound and, for a moment, wondered if it was a mouse or – horror of horrors – a rat in the walls, before she realised it was the front door. Who could it be when they'd just arrived, knew no one here and there were no near neighbours?

She opened the door to a ferrety little man, bald as a coot, and probably about their own ages.

'Evenin'!' he said, handing her a grubby card. 'Dave Turner at yer service.'

Tess glanced at the card: 'General Builder'. 'We've only just *arrived* a couple of hours ago,' she said.

'Yeah, so you'll be needin' some work done,' he said. 'The roof and that.'

'Well, we haven't had time to look at the roof yet,' Tess said.

'You'll be needin' me when you do,' said Dave Turner, giving her a cheeky wink, 'so give us a ring.'

Later that evening they settled for a pub meal at The Portmerryn Arms, aware of being stared at by some of the locals as most of the holidaymakers had left the area by now. They seated themselves on bar stools and studied the not-very-exciting menu.

'Thought you'd gone back 'ome,' said the large beefy landlord. He looked to be well into his seventies.

'We've just moved into the area,' Simon said as he surveyed the menu. 'We'll have a bottle of that Merlot to celebrate, please.'

'So where 'ave you bought, then?'

'Over and Above,' Simon replied.

There were gasps all round the pub.

'You 'ave? Never thought anyone'd be buyin' *that*!'

'Well, we have. I'm Simon Sparrow, and this is my wife, Tess.'

'Fancy that.' He stared at them for a moment. 'Jed King's the name.' He extended a large hand. 'Pleased t' meet you. Been runnin' this pub for nigh on fifty years so, you need to know somethin', you ask me.' He tapped his nose, which seemed to be a habit down here. 'That there's Gideon, me son.' He indicated a large man in his forties, Tess reckoned. 'Ye'll be needing a builder then?'

'We don't really know what we need yet,' Simon replied. 'Anyway, we've already had a builder come round offering his services.'

'And who might that be?'

'Dave Turner, I think he said his name was. You've got his card somewhere, haven't you, Tess?'

'*Dave Turner!*' exclaimed Jed loudly. There followed much guffawing around the bar. 'Wouldn't touch Dave Turner with a bargepole!'

'Oh?'

''E's not a builder! 'E's just an odd-job man and 'e's no bloody good at that! You want Tom Tallon, you do.'

'That's yer missus's brother!' snorted one of the locals, shuffling his dominoes.

'So what if 'e is? 'E's a bloody good builder!' Jed yelled back at him.

Just then a short, very fat grey-haired woman emerged from the kitchen. 'Who's a bloody good builder?' she asked.

'Yer Tom is, that's who.' Jed turned to Tess and Simon. 'This is Annie, me missus.'

''E's a right good builder is Tom,' Annie confirmed, wiping her brow.

'Good,' said Simon. 'Any chance we could order some food?'

'Probably best to look for a builder or a roofer online,' Simon said as they climbed up the lane to Over and Above. 'In a little place like this you're bound to get people recommending friends and family and, if they're no good, we'll be forever falling out with the neighbours.'

It was a ten-minute walk in the dark, Tess shining her torch on the lookout for the potholes. 'Never mind, the lasagne wasn't too bad, was it?'

'Passable,' Simon said.

'But I think we'll have to make an expedition to a decent super-market somewhere to fill up the freezer,' Tess said. 'And I fancy a double-range cooker if I'm going to be cooking anything!'

'We'll need to get the electrics checked first, and a few more power points,' Simon said, being practical for once. They stopped and stared at Over and Above's black silhouette against the rapidly darkening sky as they walked up the drive. 'I just cannot believe that this great big house is all ours!'

CHAPTER 4

REALITY

Their first night in the house wasn't – for Tess – romantic or even entirely restful. They collapsed into the hastily made up bed in a state of exhaustion. Simon was asleep in minutes, but not Tess. She kept hearing strange noises: clicks, squeaks, creaks, moans. She hoped they emanated from the wind which rattled the windowpanes for most of the night. They'd get used to these sounds in time, of course; all houses had them to some degree but this house looked like it had them more than most. This would become the principal guest bedroom anyway and they themselves would sleep in what was now the dining room, at the front, downstairs. Then Dylan had decided he didn't particularly like the new bed she'd bought for him and moved in between them. Fortunately, Simon didn't stir.

At 6 a.m., as Simon slept on, Tess tiptoed across to the window to gaze at the now- grey Atlantic. The cat jumped up on the windowsill and stared out as well. He must have wondered where on earth he was. Tess felt both exhilarated and apprehensive at the thought of there being nothing between them and North America except for three thousand miles or so of temperamental ocean. Had they put double-glazing on their list?

Giving up on sleep, Tess wandered into the kitchen and looked around in despair. Where to start? They'd plugged their fridge into one of the two power points, so were OK for milk, cheese and butter. She found the box which contained some of the packets and tins, and she unpacked the muesli and cornflakes so at least they could have some cereal and a cup of tea. The electrics had to be a priority and, in the meantime, they'd have to survive on sandwiches, salads and visits to The Portmerryn Arms. She shivered. It would soon be October and there was no central heating, and no gas. So, did they go electric or get some kind of portable gas supply? Or oil? Decisions, decisions!

Simon shuffled in. 'Why did you leave me?' he bleated. 'We should be christening this new house!' He gave her a hopeful hug.

'Because you were asleep when your head hit the pillow last night,' Tess replied. 'And you were still snoring when I got up this morning. Now, I've had an idea.'

'Oh yeah?' Simon sat down at the large oak dining table they'd brought in here, along with an assortment of chairs. He poured some cornflakes into a bowl.

'I was thinking we could perhaps buy a big, old caravan and stick it over there among the trees.' Tess waved an arm at the window. 'We could live in it while we get this place sorted out.'

'What, and lose our sea views?'

'Simon, get real! The sea views are going to be for the guests. There are going to be workmen drilling and hammering in this house for months to come and I, for one, don't wish to be freezing or covered in layers of dust.' She saw Simon shaking his still-dark head. 'Yes, I *know*, but after we've finished with it, it'll make additional accommodation for when family and friends come to stay. After all, the rooms in the house are going to be occupied by all these filthy-rich guests we're planning on having. And, heaven only knows, we're going to need them at the rate we're spending money!'

'I suppose you have a point,' he said grudgingly. 'Anyway we can think about that later.'

It was with some relief that Tess discovered the mobile phone signal was good at Over and Above. All the more so because there was no landline, although she supposed they should apply for one if they planned to run any kind of business. They'd need to use the laptop rather than their phones and they could hardly spend their days looking for WiFi outlets elsewhere. Simon contacted a professional-sounding roofer via his mobile, knowing they needed to get the roof checked and any repairs completed before the weather worsened. They were aware that they were definitely going to need paying guests to cover costs and so wanted to be able to offer drinks. They discovered that the young couple that owned the property before them had already applied for a licence to sell alcohol, which now had to be transferred from their name to the Sparrows' and should be granted in time for their opening in the spring.

They spent the day unpacking and moving their furniture around in a futile attempt to fill up some of the vast spaces. Two bedrooms remained empty, as did the so-called dining room. The large room at the rear was only half-filled with their sitting room furniture and Tess reckoned they'd need some enormous settees. More expense. But she cleaned the windows and then sat and drank a cup of tea admiring the unforgettable view. Bi-fold doors would be wonderful. She didn't think they'd spoil the character of the house too much because all the windows at the back had obviously been replaced at some time and didn't appear to be out of place, whereas the ones at the front and sides were the originals and fortunately hadn't taken such a battering from the Atlantic storms.

Ron the Roofer and his acned apprentice Joe spent most of the following day tut-tutting their way perilously across the roof of Over and Above.

'Truth be known,' said Ron later, standing in the kitchen with his second mug of tea, 'most of the roof could do with re-slating.' He rolled his eyes. 'Could cost you a fortune.' He paused for effect.

Tess, beginning to feel faint, plonked herself down on one of the chairs and Simon clutched the edge of the table. 'We haven't got a fortune,' he said.

'However,' Ron continued theatrically, 'looks like somebody made a start on it and then gave up. I suggest we just do a couple of the really bad bits for now. Make you rainproof at least, and we can do the rest as and when it needs doing.'

Joe fiddled with his phone and scratched his spots, avoiding eye contact.

'We could make a start directly,' Ron said, placing his mug carefully in the sink. 'Nice old sink that!' He looked around and sighed. 'You've got a fair bit of work to do in here!' They were to become very familiar with the 'fair bit of work' that needed doing and also with the word 'directly', pronounced 'dreckly' down here, and which merely hinted at some future date.

Ron gave them a rough estimate. 'Could be more because there's no knowing what we might find up there, do we, Joe?'

Joe shook his head sadly and they both departed.

'Don't look so worried!' Simon said, putting his arm round Tess. 'We'll get through this, you and I. Just keep imagining how great this place is going to be!'

'Oh, Simon, I love you and I love your optimism!'

'I love you, too, you daft Scotswoman! Come on, let's take a drink through and sit on a box to admire our view. That, at least, doesn't cost anything – yet!'

The electrician was called Tom. Simon had selected him from 'Registered Electrical Engineers in North Cornwall' on Google. He was fortyish and came alone, spending two days going from room to room and giving them what Tess hoped was a thorough testing.

'Most of it's safe,' he summarised, clutching a mug of coffee. 'The upstairs appears to have been done. Bit of rewiring needed downstairs, though.' He set the mug down on the table and gazed at the 1950s cooker. 'Fair bit of work needs doing in here.'

'We're aware of that,' Tess said. 'Now, power points. We're going to need masses of extra power points.'

Tom scratched his nose. 'I've got months of work ahead. Don't know when I'd be able to start. Give me a buzz when you know when you want me and I could probably send a couple of my lads along. How's that?' No definite time, not even dreckly.

'Sounds uncertain,' Simon sighed, after he'd accompanied him out of the door.

As he left Tom turned round and said, 'Did you know you had a cat shut in one of the bedrooms? Poor little devil. But don't worry, I let him out.'

'Oh my God!' Tess reckoned Dylan could be anywhere by now. Her poor cat! She searched the house in vain, cursing the stupid Tom, and hours later found her beloved cat sleeping peacefully on a pile of old blankets they'd used for wrapping round some of their furniture.

It seemed Dylan had no intention of going anywhere.

Then there was the builder who came the following day. He was around sixty and his name was Nick Norris and he was more optimistic than the other two. 'Well-built these houses were,' he said after he'd spent an hour or so looking around. 'The airbricks front and back are nice and clear, so you're lucky there. Sometimes, believe it or not, the level of the garden rises and blocks the flow of air. You need to cut away these plants and trees close to the house and I need to check the internal walls 'cos there's some condensation, but that might sort itself out with a good airing. A couple of the chimneys need attention. Now, what about this bathroom business?'

The bathroom business would involve knocking doors through from the two smaller bedrooms to two of the larger ones to provide en suite bathrooms, and the existing large bathroom divided into two to provide for the other two bedrooms. That, he said, shouldn't present any problems, except to the plumber, ha ha! He could recommend Pong and Pip Parker, hardworking, straight as a die, honest as the day is long. Worked with them often; great guys.

'Yes,' said Tess, 'we have met.'

In fact a few days previously Simon had brought back Pong Parker from the pub.

'Don't you go worryin', Mrs Sparra, I've flooded better places than this!' said Pong. His name did not fill Tess with a great deal of confidence either. 'I can turn your house into the cataracts of the Nile, and have salmon leapin' up the stairs, all in a couple of hours! You're in safe hands, Mrs Sparra!'

In the background Simon was doubled up with laughter. Was this guy serious? Tess didn't know whether to laugh or show him the door.

'Do you have public liability insurance?' she asked nervously.

'Wot's that then?' asked Pong.

'Well, how long would the guarantee be on the job?'

'As long as it takes the ink to dry on the cheque, Mrs Sparra!' Pong winked and grinned. 'Now don't you go worryin' about this 'cos I shan't have no problem. See, there's only *one* problem I come across when I'm workin'.'

'What's that?' Tess asked.

'Customers who ain't got no sense of humour! It puts the price up, Mrs Sparra!'

Tess's laugh was genuine.

'Whyever did you bring him here?' she asked Simon as Pong headed down the drive.

'Because Jed at the pub said he was cheap, he was good, he was available, and we need a plumber.'

Pong returned to have a second look and said he'd get to work 'dreckly' after Nick Norris had done the walls and doors and things, and why didn't they have a toilet downstairs as well while they were at it? Plenty of room in that scullery place. And what about an en suite in their own bedroom? Couldn't keep nipping upstairs every time you needed a pee, could you?

'Then there'll be the decorating,' Simon sighed, 'after they've all gone.'

That, to Tess, seemed such a long time ahead that it was hardly worth thinking about. 'We'll just need to get gallons of Dulux,' she said, 'and discounts everywhere for everything. We need to be in the know. Time we had a chat with the locals.'

'Fair bit of work'll need doing up there, I reckon,' Jed said cheerfully as he passed a pint of Doom Bar across the counter to Simon.

Tess, sipping a lager and lime, muttered, 'If anyone else says that…'

'We've got an army of workmen coming in over the next few weeks,' Simon said, taking a large gulp. 'Going to be costing a fortune. Shouldn't think I'll be able to afford much of this,' he waved his glass in the air, 'after all that lot's been paid.'

Jed sniffed. 'Do you know that's 'ow yer house got called Over and Above?'

'What do you mean?' Tess asked.

'Well, the reason's obvious,' said Simon, 'because of its stunning position.'

'Nah,' said Jed, putting down his own pint and wiping his mouth with the back of his hand. ''Twas always called the Cliff 'Ouse. Belonged to an old lady, Granny Gumm she was called.' He paused. 'Ninety-nine she was when she died. Been born up there an' died up there in the Cliff 'Ouse. Don't know why her was called "granny" 'cos her never did marry or have a family like. That 'ouse never did belong to anybody but 'er and 'er parents. Anyhow, a few year back this young couple come along with all them fancy ideas and bought the old place and, just like yerselves, got all them quotes. Got a bit of the roof done and the roofer says it's going to cost X amount of money over and above wot 'e'd said in the first place, 'cos of somethin' or another 'e 'adn't reckoned on. Then they 'ad Fred Wot's-'is-name…'

'Fred Belling,' prompted Annie, who'd appeared behind him. 'Flamin' Fred.'

'Yeah, Flamin' Fred, the electrician. Got 'is wires crossed when 'e were doing the village 'all and set 'imself alight. Just as well the old vicar was there with the bucket of sand.' They both snorted. 'Well, anyway, Fred got going on their wiring, and it were a whole lot worse than 'e thought so 'e said 'e'd 'ave to charge them a bit over and above wot he first thought like, if they wanted the wiring chased into the wall instead of running along the skirting boards. Someone else said much the same but I can't remember who that might 'ave been. But every bleeding thing was way over and above wot they thought they was going to be paying and that's the reason they changed the name of the 'ouse before they scarpered off abroad someplace.'

'Well, that doesn't exactly fill me with confidence,' Simon said. 'But it explains why some of the jobs are half done.'

'That 'ouse was so bleeding cold they were living in a caravan,' Jed continued, warming to his theme.

'A caravan!' Tess exclaimed. 'We thought of doing something like that while the work was being done.'

'In that case you'll be needing Jacko Jones. Jacko's got all them caravans on the Wadebridge Road, and 'e does up the old ones and sells them on cheap. 'E's OK, on the level. Yeah, you want to see Jacko.'

Somewhat perturbed by the origin of their house's name, the next day Tess and Simon set off towards Wadebridge and Jacko Jones.

'He's probably a relation of Jed's, or something,' Simon muttered as they pulled into a muddy farm gate to let an oncoming tractor and trailer pass on the narrow single-track lane. 'That's if we ever find the bloody place. It would help if we could see where we were going.'

'It'll be easier when the leaves drop off and the hedges are bare,' Tess consoled as they drove cautiously round the blind bends bordered by high hedges. Although both she and Simon were confident drivers in city traffic, the country lanes took a bit of getting used to. They felt like they were taking their lives in their hands every time they swung around a bend, blind to any tractors or school buses bearing down on them.

Then the road widened a little and, on a narrow turning on the right, a board proclaimed modestly, 'Jones Caravans – Best in the West – 200 yds!' with an arrow pointing down the lane.

As Simon turned into the lane he said, 'I don't fancy towing a caravan round here.'

'Well, we probably won't be buying anything here,' said Tess. 'We should really be looking at big established dealerships.'

'That's all very well, but this guy's supposed to be cheap, and we've got very limited finances,' Simon reminded her.

They rounded the third hairpin bend and there, in front of them, was an open field with what looked like dozens of caravans of every shape and size. There were touring caravans, mobile homes, traveller-type caravans, and even the office was housed in a mobile home, from which emerged a small, swarthy, elderly man with dyed black hair, a gold earring and very tight jeans. This, presumably, was Jacko Jones.

A burly Staffordshire bull terrier, tethered to a chain attached to a post next to the office, was growling in anticipation of their arrival.

'Mr Jones?' Tess asked politely.

'Yeah, but I get called Jacko.' He turned towards the dog. 'Shut up, Satan!' The dog continued with some low growling. 'He don't like people much.'

That much was obvious; Tess shivered.

'So wot can I do fer you?'

'Jed, at The Portmerryn Arms, suggested we see you,' Simon said, 'because we're going to need something to live in while our house gets renovated.'

Jacko stroked his chin. 'How's old Jed these days? Not seen him in months.'

'He's fine. We're looking for a caravan of some sort,' Simon persisted.

'OK, then, so how much you lookin' to spend?'

'As little as possible,' Tess said, 'So long as it's weatherproof.'

Jacko looked at them up and down. 'Just the two of you?'

'Just the two of us.'

He led the way past a ramshackle shed – which appeared to serve as a workshop – to where there was a cluster of about a dozen small touring caravans.

'Right, well, I've got a nice little tourer here. Seats make up to a double bed. Gas heater, sink, fridge, chemical toilet. Dirt cheap.'

Tess and Simon looked at the caravan, and then at each other. It reminded Tess of a mushroom.

'I think we were planning on something a little larger,' Simon said, 'as we're both quite tall. Have you got something where the sleeping quarters are separate from the living area, so we don't have to make the bed up every night?'

Jacko sniffed. 'I got every size here. Wot you plannin' to do with it afterwards?'

Simon shrugged.

'I thought we'd keep it as extra accommodation for family and friends,' Tess said.

'In that case,' said Jacko, 'Ye'll be needin' a four berth with a shower an' all.'

'We do?' Simon asked doubtfully.

'Yes, we do,' Tess confirmed, thinking of Matt, Lisa and the grandchildren.

Jacko rounded the corner, beckoning them to follow, to where half a dozen large models were parked in a semi-circle.

'This one here,' he said, pointing to one in the middle, 'is a lovely van, but an absolute bugger to tow. You wouldn't be towin' it, though, would you?'

'So how would I be able to get it out of here?' Simon asked.

'Aw, we can arrange that. Nothin' wrong with it, you understand? Been on a holiday site for years. I can let you have it dirt cheap.'

'What about planning permission?' Tess said.

'No need, as long as you keep the wheels on and move it about a bit occasionally it'll be OK. Temporary accommodation and all that; everyone does it,' Jacko reassured them as he headed towards the door which was situated in the centre. 'Follow me!' He pulled down a couple of steps, jumped in and turned left. They followed him into what was apparently the lounge, with a padded seating area round the front window and a table in the middle. 'Makes into a double bed,' he informed them.

There was a small compact kitchen comprising a sink, some work surfaces, a hob, an oven and a built-in fridge. It appeared to be clean and functional, if not spacious. Then, at the rear, was a tiny toilet and shower room, and a bedroom complete with double bed and a fair-sized wardrobe.

'Everythin' you could want,' said Jacko.

Tess had already mentally got out her sewing machine, replacing the ugly curtains, making cushion covers and bedspreads. It could, she felt sure, be made cosy and comfortable.

'Hmmm,' Simon said doubtfully. 'What about facilities?'

'You can connect it to your mains water with a hose,' said Jacko. 'You got a great storage tank so you can keep it topped up. I got some good hoses here, special price.'

'No, we've got one somewhere,' Simon said, stroking his beard.

'It all runs on bottled gas,' Jacko continued. 'I've got them cylinders here. Tell you what, you buy this and I'll throw in a gas cylinder for free. And you can connect to the electricity supply for a heater and the telly and all that. It'll heat up ever so quick.'

The price was manageable. Just. Tess looked at Simon who sighed and said, 'Well, we can't afford to spend a penny more than this, not with all the bills we're going to be paying.' He turned to Jacko. 'Any chance of a discount?'

Jacko sucked his teeth. 'It's rock bottom price already. Tell you what, as well as the gas cylinder I'll get it delivered to you for free. How about that?'

There followed several minutes of haggling, humming and hawing, but Jacko wouldn't be moved an inch. 'Delivered to your door,' he repeated. And, since there was no way they could even begin to imagine towing this great big thing along the country lanes, they accepted the deal.

'We'll freeze to death,' Simon predicted gloomily.

'Like I told you; run a cable out from the house and you can have electric heaters as well as the gas fire. Ye'll be snug as a bug in a rug.'

'We're bloody mad!' Simon said as they drove back towards Portmerryn.

'No, we're not!' Tess retorted. 'You know we can't live in the house all winter with no heating and an army of builders and plumbers and electricians. And like I said, we can make the caravan nice and afterwards it'll be extra accommodation. And there's a concrete base on the far side of the garage, behind the trees, where we can park it and it'll be out of sight.' Tess looked thoughtful. 'We must give it a name.'

'I'm sure we'll think of something,' said Simon.

*

Two days later the caravan arrived, delivered on a low loader by Windsor Brothers Transport Services.

A giant appeared on their doorstep at 11 a.m. He was at least seven feet tall, Tess reckoned, and built like a weightlifter. The type you see on TV pulling a bus or something and not necessarily someone you'd want to annoy.

'Where's this bleedin' caravan supposed to be goin' then, missus?'

Before Tess could reply, Simon appeared. 'Follow me,' he said.

As the giant trudged after Simon into the undergrowth, a second giant appeared and followed them. Tess stared in amazement; were they twins? Her husband was over six feet tall but he was dwarfed by these two. Slightly concerned for his safety, she followed them along the newly cleared path.

'I've taken out some bushes,' Simon said, 'so you should be able to get it in all right. There's a bit of a hard standing here, you see.'

The first giant growled. 'We'll have to take out a bit more.'

The second giant said, 'I'll get the chopper.'

'Won't you need a spade or something?' Simon asked tentatively. 'I've got some tools and gardening stuff in the garage.'

'No worries, mister,' said the first giant. 'Ed'll bring the chopper.'

As if on cue, Ed reappeared with an enormous axe, causing both Tess and Simon to gravitate together nervously and step well out of the way.

'This should do it,' said Ed and, with one almighty swipe, an enormous holly bush was felled, flattened to the ground.

'That's better,' said the first giant.

Tess had rather liked the holly bush but thought it politic not to mention this.

'Should be able to get it in easy now,' said the second giant, Ed.

'I'll go get it then,' said the first giant, and they both headed towards the trailer.

Tess stifled a giggle. 'Do you think they're going to *carry* it in?'

'It wouldn't surprise me,' Simon muttered.

In fact, the giants had a sturdy little tractor-type machine with which they expertly manoeuvred the caravan onto the hard standing. Ed lit a cigarette and said, 'Anythin' you want movin', just give us a call!' He handed a card to Simon and then went to help his brother stabilise the caravan. It was all done in a matter of minutes, and then the little truck was delivered back onto the trailer. Tess offered tea.

'No thanks, missus. We got some dodgy cars to pick up from Bodmin and we're running late.'

With that, Al got into the driving seat while Ed shouted instructions: 'Woah! Right a bit!' and 'Straighten up!' and 'Left hand down!' Then he jumped into the passenger seat, gave them a cheery wave, and the Windsor brothers were gone, rattling their way to Bodmin.

Tess could hardly wait to inspect their new acquisition. 'Well,' she said, 'welcome to Windsor Castle!'

'Am I supposed to carry Your Majesty over the threshold then?' Simon asked.

'Probably not a good idea. The door's a bit narrow. I think we should christen it, though.'

'I'll check the booze in the garage,' Simon said, 'and find a bottle of something fizzy, if you can dig out a couple of glasses.'

He reappeared a few minutes later clutching a bottle of Prosecco. 'There's some Moët in there somewhere,' he said, 'but perhaps we'll save that for later.'

'Prosecco will be fine,' said Tess as the cork popped.

CHAPTER 5

GETTING IT TOGETHER

Over and Above was never going to be cosy but Tess hoped it could be made elegant and beautiful once the roofer, the builder, the plumber, the electrician and the interior designer (herself) had done their bit – and one thing was for sure, there was a lot of bits to be done. They soon learned time was of little importance down here: 'be with you dreckly we've finished wot we're doin' now' was a standard answer. 'Dreckly' could only be compared to the Spanish '*mañana*', but without the urgency.

Ron the roofer, due to commence work on a Monday morning, arrived on Wednesday afternoon. No proper explanation was offered, just a few grunts about emergencies. After the building work was completed the plumber and the electrician would move in. Plumbing would be a major operation as, apart from the new bathrooms, central heating had to be installed. There was of course no mains gas, so they decided on oil-fired heating, which would involve having an oil storage tank somewhere in the garden. Meanwhile, Simon found a tap outside the garage to which he attached a long hose to simplify replenishing the supply of water at Windsor Castle. He then went in search of an equally long outdoor cable with which to transport electricity. And, while all this was taking place, Tess spent an entire day measuring windows and finally took herself off to Truro in the hunt for metres of furnishing fabrics, hoping that somewhere in the house she might find a quiet corner near one of the precious power points where she could plug in her sewing machine and begin weeks of curtain making.

But first she needed to liven up the drab interior of their temporary home with bright curtains, cushions and rugs. And so began the arguments as to who could have the car; whose need was greater, whose shopping was more urgent.

'You can't have the car today,' Simon announced at breakfast one morning. 'I've got to go to the builders' merchants.'

It was the day Tess had planned to pick up a mountain of fabric she'd ordered. 'But I've *told* them I'd collect it today!'

'Well, I'm sorry, but the building materials are far more important.'

Not for the first time Tess wished she'd kept her old Ford Focus. When she and Simon got married they decided one car was quite sufficient in London, particularly as they had neither garage nor allocated parking space. She wondered if she dared suggest buying another car, but that didn't seem too brilliant an idea when they'd just bought a caravan and money was tight anyway. But much as she loved their sporty old Stag, the car was not practical for country living, for potholed roads and for transporting building materials. They should trade it in for an off-road vehicle, a sturdy four-by-four with a seat high enough to see over the top of the hedges. Surely Simon would realise this himself sooner or later?

In her innocence she'd asked Jed at the pub, 'Are there any buses from here to Truro? From here to *anywhere*? Wadebridge? Bude?'

'Buses!' snorted Jed, which drew much guffawing all round. 'Yeah, you can get one Monday, Wednesday and Friday wot'll get you to Wadebridge and you can get a connection from there to most places. Just as long as you don't want to come back on the same day!' More gales of laughter.

Tess phoned the fabric shop and explained that – due to her domineering selfish husband – she would not be picking up the fabric until later in the week. And, for the first time since they married, she was aware of friction between herself and Simon. Their blissful honeymoon period was beginning to wear off.

They'd been at Over and Above almost a month and it was an occasion when Simon had gone off with the Stag to the builders' merchants that Tess decided to check out the village shop. She'd driven past it on the coast road half a mile or so beyond The Portmerryn Arms, and she reckoned it was a walkable distance. In fact, it took the best part of thirty minutes and was run by a generously proportioned lady in her sixties, with corrugated grey waves in her hair, and a penchant for hand-knitted cardigans. She was known as Pearly.

'As in pearly gates,' Simon had scoffed when they first heard of her existence.

This Pearly was the gateway to all local gossip and goings-on which she related in detail to anyone who cared to listen. Pearly not only sold groceries, but she sold paraffin and firelighters as well, ran the post office, sold lottery tickets and took in dry-cleaning.

Tess pushed her way past the usual collection of buckets and spades, crab lines, cheap body boards and all the luridly coloured paraphernalia required by holidaying families. The shop seemed rather dark inside, brightened mainly by Pearly, in a lime green knitted cardigan, erecting a pyramid of baked beans on one end of the counter. On the other end was a large, slightly cross-eyed teddy bear which was one of the sought-after prizes in the local raffle.

'Only one pound each,' said Pearly, waving the book of tickets hopefully at her new customer.

Tess could decipher a faint smell of paraffin mixed with TCP as she introduced herself.

'You'll get all the weather up there on that cliff,' Pearly informed Tess cheerfully. 'Comes in 'orizontal it does, right off the sea. Not so bad down 'ere, thank the lord. Someone said your 'usband's an actor, is that right? Wot's 'e been in? Not in *Coronation Street*, is 'e? Or *Emmerdale*?' When Tess shook her head Pearly immediately lost interest in actors. 'So wot you going to be doing down 'ere? B&Bs? Well, you'll need plenty of bacon and sausages and all that so we can set up an arrangement dreckly and I'll do you a good price.'

Tess, who'd planned to stock up the freezer with breakfast fodder from the nearest Cash and Carry, nodded politely, noting Pearly's inflated prices. As she backed out of the door, Pearly asked, 'You been in the pub yet? My cider's cheaper than theirs. They're all right, though, Jed and Annie, but that Gideon's forty if he's a day and still livin' off his parents and doin' next to nothin'. Still. You got family?'

And so on, and so on. Tess vowed to give Pearly a wide berth. Emergency use only.

*

When she got home Tess realised she was desperately in need of a chat with Orla. She missed her friend and the banter they always enjoyed.

'Hi, it's me!'

'Well, well,' said Orla, 'if it's not a voice from the wild west! How is it down there?'

'Oh, it's fine,' Tess replied. 'Just a bit fed up with my husband at the moment.'

Orla snorted. 'So the honeymoon is finally over, is it? What's the smarmy bugger up to?'

'He's *not* a smarmy bugger, Orla, and he's not up to anything. Just being a bit selfish, particularly about the car.'

'Ah well, he's a fella. They're all selfish,' said Orla. 'You should know that by now.'

'It's just that living here you need to have a car all the time. And we keep arguing about whose need matters most. Oh, it all sounds so petty when I talk about it to you!'

'Well, it's hardly world-shattering stuff, Tess. And all you need to do is get yourselves another car, isn't it? Couldn't you write it off to tax or something? After all, you are supposedly running a business.'

'We will be,' Tess said, feeling a little better.

'Now, tell me about all the cowboys who're knocking your house to bits!'

And, as Tess told Orla about the workmen's comings and goings, about the caravan, and about the village shop, she found she was giggling and she felt better.

*

There followed weeks of banging, crashing, shouting and intermittent swearing, with masonry dust everywhere. They abandoned their sea view bedroom, Tess stripped the bed, covered it in plastic sheeting and moved into Windsor Castle, her idea of a quiet sewing corner in Over and Above swept away with the layers of dust. The needlework would have to take place in Windsor Castle if Simon ever got the electric cable in position.

It was wet and windy on the first night and, although situated in the trees, the caravan rocked a little at times. Tess sat up in their small double bed and listened to the rain drumming on the roof while the candles flickered.

'Isn't this cosy?' Simon said, snuggling up to her.

'It's scary,' Tess said. 'This thing is *swaying*!'

'It's quite safe,' soothed her husband. 'And I do think we should christen our little castle, like *now*!'

Afterwards Simon asked, 'Did the earth move for you, my darling?'

'Well it's for sure something moved,' Tess replied truthfully.

Two days later, Simon finally succeeded in connecting the bright orange electric cable from the house to the caravan, thus providing light, heat and television. It gave Tess the ability to sew during the day while Simon made endless sketches of kitchen layouts when not getting in the way of the workmen. And luck was with them as far as Tess's desire for a range cooker was concerned, because Annie at the pub knew someone who was selling her B&B and most of the stuff it contained.

'You go over there an' have a look,' she told Tess. 'Sale starts Thursday so you want to go over there Wednesday an' make some excuse about not bein' able to get there next day. That way you'll get the pick, if she agrees to sellin'.'

It was certainly worth a try. 'Over there' was about six miles away inland and Tess persuaded a reluctant Simon to accompany her.

They found a house not dissimilar to their own, minus the sea views, with six letting bedrooms and an elderly owner called Myra, who was tiny with white hair piled on top of her head and beady little eyes.

'We understand you might have some furniture and kitchen equipment for sale?' Tess asked tentatively.

'Sale starts tomorrow, 10 a.m.,' snapped Myra.

'Thing is,' Tess continued, 'we really can't make it tomorrow due to domestic problems.' And that was only half a lie, she thought, because there were *bound* to be some. 'And we're *so* in need of things for the B&B we're just setting up at Portmerryn. Annie at the pub said what a lovely place you'd got and that you might have some tips for us.'

Myra pursed her lips but said nothing.

Then Simon stepped forward. 'We should introduce ourselves. I'm Simon Sparrow and this is my wife, Tess, and we *so* need the expertise of a professional such as yourself.' This was Simon the actor playing his part, bestowing on her the kind of disarming smile that had Tess weak at the knees when first they met.

'Haven't I seen you somewhere before?' asked Myra, visibly softening.

Simon shrugged. 'Depends on which soaps you watch and which films you've seen,' he replied airily. 'The original *Poldark* perhaps?'

And if you blinked you'd have missed him, Tess thought, trying not to smile.

'Oh my word, you're an *actor*! I *knew* I'd seen you somewhere before!' Myra exclaimed. 'Fancy that now! Well, you'd better come in!'

As they entered a hall similar to their own, Tess was taken aback by the violently patterned carpet and began to wonder if they'd want to buy anything here, recalling Simon's earlier forecast. 'It'll just be a load of old junk,' he'd said. 'We should be looking to buy *new*.'

In fact, it was anything but a load of old junk. There were several pristine divan beds, bedside tables and lamps.

'I'm not leaving any of that stuff here,' Myra informed them. 'It's all far too big for where I'm going and I'm damned if I'm leaving it for the madam that's buying this place and giving me no end of grief. I'm not leaving *her* a bloody thing!'

For all her age and size Tess reckoned that Myra would be no pushover.

'Trouble is,' Simon continued in his most impressive thespian tones, 'I don't do so much acting these days so we're trying something completely new and we're pretty clueless. We need a lovely lady like yourself to give us some advice.'

Myra had plenty of that. She and her husband had run this place for nigh on forty years and they'd just updated everything shortly before he died. She was seventy-seven now, she said, and didn't fancy soldiering on alone; she'd got her eye on this nice little retirement flat near her sister in Hayle, so all this stuff had to go.

Myra, now completely disarmed, asked, 'Would you like a cup of tea?'

'If it's not putting you to too much trouble,' said Simon.

'No trouble at all,' said Myra. 'Come into the kitchen.'

As Myra filled up the kettle Tess looked around at the pine kitchen units, dated now but immaculate nevertheless. And there was the double-range cooker, gleaming in the morning sun.

'I'd prefer the cooker went to someone like yourselves,' Myra said, beaming at Simon, 'rather than some second-home owners coming down here in their Chelsea tractors. And most of the time they eat out or microwave stuff, so what do they need a cooker like this for? For *show*, that's what, Simon!'

'I couldn't agree more,' Simon said, sighing dramatically.

'And will you be needing a coffee machine?' Myra asked.

'We have a little one,' Tess said.

'I've got a big one here,' Myra said, lifting the cover off a large gleaming Italian machine. 'Just like they have in Costa!' she added proudly. 'And you bet some poncey second-home owner will want that, too; you won't catch *them* sticking a spoonful of Nescafé into a mug of boiling water now, will you?'

Myra's intense dislike of second-home owners could be very much to their advantage, Tess hoped, although money, of course, had not yet been discussed.

'I'd make you a coffee with it,' Myra continued, 'but it's all cleaned and polished up, see? For the sale tomorrow. But if you fancy buying it, well, I'll make you one now. Cappuccino, latte, mocha, anything you like.'

'No, thank you, Myra, tea will be fine,' Simon replied.

Myra narrowed her eyes. 'You haven't got a place up in London as well, have you?'

Simon sighed dramatically again. 'I *wish*! Oh, Myra, we've invested every penny in a lovely house very similar to this. But, if you could *see* the work that needs doing to it! We're living in a haze of builders' dust at the moment.'

'No good for your poor lungs,' said Myra, gazing adoringly at Simon. 'You've got to take care of a lovely voice like that.'

Never mind me, thought Tess, stirring a sugar lump into the cup of tea Myra had placed in front of her. Tea was served in utilitarian white cups and saucers which she'd presumably used for her guests. In spite of playing gooseberry to the flirtation between Myra and her husband, Tess hoped this would prove to be to their advantage financially, particularly as she'd like a couple of the beds as well, not to mention the coffee machine, depending on the cost.

Myra wasn't finished yet. 'Some people come down here to Cornwall with all these fancy ideas about B&Bs, guesthouses and all that, and then find out it's manic all summer with one- and two-nighters, so you end up washing sheets and towels every five minutes, and then there's hardly anything at all in the winter.'

'Well, I must confess we'd hoped to make ours a little bit special,' Tess admitted, wondering if they should be buying an extra washing machine instead of a coffee machine.

'Everyone says that,' Myra said dismissively before turning her attention back to Simon. 'How many rooms you going to be letting out?'

'Four,' said Simon.

'Only four? I've got six up there, and two bathrooms.'

'Four with en suites,' Tess pointed out. 'Or there will be.'

Myra sniffed. 'If I was doing it all over again I'd go for long-term guests. Make them stay a week or two. Less chance of them taking off with your towels when they get to know you.'

'We'll bear that in mind,' Simon said, grinning at Tess.

But Myra wasn't finished yet. 'And that's not all, Simon. No, siree. I've had two women come here looking for a double bed. A *double*, not two singles! I tell you, my Arthur wouldn't have let them through the door! He'd have turned in his grave!'

'Yes, well, Myra, we've moved on now,' Simon said soothingly.

'We'd better talk about money then,' Myra said, producing a box of biscuits. They were plainly coming to the crunch in every sense of the word. Tess took a chocolate digestive and Simon a custard cream.

'And be sure to get a deposit off everyone,' Myra added, chomping on one of the custard creams. 'Are you going to be doing dinners?'

'I think we'll have to,' Tess said. 'Although the pub's within walking distance their menu's a bit limited.'

'It's a palaver,' Myra said. 'And you'll get blooming vegetarians, and *vegans*! You won't want to be having vegans!'

'Well, I guess they'll be one of the many groups we won't be able to discriminate against,' Simon said, diplomatically, 'but we'll cross that bridge when we come to it. Now, let's talk about money, Myra.'

Myra offered the biscuit tin again. Both Tess and Simon declined politely, while Myra chose a bourbon and dunked it in her tea. There followed a long monologue on how much everything cost, what bargains they'd be getting and remember, she wasn't a rich woman because there was no company pension for the likes of her and she'd got a rock-bottom price for her house. This proved to be a prologue to asking for some silly prices for everything.

Simon gave another sigh. 'I rather fear these second-home owners can probably afford these prices more than we can, Myra. Which is such a shame, but there it is.'

There was a silence while Tess held her breath.

'Well, maybe I could lower the prices a little,' Myra said, sighing. 'More tea?'

'Oh no, thank you,' Simon said sadly. 'We must move on because, if we aren't buying your lovely things, then I'm afraid we must look elsewhere. There are some bargains online, so we need to start looking.'

Another silence. Then Myra quoted some more down-to-earth prices.

Simon sucked his teeth. 'If you went a tiny bit lower we could probably manage that, couldn't we, darling?' he asked, turning to Tess.

'Just about,' agreed Tess.

'I'll want cash,' Myra said, 'and I'll want it all collected by this afternoon latest.' She stood up and peered out the window. 'That little yellow thing's no blooming good!'

Simon balked visibly at her description of his precious Stag. After a minute he said, 'Jed's got a van he said we could borrow. So, if we came back with the van and the cash at about three o'clock, how would that be?'

'That would be fine,' said Myra.

'She's not too keen on vegetarians,' Simon remarked as they drove home.

Tess giggled. 'Even less keen on vegans!'

'But I think her pet hate has to be second-home owners!'

'Just as well she's packing up,' Tess remarked, 'And at least we're getting some great bargains out of it.'

'Thanks to my irrepressible charm,' said Simon. They both laughed as the yellow car navigated the twists and bends of the lane, bordered by clumps of early primroses, which took them back to the two-lane road leading to Portmerryn.

CHAPTER 6

ABSENCE MAKES THE NIGHT SEEM LONGER

They drove home via the pub. Tess wondered how they could possibly fit two double divans, two bedside tables, the range cooker and the coffee machine into Jed's dilapidated old van.

'Might 'ave to tie somethin' on the roof, I s'pose,' said Jed, stroking his chin. 'Better take Gideon with us; 'e's strong as an ox. 'Elp carry everythin'.'

'That's very kind,' said Simon as Gideon appeared wearing a pink T-shirt and nodding enthusiastically.

'Be glad to help,' he said. They hadn't heard him speak before. And Tess, seeing him properly for the first time, noted what a good-looking man he was.

And so that afternoon Simon, Jed and Gideon set off to collect the new purchases, with a stop en route to withdraw the cash for Myra. Tess, in the meantime, wondered where the items could best be stored until such time as upstairs was ready. The sitting room – at present piled high with boxes – was the largest area able to be sealed off from the ever-infiltrating dust. The range cooker would, of course, have to be placed somewhere close to the kitchen for the time being, probably in the so-called boot room although this was due to have a toilet installed in it eventually. It was like a three-dimensional chess board, trying to work out where the next move should be.

At the moment there was a gaping hole in the kitchen wall which would be the doorway to one of the two rooms at the back, designated to be the new dining room, with sea views. The original dining room, opposite the kitchen on the other side of the main door, was to become their bedroom, much to Simon's disgust.

'I don't like sleeping downstairs,' he'd wailed, 'and we won't have our lovely views!'

'The lovely views are for our visitors, Simon,' Tess had insisted patiently. 'They're going to be paying a lot of money to look at the sea, which is how we hope to make our living.'

For all Simon's laidback nature and his undoubted charm, there was also an almost childlike petulance about him, particularly when he didn't get his own way. The trouble was that he usually *did* get his own way because he was good at winning people over, Myra being the latest example. He'd won Tess over in exactly the same manner, more or less proposing to her within minutes of their meeting. He came across as exciting and one hundred per cent different from the succession of weird men she'd met on the online dating site.

When Simon, Jed and Gideon arrived back with the van and their acquisitions, it was Gideon who wielded the sack-barrow and did most of the heavy lifting. It was late afternoon before they'd finished and everything had been carried safely inside.

'Would you like a drink, guys?' Tess asked. 'Tea? Coffee? Something stronger?'

Gideon looked at his dad, who shook his head. 'We've got to be getting back,' he said, and smiled broadly when Simon pressed a £20 note into each of their hands, saying, 'Thank you for all your hard work.'

Jed was pleased. 'Any time you need a bit of help,' he said. Then, indicating Gideon, he added, ''E can help you with any heavy lifting and that, can't you, Gideon?'

Gideon nodded, smiling and blushing. And Tess realised then that Gideon was shy.

Ron the Roofer and Joe, his apprentice, were the first to finish. The work lasted three weeks off and on, and more often off than on. 'Too windy', 'Too wet', 'Too something-or-other...' But now Ron promised that the damp wouldn't get in and grudgingly admitted that 'the roof ain't as bad as I thought it would be' which, translated, probably meant that there hadn't been much wrong with the roof in the first place.

Pong, with his endless repertoire of jokes and witticisms, and his son, Pip, had put in the pipework around the walls, and were waiting for the builders to finish off the doors.

'I just want it all to be finished,' Tess sighed.

'Dreckly,' said Simon.

It was now late October, the shops in Wadebridge and Truro already brimming with Christmas trees and baubles. And even Pearly had stuck up a bit of tinsel. Tess didn't think there was much hope getting the house finished before March at the earliest, but knew they had to be up and running before the first hordes of tourists descended on the South-West.

Cosy and compact as the caravan might be, Tess was very much looking forward to being back in the house to decorate, hang curtains and buy any necessary furniture. Then they'd take photos, sort out a website and hope to get some bookings. And money! Because everything was costing far more than they originally anticipated. Over and Above was certainly living up to its name. They hadn't planned on buying Windsor Castle, of course, and, just to add to the expense, even Simon now admitted that the Stag was not a practical machine for potholed lanes and for transporting bags of cement. They needed something newer and sturdier.

'Someone will pay a lot of money for this,' Simon insisted, patting its yellow bodywork. 'It's a classic, you know.'

Tess had thought fondly of dear David, the man who'd been her soulmate for some years after her divorce from her first husband and father of her children, Gerry. David had had a business selling classic cars. Unfortunately, he and his E-type Jaguar had come to one hairpin bend too many. Tess had been heartbroken. It all seemed a very long time ago now.

'I'll take it to Plymouth or somewhere,' Simon continued, 'because no one round here would be likely to buy it and, anyway, I couldn't bear to see anyone else driving it around.' His voice wobbled; he loved that car.

Tess put her arm round him. 'I know it's hard, darling, but we really *need* to do it.'

The problem was solved in an unexpected fashion when Simon got a call from his agent in London. 'I know you're semi-retired, old chap, but we've had this amazing offer of a commercial and some voice-overs and wondered if you'd be interested? It would mean you coming up to town, of course, but it would be well worth it financially. But the beard will have to come off.'

'They've made me an offer I can't refuse,' Simon said, stroking his beard, 'even though I've got to shave this off.'

'Let's face it, we can't refuse *any* offer,' Tess said. 'And that damned thing was giving me a rash!'

'I'll have to fly up or something,' Simon said, 'because you'll need the car while I'm away.'

'Or you could get a train or a bus,' said Tess, thinking of the expense.

Simon sighed dramatically. 'The trains are always being cancelled; it's on the news every night. And who needs to sit five or six hours on a bus?'

Tess thought for a moment. 'I could manage without the car for a few days if you'd prefer to drive.'

'Could you *really*?'

'I'll stock up on everything I need before you go, and I can always walk down to Pearly's if I run out of something.'

'That is *so* lovely of you, darling!' Simon kissed her with gusto. 'I should only be gone a couple of days.'

And, as the yellow Stag disappeared in a cloud of dust down the drive, Tess thought how good it would be to have a couple of days on her own, with minimum cooking and lots of sewing. It wasn't until Pong and Pip knocked off to go home at five o'clock that it hit her. Here she was, on her own, one woman isolated on the side of a cliff, in a wobbly caravan, a large empty house opposite and a long, dark night looming ahead. She'd never been nervous about being on her own before because there were always people around, close neighbours. And there had been street lights and the comforting sound of traffic in the distance. But now it was only six o'clock and already almost dark, deathly silent, no street lights, no traffic, no neighbours. Just the howling of the wind and the rustling of the branches. Tess hoped they were branches, these unidentifiable noises, and not mice. Or rats! Or worse, *prowlers*!

As she locked herself into Windsor Castle she thought fondly of her cottage in Temple Terrace, up in leafy Surrey. She'd wept when she sold it to move in with Simon. And then she thought about Orla. They'd lived next door to each other during Orla's marriage to Gavin and hers to Gerry. Then Tess, divorced, and Orla, widowed, had remained friends and set up their boutique where Tess slaved to make large outfits for large ladies and Orla did the selling. ('That woman could sell a sunlamp in the Sahara,' her daughter had once quipped.)

Orla's daughter-in-law had changed her mind about taking over the shop. They couldn't do made-to-measure outfits any more now that Tess had gone, for one thing, and for another, Orla and Lauren had never really got on, so they had decided to close down the business, and the shop was now up for rent. Tess had felt very nostalgic for some weeks, but had come to accept that changes happen and life moves on. However, Orla had wasted no time in finding a job for two days a week in Milbury's one and only department store, selling hats. And so successful was she in the short time she was there that they'd asked her if she'd consider working full time, in spite of being sixty-five. But Orla liked working two days a week and had said to Tess, 'Sure, now I'll be able to pop down to the wild west occasionally and give you a hand.'

Tess missed Orla's banter, her arguing and her humour. With Simon away this would have been an ideal opportunity for Orla to keep her company – if only there was somewhere she could sleep. Tess didn't think Orla would relish a few nights on the rock-hard settee that served as the extra double bed in Windsor Castle. Neither was she likely to relish dashing across to Over and Above in the early morning for a half decent shower before the workmen arrived at eight o'clock. If it hadn't been for the workmen and her constant duties as tea-maker, she could have gone up to London with Simon and spent a few nights with Orla. And seen her family. She missed Amber, and Matt, and the grandchildren.

Now, as Tess lay in the dark listening to the strange noises in the night, for the first time she began to wonder why on earth she'd ever agreed to come down to this godforsaken place. She was missing Simon dreadfully; she hadn't realised quite how much she'd come to need him. But, never mind, he'd be back soon, and between them they were going to make a success of Over and Above.

In spite of feeling positive, it still took a very long time to get to sleep.

CHAPTER 7

HOMECOMING

Tess spent the best part of a week sleeping badly, jumping at every unfamiliar noise in the night, waiting to be murdered in her bed. Days were spent attempting to clear away some of the dust and debris in the kitchen, where the door opening into the new dining room was now complete. At some point the electrician would come in to connect the cooker and wire in power points for all the kitchen equipment. And more dust and debris was floating around upstairs because Pong and Pip were still hammering and drilling away.

Simon, in the meantime, was doing a TV commercial for gin, with doubtless much sampling of the product, plus voice-overs for a holiday company and a double-glazing firm. All involved drinks and dinners in the evenings. He was having a whale of a time.

On the third day of his absence Tess decided she'd need to visit Pearly's as she'd run out of teabags and milk. It was a pleasant walk down to the shop, although Tess rather dreaded the uphill return journey.

As she walked through the door of the shop she was aware of a heated argument taking place between Pearly and a small dark-haired woman who was waving a box of cornflakes in the air. This woman was yelling, 'You've put your prices up again, Pearly! And it's not *on*! Do you know, it's cheaper for me to go on the bus to Tesco and back, even if I have to spend the night at my brother's, than it is for me to shop here?'

'Well, go to bloody Tesco's then!' Pearly yelled back, red-faced, her grey corrugated waves quivering with anger. 'See if I bloody—' She stopped in mid-flow and switched on a smile. 'Oh, Mrs *Sparrow*, how nice to see you! Now, what can I do for you?'

'What can she *do* you for, more like!' the dark-haired woman said to Tess.

Tess felt embarrassed. 'Um, perhaps I've come in at the wrong time?'

'Not at all,' said Pearly. 'Mrs Pengilly was just off to Tesco's.'

With that, Mrs Pengilly slammed the box of cornflakes back on the counter and stomped out of the shop.

As Tess bought the items she wanted she observed Pearly's nostrils were still flared in anger and her large bosom – today clad in a bright pink hand-knitted cardigan – was heaving. She kept throwing evil looks at the door. For once Pearly wasn't in the mood for gossip other than saying, 'Don't pay no attention to that miserable cow! How am I supposed to survive when my deliveries have to come all the way from Plymouth and they charge me a fortune 'cos I live here. Of course I've got to charge more than bloody Tesco! "Convenience Store" it says above the door, don't it? And that's what people have to pay for: the *convenience*.'

'Quite so,' agreed Tess, looking to make a quick escape.

As she left the shop she found Mrs Pengilly waiting outside.

'Don't tell that woman a thing!' she instructed Tess. 'She'll have it all round the village in no time. And as for her prices – *well!*' She shook her head in despair.

'I only come down here very occasionally,' Tess said. 'I'm not really a regular customer but my husband's away on business with the car and needs must.'

'Greedy old bat she is,' said Mrs Pengilly. She held out her hand. 'Gina Pengilly.'

'Tess Sparrow.'

They shook hands and Gina Pengilly said, 'Are you the folks that's bought Over and Above?'

'That's us,' replied Tess.

'Well, you can't be walking up that lane with all that heavy shopping. Bob'll be here in a minute and we'll give you a lift.'

'Oh, I'm fine, Mrs Pengilly, really…'

'Nonsense! We live up at the top of Seagull Hill so we're going right past your place. And you call me Gina.'

At that moment a large white van, with 'Pengilly Electrics' emblazoned in blue paint on the side, drew up.

'You sit in the front there with Bob,' ordered Gina. 'There's a little seat behind I can squeeze into. Bob, this is Tess, who's bought the old Cliff House – Over and Above, or whatever they call it these days.'

Bob, who appeared to be in his sixties, was bald as a coot but sported a luxuriant moustache.

'We're passing by the end of your drive anyway,' he said.

As Tess got gratefully into the front seat, her groceries balanced on the floor between her ankles, he asked, 'How are you settling in?'

'Well, we're not actually in yet,' Tess replied. 'We're having masses of work done and so we've got ourselves a little caravan to live in while the house is being ripped to pieces. And my husband's had to go up to London so I'm without wheels at the moment.'

'It's never been looked after proper, that place,' said Bob as they headed towards Seagull Hill. 'Shouldn't think the electrics have been updated in years. The old girl who spent her life there never did a thing and then some young couple bought the place and hardly ever came near it.'

'They did begin to update the electrics,' Tess said, 'but they didn't get very far.'

As he pulled up opposite the driveway to Over and Above she said, 'You're very welcome to come in and have a look if you'd like to. If you don't mind dust, that is.'

'Quite used to dust,' said Bob, making a quick right turn up the drive.

'Nice old house,' commented Gina as they got out of the van.

As Tess led the way through the front door and turned right into the kitchen, she said, 'This is the only room we're using because the other downstairs rooms are piled high with furniture.'

'You haven't got any units,' Gina said, looking around.

'We're going to order them just as soon as Simon gets back. But we've just bought a lovely double-range cooker and, once I get that installed, at least I can begin to cook properly.'

Bob was scratching his head as he studied the two power points. 'You're going to need a load more of these,' he said. 'You got someone lined up to do it?'

'Well, I know Simon was talking to someone called Tom, but I don't think they agreed a date or anything.'

'You don't want *him!*' Bob said. 'He'll have the place up in smoke. Now, I'll be free dreckly, most likely in a couple of weeks, so perhaps I can have a word when your husband gets back?'

'And you might need a hand with the cleaning,' Gina put in. 'I do early mornings down the pub but I could come in afterwards. If you wanted me, that is.'

Tess felt overwhelmed by these offers of help, but she and Simon had to discuss money with them before any decision could be made. But she liked them both and felt sure they wouldn't overcharge. She opened the door to what Simon insisted on calling the boot room.

'This,' she said, 'will be the utility area and laundry room and we're having a toilet installed as well. And *this,*' she indicated with pride, 'is my lovely new big cooker.'

'Want me to wire that in for you?' asked Bob.

'That would be wonderful. When could you do it?'

'No time like the present,' said Bob. 'But I'll need a bit of help to move it. You know where it's to go?'

'Oh yes!' Tess replied. 'I know exactly where I want it to go.'

'You got someone working upstairs?'

'Yes, Nick Norris and his brother are making doorways and things.'

Bob rolled his eyes. 'As long as you're not in a hurry. Not known for speed, that pair. Anyway, I'll get those two buggers down here and we'll have your cooker in place in no time.'

With that he headed towards the stairs and Gina said, 'You got hot water here?'

'Yes,' Tess said. 'There's an immersion heater.'

'Right, I'll give that floor a bit of a wash before they put the cooker on it.' And without further ado Gina had spotted a pail and was filling it up with cleaner and hot water.

'I can't let you do this,' Tess protested.

'Yeah, you can. You just put the kettle on because we're all going to be needing a cup of tea when we've finished.' And she began to mop the floor.

An hour later the cooker was in place, duly connected and working, and everyone was sitting round the table drinking tea and eating chocolate biscuits. For the first time Tess felt she'd made some friends and she had the beginnings of a kitchen.

She thanked the Pengillys profusely and, as they left, she took Bob's card and made a note of Gina's mobile number.

Simon's 'few days away' had stretched to a week. Tess wondered why on earth she hadn't let him fly up to London as he'd originally suggested as she not only missed him, but she missed the car. She felt marooned and lonely, and not a little frightened at night. In his absence, though, Tess had finished making curtains for the sitting room and dining room, and was studying paint charts in detail so that they could begin to decorate. She'd christened the cooker and worked out exactly how many kitchen units they'd need. And when he got back – if he ever got back – the house should be ready for the plumbing and electrics. More dust and more chaos. And, as Christmas was fast approaching, every tradesman around would down tools for the two-week break. Would they ever be able to welcome guests in the spring? she wondered.

Then, on Day Six of his absence, she had a call from Simon mid-morning.

'Darling, I've just left London behind, and I've stopped for fuel on the M3. I should be home by early afternoon. *Lots* to tell you!'

'And I've lots to tell you,' Tess replied with feeling, vowing never again to be without transport on her own in this place. Or lie tossing and turning half the night in Windsor Castle listening to weird night-time noises, terrified that someone was prowling outside preparing to murder her. She could laugh at herself during the day but it was altogether different at night. And not helped by Dylan, who, in the manner of all felines, would suddenly stare wide-eyed at a window or the door. What was he seeing or hearing? A massive rat, a peeping Tom or an axe murderer? But Dylan just yawned and settled himself down again to sleep.

And so, for all these reasons and not least because Tess loved and missed her husband, she waited anxiously for the yellow Stag to reappear in the drive. Instead, just before three o'clock, a large dusty blue Land Rover pulled up outside. Who was this? she wondered, as she popped a casserole into one of her ovens. Whoever it was had parked in the exact spot where they parked the Stag and Simon would be back any moment. Tess wiped her hands and headed out of the door.

And there was her husband, leaping out of the driving seat, grinning from ear to ear.

'Simon! What on earth…?'

'Like it?' Simon asked as he hugged and kissed her. 'Great to be home! I've missed you *so* much!'

'Not as much as I've missed you,' Tess said as she extricated herself from his embrace. 'But what's with the Land Rover? Where's the Stag?'

'I've left the Stag in Twickenham,' Simon replied. 'One of the sound engineers fell madly in love with it and wants to do it up. He offered me a ridiculous amount of money – an offer I *really* couldn't refuse. But I must admit I shed a tear. Still, I know it will be loved by this guy. Evan, he was called. Welsh.'

'But, where did *this* come from?' Tess ran her hand along the Land Rover's dusty blue bodywork. It looked lofty and rather forbidding after the Stag.

'Ah, yes, well.' Simon put his arm round her waist. 'The girl who was doing my make-up for the commercial was telling me all about her sister and family who're leaving to live in Australia. Apparently, the husband's landed a fantastic job and the company want him out there *pronto*! Like *yesterday*! So everything's had to be packed up and sold off double quick. And this motor, would you believe, was only used to ferry the two kids around. I ask you, in *London*! These people with their Chelsea tractors! It's a few years old but, look, it's built to last and it's almost immaculate apart from a few dents here and there. School parking, most likely. It all adds to the character, and what's a Land Rover without a few dents?'

'Wow!' exclaimed Tess, wondering how much of a hole in their budget this purchase had made.

'With what I'm getting paid for the commercials, plus what I got for the Stag, we should only be a thousand or so poorer,' Simon said airily.

A thousand or so, thought Tess. It was the 'or so' that worried her, particularly added on to what they'd paid for Windsor Castle, bearing in mind they couldn't afford to spend *anything* that didn't contribute to the costs of renovating the house. However, they did need sensible transport and this certainly looked sturdy.

'Hey!' he said, as he followed her into the kitchen. 'The cooker's installed! And you've got something cooking in there!'

'Yes – and yes,' Tess replied, and went on to tell him about her encounter with the Pengillys. 'I think we might ask Bob to do our electrics,' she concluded.

'They sound heaven sent,' declared Simon.

Bob Pengilly said he'd be delighted to do their electrics if they could wait another couple of weeks. And he'd try to get most of it done before Christmas. However, the plumbing was the next major job with two bedrooms waiting to be transformed into en suite bathrooms, plus a downstairs toilet – and now they'd decided to have a small en suite of their own installed in what was to become their bedroom. More drilling, more hammering, more dust.

Tess decided it would be a good idea to invite Gina and Bob down for coffee on the Sunday morning and hoped that Simon and Bob would get along. She thought they would.

They duly arrived, Gina producing a box of ginger snaps. 'We love them,' she said as she handed them to Tess. 'We dunk them in our tea, coffee, anything.'

And Tess was right. Simon and Bob struck up an immediate rapport, due in no small part to the fact that Bob was a TV addict and Simon had worked with several of the actors that Bob was particularly in awe of. In fact, it took some time before electrics were discussed at all. And, while the men were discussing TV, Gina was telling Tess that they had four sons, three of whom had moved away up to the South-East because there was little work in Cornwall. All except Denis, who was an electrician, too, and who lived 'up in Devon'. She made Devon sound like a foreign country and the South-East akin to the moon.

After a further half hour of constant chatter, Simon produced a bottle of wine and Tess made some cheese omelettes.

'We didn't mean for you to do all this,' Gina protested. 'We're having a roast later.'

'So are we, it's only a snack,' Tess said.

More chatter followed. Gina said that she and her brother had been born in Falmouth where their father was a boat builder and their Spanish-born mother had come to work as a chambermaid in one of the big hotels. Gina had married young, having met Bob at a dance in Truro, and had had countless cleaning jobs while the boys were growing up. 'If you ever need a hand round here…' she added.

Do I need a hand round here? Tess thought. I could do with an army of hands round here!

All in all it had been a very successful visit. And this was more like the new beginning she had been hoping for.

CHAPTER 8

A CORNISH CHRISTMAS EVE

Somewhere, at some time, Tess had a vague recollection of having said to Matt and Amber – and possibly Orla, too – something like, 'You must all come down to us for Christmas, see what we've saddled ourselves with!' In her innocence she'd been sure that most of the work would be well under way, if not finished, and she had visions of an enormous tree, laden country-style with little red apples and pine cones perhaps, and aglow with lights. Positioned, of course, by the French windows in the sitting room. Yes, the old windows would probably still be there but she'd made heavily lined and insulated curtains for those rooms and so, with the open fire, it would be cosy. That was what she'd thought.

What she'd actually got was a sitting room piled high with boxes and furniture, an icy draught wending its way in through the ill-fitting French windows, a kitchen without any units, and one freezing cold bathroom upstairs, with limited hot water and a great deal of dust.

At least Nick and Jim were finished, but Pong the plumber couldn't come back until after New Year and he couldn't specify a date. And good old Bob had done most of the downstairs wiring, including the kitchen, which was now ready for the units to be fitted. The units, too, would arrive sometime in the New Year. Therefore, until the work was completed, these two rear rooms remained packed with beds, boxes and assorted furniture.

So, when Matt rang up during the second week of December and casually asked, 'Are we still coming to you for Christmas?' Tess was taken aback.

'Well, the thing is,' she said, 'we're in a bit of a state here. Everyone's about to knock off for Christmas and we're left with a house without heat, without a kitchen and with only one antiquated bathroom.'

'But we need to see the "before" so that later we can rave about the "after". Come on, Mum, we don't mind roughing it for a few days.'

He might not mind but Tess didn't think Lisa would be particularly smitten with the idea. And there was no end of exposed brickwork and sharp edges where young children could come to grief.

'And Amber won't be coming,' Matt went on, 'because she and Peter are off to Thailand; Phuket, I think she said. And we could give Orla a lift down if you wanted.' Tess's mind was in a whirl and she could scarcely believe she was saying, 'Well, yes, of course, that would be lovely…' wondering what Simon would have to say and how they could cope with three extra adults and two young children.

She found Simon scraping the paint off the window of what was to become their bedroom.

'We need to replace some of this wood,' he said, 'half of it's rotten.'

'About Christmas,' Tess said, 'I've just had a call from Matt.'

'And,' Simon said, 'they all want to come down here?'

'However did you guess?'

'Because,' he replied, 'I can clearly remember you prattling on about lovely Cornish Christmases, huge Christmas trees, roaring fires – the whole nine yards. They do say you shouldn't advertise what you can't deliver.'

'And that's just it, Simon, we *can't* deliver!'

'Oh yes we can.' He laid down his paint scraper. 'The kitchen's functional, if not glamorous. This old dining room, which you're hell-bent on making into our bedroom, has a fireplace of sorts, so we could open that up, we could drag a couple of sofas through and, hey presto, we have a sitting room, albeit temporary.'

'But where are they all going to sleep?'

'They're spoilt for choice upstairs. I think the dust has pretty well settled now and there won't be much more until after Christmas. So we could put Matt and family in the one we originally chose for ourselves; after all, our big bed is still in there, and we can rig up something for the kids. And did you say Orla might come? Well, she could take her pick of the others, and we can move a divan up for her as well.'

Tess scratched her head. '*One* bathroom for *five* adults and *two* kids!'

'We used to manage perfectly well years ago,' Simon said, 'before we all became obsessed with having our own loos. And it's only for a few days, darling. It'll be fun! Tell you what, I'll quit the paint-scraping and go in search of a lovely big tree! How about that?'

*

Even Orla had seemed delighted at the prospect of a chaotic, chilly, Cornish Christmas.

'Both my boys are duty-bound to take turns to ask me over for Christmas Day,' she said to Tess on the phone, 'but one of them's away this year, and the one that isn't had me over last year, so I'd quite like to be able to say, "please don't bother because I'm going to Cornwall"!'

'You could live to regret that,' Tess said. 'Just bring plenty of warm clothing.'

She was aware that it was *her* family and friend who was coming, and so felt she had to offer some sort of invitation to Simon's son.

'Don't worry about Damien,' Simon said, 'I'd already suggested to him that he come down, but apparently he's spending the festive season with some girl he met in Coventry. Said he might pop down in the New Year, though.'

Well, Tess reckoned, that was a temporary relief at least.

Simon was as good as his word because, the very next morning, he set out and came back a couple of hours later with a tall, well-shaped tree, complete with roots. 'We can plant it out the rest of the year,' he said, 'and just bring it in for Christmas. It's going to look great in the hall.'

And, although the fire surround had been removed from the old dining room, they'd established that the flue was still functioning and Simon had discovered a rusty fire basket at the back of the garage which he'd cleaned up sufficiently for use temporarily. Meanwhile, Tess was doing her best to create the Christmas spirit by decorating the staircase with evergreen branches woven into the bannisters, boughs of holly, arrangements of ivy and mistletoe and lots of candles. She even managed to locate the box which contained the baubles and lights and so was able to decorate the tree properly – and had to admit that it looked very impressive indeed in the hallway.

Both Gina Pengilly and Annie in the pub recommended buying a turkey from Tremerron Farm at the top of the hill. Beautiful birds they were, and you could get most of your vegetables there, too. A quick trip to Tesco provided everything else. Suddenly, Tess began to feel excited. Matt and the family! Orla! So much to chat about, so much to catch up on! And Matt was right; they needed to see this house in its embryonic state to best appreciate the work done when it was finally complete, although Tess did sometimes wonder if that day would ever come.

As Matt's large estate car drew up outside Over and Above at 10 a.m. on Christmas Eve, Ellie was the first to come running to Tess and hurl herself into her grandmother's arms. 'I've *missed* you, Nana!' Then she beamed when she spotted the tree. 'That's the biggest tree *ever*!'

Next was Orla. 'Jaysus!' she said as she hugged Tess. 'Aren't you a million miles from anywhere!'

And then there was Matt, giving his mother a bear hug and saying, 'This is some place you've got yourselves here!'

Lisa, carrying a half-asleep Josh, was the last to come in. 'Rather you than me,' was all she said, her eyebrows arched high.

'Welcome, everyone! We'll start with the apologies,' Simon said, emerging from where he'd been fixing some skirting boards. 'Apologies for any dust we might have missed, for the lack of heating, for the barren bedrooms and for there being only one bathroom. *One!*

'So we must form orderly queues,' Matt quipped. Matt looked like his mother, with his green eyes and dark brown hair, but had inherited Gerry's height, which was six feet two inches.

'I've had to pee behind a tree before now,' Orla laughed. Tess realised how much she'd been missing Orla's unique laughter, which involved a sort of snort in the middle of a giggle.

'There's no furniture up here other than a couple of beds,' Tess said, as she ushered them into the two back bedrooms. 'We've brought a double up for Ellie and Josh because you said he'd outgrown the cot now.' But no one was listening as they were all glued to the windows gazing at the sea.

'That's some view!' Matt exclaimed.

'And this room will be lovely,' Lisa said, looking around with a critical eye. 'You'll make it nice, Tess.'

Tess was relieved; Lisa was the one she thought would not enjoy roughing it. But of course it was early days yet.

They'd set off at 5 a.m. in the hope of avoiding a last-minute Christmas rush to the West Country and so Josh, who'd been asleep for most of the journey, suddenly came alive and began running around the room and jumping on and off both beds.

'And watch *him*,' Tess added, 'because there are no end of places where he could hurt himself.'

She then explained that the empty adjoining rooms were about to become en suite bathrooms and showed them the existing bathroom where the only shower was a hand-held one attached to the roll-top bath.

They'd arrived laden with presents, which they spread out under the tree, all over the hall floor. Both Lisa and Orla unloaded a mountain of groceries in the already packed kitchen; enough to feed a regiment: soups, pâtés, panettone, stollen, shortbread, mince pies. And bottles and bottles of champagne, Prosecco and wine. And, the *pièce de résistance*, Orla had made her Christmas pudding. She was famous for her Christmas pudding, which she claimed was from an ancient secret Irish recipe, the details of which she flatly refused to divulge.

Then everyone congregated in the kitchen to admire the cooker standing in solitary splendour, surrounded by an assortment of old tables and cupboards. No one wanted a cooked breakfast, just bacon sandwiches and lots of hot drinks. The children, in the meantime, chased each other round the hallway with regular forays into the kitchen.

Tess was relieved to see that they'd all taken her advice and were wearing several layers of clothing. The electric convector heater had been plugged in all morning, but it was a large room and the door was frequently open or ajar.

'You don't need to make a decision as to what you're going to wear each day,' Simon said, 'because you wear *everything*.'

Matt had gone off with Simon to see the work in progress and what still had to be done outside, while Tess explained to Orla and Lisa how they hoped to finish off downstairs. She showed them briefly into the rear rooms stacked high with assorted furniture and boxes, and as she opened each door she could feel the cold draught sneaking its way in through the French windows.

'Well, I think you're both nuts,' Orla summarised as, back in the kitchen, they sat round the table with mugs of hot coffee. 'You'd have to be nuts to be doing all this in your twenties or thirties, but in your *sixties*…!'

'But we love it, Orla! And, honestly, you're seeing it at its worst at the worst time of year. You come back next summer and you won't think we're mad then!'

Orla snorted.

'I can see the potential,' Lisa said, 'but then you'll be slaving away looking after guests. How will you ever get a break? Catering's a full-time job.'

Tess produced a bottle of brandy and poured a generous measure into each of their coffees.

'We're only letting four rooms,' she said, taking a sip. 'They'll be here for a minimum of two or three weeks and hope we may persuade them to stay longer. We're advertising it as a retreat, somewhere to come to get away from it all. We'll do breakfast and dinner, with lunch available as an extra, on request. Simon'll share the cooking with me and I'm hoping to have some help with the cleaning, if money permits.'

'What about their washing if they're here for weeks on end?' asked Orla.

'Well,' Tess replied, 'we'll obviously do the bedlinen and towels each day but we're having two washing machines installed through there in what we now call the laundry room, along with a tumble dryer and an ironing board, so they can do their own personal things. I'm also putting hand-wash detergent in each bathroom so they can wash out their smalls.'

'So, where are you two going to be sleeping?' Lisa asked.

'Oh, we're in Windsor Castle. We've got quite used to it now.'

There was a brief silence, broken by Orla, who asked, 'Did you say *Windsor Castle*?'

'Ah, that's our little caravan,' Tess replied quickly, 'delivered by a couple of giants called the Windsor Brothers.'

Just then there came a wailing from the hallway, and Ellie burst in to say Josh had fallen over, which necessitated Lisa having to rush to his aid and Orla to add some extra brandy to her coffee.

'You'll like Portmerryn, Orla,' Tess said hopefully. 'Matt and Lisa were talking about taking the children for a walk along the beach and you must go with them. You'll need fresh air after that long drive.'

'There's quite enough fresh air in here for me,' Orla said, as the door swung open yet again. 'Let's you and me catch up on the gossip, beside that fire you were talking about!'

Simon escorted Matt and family down to the beach and, Tess suspected, an introduction to the pub. She was glad to have some time with Orla to catch up on the news.

'This is more like it!' Orla proclaimed as she lowered her bottom onto the chair nearest the fire. 'Jaysus, this reminds me of Christmases when we were kids: cold house, one fire, the mammy yelling at us to put on our paper hats and come eat in the kitchen! What was yours like?'

Tess had recollections of herself and her sister, Barbara, in their best dresses, sitting primly at the table for Christmas lunch while their father thanked the Lord for what they were about to receive. It was always cold because there was no central heating, the one-bar electric fire only warming the cat, who wisely plonked herself in front of it. No, in retrospect, Tess decided this was definitely more relaxed, if not a great deal warmer.

'How's Ricky?' Tess asked as they sat down.

'Oh, he's fine. He's actually working today. And going to his sister's tomorrow, and wanted me to go, too but, do you know what? That woman has *six* kids and they run around screaming like banshees. Then he said something about coming down here with me and I said, "No, thank you very much," because I need a break from him. I'll have a drop more of that coffee, please.'

Orla had met Ricky a couple of years previously on the same Internet dating site which had produced only a series of disasters for Tess. Ricky was the proud owner of a large articulated truck in which he transported anything and everything to every corner of the UK. He'd now become the owner of a second truck, which necessitated employing another driver and having someone to 'do the books' which, of course, was Orla.

The relationship suited Orla, who wasn't looking for any sort of permanency; she was completely happy with her own company, and her two days a week selling hats, while he was away.

'Like I said, Ricky's fine,' Orla said. 'And how's the thespian?'

'The thespian's doing his best to charm half of Cornwall,' Tess replied.

Orla rolled her eyes. 'Good luck to him. And how are *you* coping with Cornwall?'

'Put it this way,' Tess said, 'we came to live here just as the weather changed so we've had lots of wind and rain, and we're living in the caravan because the house is being knocked to bits, and I'm missing you guys like hell!'

'Oh,' said Orla.

'But,' Tess continued, 'when the sun comes out and we walk along the beach, or climb to the cliff top, or even just look out of our windows at the sea and the surf, there's nowhere else I'd rather be. The natives are friendly and helpful, most of them, anyway. And the rush hour in Seagull Hill consists of the Pengillys driving up or down the hill to work, or our workmen hurtling up the drive.'

Orla warmed her hands at the fire. 'Well, it certainly sounds different. Reminds me a little of home.'

'Reminds me of my old home in some ways, too. When I think how desperate I was to leave boring old Strathcoy and head for the bright lights of London! Now it's gone full circle, and I'm relishing the peace and quiet of rural living again.'

'We must be getting old,' Orla muttered, 'although I don't think I'm ready to be put out to grass yet.'

'Would you ever consider going back to Ireland?'

Orla shook her still-dark head. 'I've been away too long. I love going back to see everyone but a couple of weeks is more than enough. Particularly when the priest comes knocking on the door saying, "I haven't seen you at Mass since you got back, Orla O'Malley!" I haven't been an O'Malley for forty years! They *never* let you go! Jaysus, I was on the next flight back!'

Tess laughed. 'Well, we don't have that problem in Cornwall. And I can't wait for the house to be finished so you can come for a proper visit. I miss you, you know.'

Orla grinned, her blue eyes crinkling. 'Yeah, I miss you, too. We had some good times, didn't we? I miss our shop and the miracles we used to make with those flattering dresses. Did I tell you it's now called Contact and they're selling mobile phones?'

'Times change,' Tess said sadly. 'Shall I make more coffee? Another shot of brandy?'

'Yes, please. And I have another grandson,' Orla went on. 'Makes five altogether. At least none of them were born in the middle of a wedding!' She was referring to the fact that Lisa had given birth to Josh in the middle of Amber's wedding, something that was as unlikely as meeting the man of your dreams at the same event. It had been, to put it mildly, an unforgettable occasion.

'I don't think there'll be any more grandchildren for me,' Tess said. 'Matt and Lisa don't plan on having any more now that they've got one of each, and Amber admits to not being very maternal. She loves her job so much; she's been nominated a couple of times for an award as the best make-up artist.'

'Good for her,' said Orla. 'Anyway, she must be pushing forty so why would she be wanting a squalling infant at this age?'

'She's only thirty-six,' Tess protested. 'But you're right, she doesn't want one. And there she is on yet another luxury holiday, so who could blame her?'

'Who indeed?' Orla agreed. 'What about the fearful Damien, or whatever his name is?'

'Fortunately, he's shacked up with some girl in Coventry at the moment, but he's threatening to come down in the New Year sometime.'

As always Tess tried to think kindly of Damien, and offered up thanks for her own two successful offspring, neither of them having had the private education or the money spent on them that Damien had. Damien's downfall had been drugs, and these were in plentiful supply in the murky one-night-stand world of the second-rate pop group.

'Simon says Damien's thinking of going solo,' Tess said. 'So who knows?'

'Sure, nobody's perfect,' said Orla.

When everyone returned some time later they'd all had drinks and crisps and, Simon said, he'd even had the forethought to line them all up at the pub toilets before they came back, 'Knowing our limited facilities,' he added.

As they gathered in the makeshift sitting room, Ellie asked anxiously, 'Will Father Christmas know that we're here and not at home?'

'Of course he will,' said Matt. 'Father Christmas knows everything.'

Ellie still looked doubtful, a frown appearing under her blonde fringe.

'In fact,' Matt went on, 'it'll be easier for him here because he can come straight down the chimney and not have to battle his way round the log burner like he would at home.'

This seemed to satisfy the six-year-old Ellie, but both children remained in a state of feverish excitement, willing the hours away so they could hang up their stockings. Lisa explained that Santa would probably unload most of his goodies in the hall, around the tree, but that they could each have a stocking upstairs beside their bed, and he'd leave a few things up there for them, too, so that they'd have something to open first thing.

Tess prepared an early supper of a lamb casserole with mountains of vegetables and potatoes, washed down with great quantities of wine, and followed by mince pies. Everyone was ready for an early night, after they formed a stately queue to visit the toilet and have a quick wash.

As they settled down to sleep in Windsor Castle, Simon said, 'I wonder what it'll be like in the morning?'

'Probably chaotic!' Tess said happily, excited for the first time in years at the prospect of a family Christmas.

CHAPTER 9

A CORNISH CHRISTMAS DAY

At seven o'clock on Christmas morning, as Tess pulled back the curtains in Windsor Castle, she espied Orla roaming around outside in her nightie and dressing-gown. She opened the outside door and called out, 'Orla?'

'Merry Christmas!' Orla shouted cheerfully. 'Just trying to find somewhere to pee!'

'Do you mean to say,' Tess said, stifling a yawn, 'that the bathroom is permanently occupied at this hour?'

'No,' Orla said, as she came in, 'it isn't. But your dear little grandson decided to swing backwards and forwards on the pull-chain which has, of course, broken off. It's a holy miracle he didn't bring the whole cistern down. Now no one can flush the damned thing.'

'What's all the fuss?' asked a bleary-eyed Simon as he shuffled along from the bedroom.

'Merry Christmas to you, too,' Orla said. 'Please can I use your chemical toilet?'

While Orla used their makeshift conveniences Tess explained the problem to Simon.

'Dear Lord,' he sighed.

Josh had had a *Guardians of the Galaxy* costume in his stocking which, at the crack of dawn, he'd insisted on putting on because he wanted to see if he could fly. With his parents both half asleep he'd launched himself at the chain dangling in the bathroom and, on one of his more daring manoeuvres, the chain had collapsed on top of him, causing some wailing on his part, and a lot of swearing from everyone else.

'I'm really sorry,' Matt muttered when Simon, still in his pyjamas and dressing-gown, appeared with a stepladder and a length of rope. 'The little devil sneaked through unbeknown to us. Ellie was supposed to be keeping an eye on him.' At this Ellie started wailing, too.

Tess watched as Simon climbed up the steps with the rope. And then Orla appeared. 'No need to go hanging yourself!' she said cheerfully.

'Very funny,' said Simon from the top of the ladder as he attached the rope to what remained of the chain and directed his gaze at a still blubbering Josh. 'Do not as much as *touch* this rope, Josh! Do you *understand*?'

Josh nodded while hiding his face in the folds of his mother's dressing-gown. Tess looked with disbelief at the trail of toys, games and wrapping paper strewn across every floor.

'He woke us up at half past four,' Matt informed his mother, 'to show us what Father Christmas had brought.'

'He's always been trouble,' Lisa said, 'ever since he arrived in the middle of Amber's wedding.'

Tess headed towards the kitchen, wading her way through the hallway, the floor of which was already covered in half-opened presents and toys, some of them amazingly large. The plan was to have a massive fry-up for breakfast, accompanied by Buck's Fizzes and then aim on having lunch mid-afternoon. As she plugged in the convector heater she heard the toilet flush upstairs, so Simon's rope must have done the trick. And both children were now running round the hallway and opening yet more presents, scattering wrapping paper with gay abandon.

Simon appeared, still in his pyjamas. 'I'm going to wash at the kitchen sink,' he announced, 'so that the bathroom is free for our visitors.'

Tess sighed as she prepared the turkey for the oven. 'Simon, you'll have to get out of my way because I need to stuff this bird,' she said.

Lisa had come down to oversee the chaos in the hallway and to help Josh unwrap his main present: a small blue tricycle, which caused screams of delight. 'He asked Father Christmas for that,' Ellie informed Tess, 'and I was worried he might not be able to get it down the chimney. 'Cos it's quite big.'

'It certainly is,' Tess agreed, wondering how much further chaos he might manage to create on three wheels. Ellie was sitting on the hall floor playing with a large doll's house which Matt and Simon had spent the previous evening fitting together with a great deal of brandy and swearing. Tess went back into the kitchen to finish stuffing the turkey, and found Simon was standing naked at the sink.

Then Orla arrived on the scene. 'Oh my God!' she exclaimed, sighting Simon.

'Cover your eyes, Orla! I think we might need Buck's Fizz,' Tess said. 'Can you do the honours?' She directed Orla to the glasses on the shelf and the relevant bottles positioned in the fridge.

Simon tied his towel round his waist to protect his modesty and grinned at Orla. 'Let me wish you Merry Christmas, my treasure!'

'Not until you've put your clothes on,' Orla retorted as she opened a bottle of Moët. 'Am I supposed to be impressed or something?'

'Yes,' Simon replied, 'you are. But try to control your lust because my dear wife is here watching us.' He gently smacked Tess's bottom, stuck his feet into his mules, and set off for Windsor Castle.

As Lisa came back into the kitchen she said, 'Apparently we're flushed with success upstairs. I've had a quick shower with that hand-held attachment in the bath, and now Matt's doing the same. Is that a Buck's Fizz I see?'

'It is,' said Orla, handing her a glass.

Half an hour later, Amber Skyped. 'Hi, everyone! Happy Christmas!' said this suntanned vision in a bright pink bikini, clutching what appeared to be some sort of exotic cocktail.

'Wish you could be here,' Tess said sincerely. Then, looking round the kitchen, added, 'You might not agree.'

'Well, that would be nice,' said Amber, 'but it's cocktail time here and I've just had a lovely swim. The sea is like a warm bath. How's it with you?'

'Freezing!' Simon hollered. 'Sea's freezing, we're freezing and your nephew has just buggered up our one and only loo.'

'Sorry I'm missing all the excitement,' Amber said, raising her glass, 'but I'd still like to be with you.'

It was about ten o'clock before everyone was dressed and congregated round the kitchen table. Tess and Simon were cooking batches of bacon, sausages and eggs, Orla was in charge of baked beans and mushrooms, and Lisa was making a pile of toast. Almost everyone was on their second Buck's Fizz by the time they sat down to eat.

Josh refused to be parted from his tricycle and Lisa attempted to spoon some food into him each time he circumnavigated the table. Ellie wanted to help, and was allowed to remove the empty plates, one by one, and stack them in the dishwasher.

Simon had got the fire going in the room across the hall, and had placed a fireguard in front of it, fearful of Josh's apparent lack of any sense of danger. 'Time to open presents,' he announced hopefully.

Orla came into the kitchen, having been upstairs, and said, 'That daughter-in-law of yours has been in that bathroom for a good ten minutes.'

'Some things take time,' Tess said, checking on the turkey.

'Not this much time,' snapped Orla. 'I bet she's beautifying herself in there in front of the one and only mirror.'

Tess realised she hadn't thought of that. The mirrors were still wrapped in cardboard and stacked away somewhere, and she should really have thought to lean one against the wall in each of the bedrooms. Perhaps she'd do it later, if she ever had a moment to herself. When Lisa eventually emerged from the bathroom Orla hotfooted it in there with exaggerated sighs of relief. In the meantime, Simon and Matt were conferring as to whether or not they should organise everyone to have a walk – after they'd opened their presents.

'Spectacular views from the top of the cliff,' Simon said. 'It's worth the climb, and at least it's not raining. Not sure about the kids.'

'Well, I can carry Josh on my shoulders,' Matt said, looking around. 'Where is he anyway?'

Somehow or another Josh had managed to open the door to the rear sitting room and was merrily riding at speed round the piled-up furniture and boxes.

'Dear God,' Simon said, 'if he knocked that lot over he'd be squashed to bits.' With some difficulty Josh was persuaded to abandon this new race track, and threatened with removal of the tricycle altogether if he went anywhere near these rooms again.

'I'll take him outside,' Matt said. 'He can whizz around on the terrace.'

Simon sighed. 'Just don't let him topple over that wall!'

Present opening was sporadic with everyone coming and going and then discovering something else labelled for them and coming back in again. Tess had a beautiful black cashmere sweater from Simon, which she was desperate to wear there and then, but didn't dare in case she spilled something on it. She'd given Simon the electric drill he'd been going on about, and she gave Orla a year's subscription to *Vogue*.

Orla presented her with a length of beautiful bronze-coloured raw silk. 'That's for you to make something lovely for yourself,' she said, 'so you don't waste all your expertise on curtain making.'

'It's beautiful, Orla, thank you.' Tess held up the silk and wondered briefly if she'd ever have the time again to make anything for herself. Perhaps next winter, when there was no sanding down to be done, no painting, no decorating, no curtain making. Would that day ever come?

An hour later they all straggled their way up Penhennon cliff.

'Wish we hadn't eaten so much breakfast,' Matt remarked as, with Josh astride his shoulders, he made his way carefully up the steep path.

It was a dry day, mostly cloudy but with occasional appearances from the sun. And when the sun did appear the sea glittered, the birds sang, and it could almost have been spring. Tess and Orla brought up the rear of the little procession, Ellie swinging between them.

'You didn't tell me this was so steep,' bleated Orla.

'You get used to it,' Tess replied. 'Anyway, if you'd known it was steep I'd never have got you out of the house, would I? And you need fresh air.'

'It's all right for you, you've kept the weight off after our stint at Slim Chance,' Orla puffed. 'And this view had better be good.'

Each time Tess made it to the top she was enchanted again by the panorama of rocky coastline with cliffs stretching all the way from Hartland Point in the north – with the silhouette of Lundy Island on the horizon – and right the way down to Trevose Head in the south. Fortunately, today it was clear enough to see most of it: the Atlantic rollers crashing against the overhanging cliffs, the coves with their stretches of sand, the crying of the ever-circling seagulls. Even Orla said, 'Wow!' and grudgingly admitted that it was probably worth her aching legs and gasping lungs. 'Another few yards and I'd be needing an oxygen tent,' she informed everyone.

'I believe Jed's open today,' Simon said, looking round at everyone hopefully. 'I could murder a pint of Doom Bar, just,' he added hastily, 'so we have an excuse to use their loo.'

There were murmured agreements as they all began their descent. Tess had never, in her entire life, seen so many people so obsessed with finding a toilet. For decades one bathroom per family had been the norm for the lucky families who didn't have to troop down to some makeshift privy at the foot of the garden. She could well remember her sister monopolising their bathroom when they were teenagers and her father hammering at the door shouting, 'What in the name of goodness are you *doing* in there?'

Jed had boasted that he opened up every day of the year, including Christmas Day, and sure enough he'd opened up. The fire in The Portmerryn Arms was blazing merrily, Annie had positioned an artificial tree close to the window, liberally adorned with tinsel, and Jed was even offering mulled wine, 'for the ladies, like.' The normal four domino players rattled away in the corner, with their pints of beer, as they did every day of the year. Simon and Matt had their pints of Doom Bar, the ladies sipped the mulled wine, and everyone used the toilet. They then headed back up the hill to continue their festivities at home.

It was almost four o'clock when they sat down to Christmas lunch. There was a smoked salmon starter followed by the turkey, which was succulent and delicious, with all the trimmings: roast potatoes, roasted winter vegetables, pigs-in-blankets and sprouts. Nobody really liked sprouts very much but all agreed it wouldn't be Christmas without the damned things. And Orla's Christmas pudding went down a treat. Even Josh was persuaded to sit at the table for a short time before demanding to be reunited with his precious tricycle, amid strict instructions to stay in the hallway, not to open any doors, keep away from the fire, and not scoot around the kitchen colliding with everyone's chairs while they were trying to eat.

It was while they were in the middle of Christmas pudding, in a state of great merriment fuelled by gallons of alcohol, that the crash occurred.

A very, very loud resounding crash. Followed by howling.

'What the…?' Matt and Lisa both rushed out into the hallway, followed closely by Tess and Simon.

The Christmas tree had crashed onto the floor, tinsel and baubles scattered from one end of the hall to the other. And, lying on the floor, the tricycle having fallen over, was Josh, yelling at full volume, '*Naughty* tree!'

As Simon and Matt heaved the tree back up into some sort of upright position, Lisa attended to her tiny screaming son. There was chaos as everyone rushed to retrieve some of the scattered baubles.

'How could a tiny boy like this knock over a thundering great tree like that?' Simon asked. 'I had it firmly in the pot.'

'I don't know,' Matt said. 'He's a one-man demolition squad. I'm so terribly sorry.'

'Perhaps he needs to have a nap?' Orla asked hopefully.

As Lisa wiped the last of his tears away she said, 'I think it might be better all round if he were to skip his nap and go to bed early so we can have some sort of civilised evening.'

Matt insisted on tidying up the hall, clearing the floor of spilled earth, assorted toys and torn wrapping paper. Both children – having exhausted themselves with their new toys and having been up since the early hours – were persuaded to go to bed at seven o'clock, Josh demanding that the precious tricycle was positioned near his bed so he could see it. As Lisa came downstairs she reported that both had fallen asleep almost immediately and she'd brought the tricycle downstairs again just in case Josh might wake up and take off on the wretched thing to do further damage.

Tess had laid out a cold food table, including seafood, a large ham and assorted salad, in the kitchen, and invited everyone to help themselves as and when they felt like it. Orla, carried away by the success of her pudding, now insisted on making Irish coffees. 'Shall we play charades?' she asked. There were groans all round.

'Listen, if it's good enough for the Queen it's good enough for us,' she persisted.

With that she began to make some weird arm movements, after informing everyone it was a book.

'Why are you making L-signs and V-signs and crosses?' Simon asked.

Orla shook her head and began again, ending up with pointing at the ceiling.

'We give up,' Lisa said wearily. Everyone agreed with much nodding.

'*Fifty Shades of Grey*!' Orla said triumphantly.

'How could *that* be *Fifty Shades of Grey*?' Tess asked.

'Because you're all thick as planks,' said Orla. 'Now, look…' She made some more elaborate V-signs and Xs. 'Five multiplied by ten, Roman numerals, equals fifty. Or L, which I think also stands for fifty. Honestly! It's *so* easy! And I'm looking up at the grey sky.'

'You're looking up at a white ceiling,' said Matt.

'Which I've just painted,' added Tess.

'You have no imaginations,' said Orla. 'I'll do another one. A song.' She then began to prance round the room waving her arms, followed by pointing at her bottom, and then grabbing an apple from the fruit bowl.

'That's cheating,' said Simon. 'You're not allowed to use props.'

'I'm *not* cheating!' Orla roared.

'So, it's something to do with an apple?' Tess asked.

Orla nodded and made a large circle with her hands.

'A *round* apple?' Lisa suggested.

Orla shook her head and re-enacted the entire ritual.

'A *big* apple?' asked Tess, to which Orla nodded enthusiastically.

'So, a song about New York?' Matt said. More nodding. '"New York, New York"?'

Orla shook her head and sighed. 'Think Christmas!' she ordered. 'Didn't you see I was being a fairy, waving my wand?'

'No,' they replied in unison.

'And pointing to my tail? "*Fairytale* of New York" – got it? You really are a bunch of thickos.'

This caused much giggling all round.

'Tell you what, Orla,' Simon said, 'stick with making the Irish coffees! We'd all like another one, wouldn't we?'

With some sighing and eye-rolling, Orla headed for the kitchen. 'Not a brain between you,' she muttered. 'Anyway, how can I make proper Irish coffee when you've only got Scotch?'

'Well, we weren't aware of your great talent,' Simon said. 'I promise we'll get some of the Jameson next time – or do you prefer Bushmills?'

'Bushmills,' Orla said, 'and until then I'll just have to make do.' She sighed as they lined up with their glasses. 'I'll just have to use more of it.'

By nine o'clock everyone was pleasantly pickled, tales had been told of Christmases past, terrible in-laws, terrible presents, disastrous food.

'But this one's been fun,' Matt said, 'if a little weird.'

'Not weird, just our first Cornish Christmas,' said Tess.

'Josh will never be allowed to forget it,' Lisa said, laughing.

'We'll incorporate it into his wedding speech,' said Matt.

By ten o'clock both Orla and Simon were fast asleep by the fire and Tess was struggling to keep her eyes open.

'We'd better let these old folks get to bed,' Matt said.

'It's been a long day,' Lisa said, yawning.

By eleven o'clock everyone was asleep.

No one got up early on Boxing Day; even the children slept until nearly nine o'clock. Josh demanded to know where his tricycle was, and was apparently given all sorts of dire warnings as to what might happen if he even *thought* about going downstairs until they were all up and dressed.

Matt decided they should head home in the evening because he had to be at work the next day, and Lisa the day after, when the au pair was due to come back on an early flight from Munich.

'If we set off around five we should be home by nine or ten,' he said. Seeing his mother's face fall, he added, 'But we'll come back, just as soon as you're open for business. And we'll rent one of those fisherman's cottages where the fishermen *don't* live – right?'

It had been a lovely Christmas, Tess reckoned, even if a little chaotic at times. She'd miss the children, too, particularly Ellie.

'I love it here with you, Nana,' Ellie said.

'When you're a little bit bigger you can come often, and even spend the summer here.'

'Oh, I'd *love* that! But *not* Josh, Nana.'

'No, perhaps not for a few years,' Tess agreed.

'He can't help being like that,' Ellie explained sadly. 'He's a *boy*.'

'That explains a lot,' Tess agreed.

They had a lazy day, eating up the mountains of food, and drinking very little. The three 'oldies' indulged in some lunchtime wine; Matt and Lisa stuck to water.

The afternoon was spent sitting by the fire, drinking cups of tea, entertaining the children. Josh was less boisterous today, and kept well away from the tree with his three wheels.

Later, as their car disappeared down the drive, everyone waving out of the windows, Tess wiped a tear from her eye.

Simon put his arm round her. 'It's been a lovely Christmas, darling – and we won't need to buy any food for weeks!'

CHAPTER 10

DISASTER

On 7 January, at two o'clock in the afternoon, Simon Sparrow fell off the ladder while attempting to paint one of the front bedroom windows. Tess heard the crash as she herself was painting the kitchen ceiling and nearly fell off her own stepladder with the fright. As she dashed out the front door, she found Simon, liberally splashed in white paint, trying to get up and clutching his arm, groaning in agony.

'Oh my God! Are you all right?'

'No,' said Simon, ashen-faced, 'I am not.'

Pong Parker had also witnessed the accident from upstairs and had dashed down to assist Tess in trying to get Simon to his feet. 'Thought I saw a bleedin' sparra flying past,' he quipped.

'Do you think you've broken anything?' Tess asked anxiously as they got him standing.

'Yes, my bloody arm,' groaned Simon, clutching his right elbow with his left hand. 'And my ankle...' He limped a few steps leaving footprints of white paint all over the stone. The plumber grabbed the paint pot which had crashed to the ground along with Simon.

Fortunately it had been almost empty but had still succeeded in splashing both Simon and more of the stonework.

Tess noted the side of his face and his hand were also badly grazed. 'We've got to get you to the hospital,' she said, 'after we've got those overalls off, and your shoes.'

Simon refused to stop clutching his elbow and groaned in pain as Tess rushed to get some scissors and cut away the overalls round the sleeve. He stood shivering in his sweater and jeans while Tess fetched his coat and then drove the Land Rover, parked just a few yards away, to where Simon was leaning against the wall by the front door. Pong and Tess, with difficulty, got him into the front seat and off Tess sped to the local clinic-cum-cottage-hospital ten miles away.

The X-ray confirmed that he'd broken his lower arm in two places but not his ankle, which was only badly sprained. He'd hit his head, too, and had to spend the night in hospital while they checked him for concussion. He'd need to go to Plymouth to have the bones set and the arm plastered but they'd take him by ambulance. Tess was advised to go home as there was little point in her going to Plymouth, but she should check next morning and, if he was all right, she'd be able to drive him home. Poor Simon! He must be in such pain! Furthermore, it was going to delay much of the work he was doing, the window-painting being just one of a long list of jobs that needed to be done. Tess sighed; at times life appeared to be one step forward, two steps back.

The following morning Tess was informed that he was ready to go home and so off she set for Plymouth.

'Six bloody weeks!' he ranted, as Tess drove him home. 'I'm not going to be able to do anything for six bloody weeks!'

Simon was not a good patient. He limped around the house, the arm in a sling, feeling very sorry for himself and continually getting under Tess's feet.

'Just sit down, darling,' she said, exhausted from hours of cleaning the paint off the stonework at the front. 'Relax! Read a book or something.'

'How can I relax,' he wailed, 'when there's so much work to be done round here? Who the hell's going to do it?'

In the end Gideon from the pub very kindly offered to finish off repairing and painting the upstairs windows while Tess concentrated on downstairs. Gideon didn't say much but he was very obliging. Tess learned that he had a brother, Michael, who'd left home years ago and had a little bar in Penzance. Gideon visited him occasionally but had no wish to leave Portmerryn. Had he ever had a girlfriend? Gideon shook his head and blushed some more. He was painfully shy, which was a great shame, Tess thought, because he was a good-looking guy and he was *nice*. Some woman would be lucky to have him.

The plumbers, Pong and Pip, had come back to resume work on 9 January. They were always cheerful, whistled while they worked and told incessant jokes to anyone who would listen. At Tess's insistence the first job they were asked to do was install the toilet and shower in their bedroom and a toilet in the laundry room before starting upstairs. This, of course, caused more hammering and more dust with the added delight of the water being turned off at regular intervals. Meanwhile Simon attempted to paint the new dining room wall with his left hand and succeeded mainly in dripping paint over the floor.

Then he hit on a new idea. 'I'm going to set up a website for our business,' he announced. At least he could sit down, out of the way, to do that. The trouble was that they really needed photographs of the interior rooms which were nowhere near completion. So he concentrated on the ones they'd taken outside when they first arrived, highlighting the views and explaining that restoration work was in progress and that this boutique guesthouse would be available for a minimum of two-week lets from 1 May.

'We aren't going to be able to open for Easter,' Simon sighed. 'There's far too much work still to be done.'

This was a setback indeed. 'We need the money,' Tess said. 'But perhaps we can get enough bookings and deposits to keep us going.' Otherwise, she thought, we'll be going to the bank for a loan, cap in hand, which was something they desperately wanted to avoid doing.

Tess felt cheered when, at the end of the month, the kitchen units finally arrived and were fitted free of charge by the supplier. It had been a dull, grey month with little or no sunshine and Simon complaining constantly. He couldn't sleep at night because of the pain in his arm and, on one occasion, Tess had inadvertently flung one of her own arms, in her sleep, directly onto the fracture. Chaos ensued with Simon insisting that he must sleep *alone* until such time as the pain subsided. This meant her decamping to one of the divans in what would become the new dining room at the rear.

Tess consoled herself by enjoying her newly fitted, newly painted kitchen with its new Shaker-style units. Better still, her washing machine, dryer and freezer had now been installed in their correct places, along with the new loo and shower in their new bedroom.

'Time to move out of Windsor Castle,' Simon said, 'and bring our nice big bed downstairs.'

They hadn't lit the fire in there again as the room had to be painted and made ready. They chose a pale yellow for the walls, in an effort to make the room feel warmer since it, like the kitchen, faced east. Tess found a clothes rail in a second-hand shop, which she installed at one end of this new bedroom. It would have to do for now, but perhaps one day they might be able to afford a wall of built-in wardrobes. One day.

Pong and Pip plus their apprentice were now hard at work upstairs, as was Bob Pengilly, who was adding a few extra power points. All in all it was a slow, laborious business and Tess felt exhausted with the endless clearing up, painting, ferrying Simon around as well as shopping, cleaning and washing. At least the tank for the central heating oil had arrived and was sited a few feet from the back door.

And then Damien phoned.

Simon cleared his throat and said, 'Thing is, Tess, he needs somewhere to unwind and practise, get a repertoire together and all that. He's really keen now on going solo.'

Tess knew what was coming.

'I mean,' Simon continued, 'it's not as if we have guests yet or anything. Heaven knows we have plenty of space.'

'And a house full of workmen,' Tess added.

'He won't care, darling. He'll have his sleeping bag and he'll doss down anywhere. After all, he's used to sleeping on the bus, in squats, any old place. It will only be for a week or so and then he'll be heading back to London.'

Tess knew she could hardly refuse.

'On one condition,' she said. '*No* drugs! If he has to smoke or sniff or snort or whatever he does with the bloody things then he does it somewhere else: on the cliff top, in the woods, anywhere he likes but not, repeat *not*, in this house!'

'I knew you'd understand,' Simon said, kissing her on the cheek. 'He'll be no trouble.'

He'd hitched all the way from London to Launceston, Damien said, and there didn't seem to be any way of getting to Portmerryn from there. No bus, no train, he moaned, what sort of a place were they living in, for God's sake? So could someone please come and pick him up? Tess downed tools and set off, with Simon in the passenger seat, for Launceston.

'He's come at just the right time,' said Simon, 'to be able to help you with the painting and everything.'

Well, that'll be a first, thought Tess.

They found Damien, with a girl, leaning against the war memorial in the main square. Both wore tight jeans, black leather jackets, and both had backpacks. Damien also had his guitar slung over his shoulder.

'What the…?' Tess muttered as she had to double park to pull up alongside.

'Hi, Dad!' Damien yelled cheerfully. 'I see you've been in the wars! Hi, Tess!'

Simon had leaped out with some amazing agility and embraced his son with his good left arm, while Tess, afraid of blocking the traffic, remained in the driving seat, staring at the girl.

'This is Liz,' Damien added. 'She's come along for the ride.'

Come along for the ride! What are we supposed to do with *her?* Tess wondered.

Damien and Liz had clambered into the rear seats, having deposited their belongings into the back. Simon, now sitting in the passenger seat again, was beaming ear to ear.

'And where do you hail from, Liz?' he asked cheerfully as Tess pulled out into the traffic.

Tess studied what she could see of Liz in the rear-view mirror. Thin-faced, piercings, nose studs, long dark hair, gum chewing.

'Southend,' replied Liz. 'Essex, like.'

'Oh,' said Tess, 'and how did you two meet?'

'Liz has a great voice,' Damien replied. 'We met at a gig in Farnborough.'

'Farnham,' corrected Liz.

'Whatever.' Damien yawned. After a minute he asked, 'What's the music scene like down here?'

'No idea,' replied Simon. 'Tess and I haven't got round to attending any gigs yet, have we, Tess?'

'No,' Tess replied through gritted teeth, 'we haven't.'

As they headed back towards Portmerryn the heavens opened. Tess switched on the windscreen wipers and stared gloomily out at the bare hedges and leafless trees forming intricate patterns against the ever-darkening sky. It wasn't her favourite time of year but there was a certain stark beauty in the countryside on a day like this.

'What a godforsaken place!' said Liz.

Tess's blood began to boil. She had to stop herself saying, 'Well, nobody asked you to come here,' when Simon said, 'Oh, but it's so beautiful in summer, Liz, and when the sun shines. Just wait until you get that first glimpse of the ocean!'

As luck would have it the grey sky merged with the grey sea in a grey haze and the ocean was completely indistinguishable. Their visitors appeared unimpressed, even when they finally arrived down on the coast road.

'That's our local pub,' Simon informed them as they drove past The Portmerryn Arms.

'Cool,' said Damien.

'They have gigs there?' asked Liz.

Tess tried to imagine Jed and Annie and the domino-playing locals swaying around to rock and punk.

'Not as a rule,' Simon replied, grinning at Tess.

As they turned up Seagull Hill, over the now barely noticeable potholes, Over and Above became just about visible through the bare trees. Simon said, 'That's us!'

Tess drove up the drive and parked next to the plumber's van.

'Bloody hell, Dad!' Damien exclaimed as he clambered out of the Land Rover. 'That's some pile!'

Simon smiled proudly.

'This great big place for just the two of you?' Liz asked.

'The idea is that we'll have guests when the work is complete,' said Tess as she led them into the kitchen. 'This room is almost finished except for the radiator to be fitted. No central heating, I'm afraid, so it's going to be a bit chilly.'

'Cool,' said Damien, looking around.

You can say that again, thought Tess.

'So where are *we* sleeping?' asked Liz, peering into the laundry room.

Before Tess could reply Simon said, 'Probably best if you two camped out in Windsor Castle,' blithely unaware of the startled looks exchanged between Damien and Liz or the sharp intake of breath from Tess.

'Windsor Castle! We passed near that hours ago!' Damien looked from one to the other. 'Is the Queen expecting us or something?'

Simon then explained to them that Windsor Castle was in fact a caravan and that they were very fortunate indeed because it was the only place round here that was warm and cosy. Tess, who frequently escaped there when the cold and the noise became too much, was furious. He hadn't even considered her!

'Well, it seemed like the obvious place to put them,' said Simon defensively when they were on their own. 'Out of our way.'

Tess had intended them to camp down in what would eventually become the sitting room at the back, among all the assorted furniture. She was hopeful that not even the view would likely compensate for the workmen arriving at eight o'clock, stomping about overhead in their heavy boots followed by hammering and banging, bearing in mind that Damien rarely surfaced before mid-morning. They'd probably only stay for a couple of days. But the caravan! They'd probably never have lived in such luxury. They'd be here forever. She could only hope that they'd be bored witless and decide to move on before long. In the meantime she had to feed them and prayed that they hadn't gone vegan.

Damien, like his father, was a good-looking man. Tess had to admit that he had a certain charisma if you concentrated hard enough to decipher it, but not in the same league as Simon. Any shortcomings that Damien might have were, according to Simon, 'just like his mother'. As she'd never met Simon's ex, she couldn't really argue with that, but she was a handy scapegoat.

Tess had stripped the bed in the caravan when they moved into the house so she now had to find some bedlinen and towels, switch on the electricity supply again and attach the hose to ensure that the water supply was topped up. All tasks requiring two hands.

Simon took on the role of overseer. 'Sorry I can't help,' he sighed, not looking in the slightest bit sorry, 'it's this bloody arm.'

'Poor Dad,' said Damien, 'you've had a rough old time.'

He's not the only one, thought Tess as she returned to the kitchen to cook supper for them all.

Her stepson was in a world of his own, which Tess suspected was drug induced. He and Liz were either asleep or 'getting an album together' which, they were convinced, they'd be able to record when they got back to 'civilisation'.

On one occasion, and one only, Damien had actually offered to do some painting. Unsure of his capabilities Tess had restricted him to a wall in the laundry room. An hour later when she looked in the door she found him swaying to some music inserted in his ears with more paint on the floor than on the wall.

'Time for lunch?' he asked hopefully, laying down the brush which he made no attempt to clean. Tess replaced the lid on the paint pot and washed out the brush. And then sorted out lunch. She was rapidly succumbing to martyrdom.

Liz, on the other hand, was a complete enigma. She rarely surfaced except at dinnertime. Damien made a daily expedition to Pearly's and came back laden with biscuits, cereal bars and chocolate, which probably accounted for Liz's unhealthy pallor.

Damien's couple of weeks stretched into a month. They slept until ten or eleven o'clock, ate like horses, played pop and punk at full volume most of the day, then strummed the guitar and sang for most of the night.

'They're very good, you know,' Simon informed Tess. 'I think they've got some great stuff together there.'

Tess, who'd been unable to decipher any sort of melody emanating from Windsor Castle, made no comment. When were they *ever* going to leave? There was little point in asking them to pay towards the cost of their food because they hadn't any money. But, apart from the cost, Tess was heartily fed up of them being there.

Her only consolation was that most of the radiators were now in place and the central heating engineers appeared to be working quickly and efficiently. The en suite bathrooms were all functioning and Pong and Phil had moved on now that their work was done. They weren't registered to install oil-fired central heating and so that was left to the specialists. There were three specialists, all extremely thirsty, requiring tea at hourly intervals. Tess couldn't wait for them all to be finished and for the oil to arrive and then, hallelujah, they'd be *warm*. She now knew without a doubt that the most important thing in the whole wide world was to be warm. They had one electric plug-in radiator in the kitchen, which was the only room with any heat in the entire house. Both she and Simon worried that a sudden freeze-up could result in burst pipes everywhere. Fortunately, the Cornish climate was rarely extreme; winters were generally wet and windy, with frost and snow restricted to the moors. But there were exceptions and Tess prayed each day for the work to be completed and for the tanker to arrive.

She was cold and she was tired. It wasn't Simon's fault that his arm was broken, but he wasn't doing a great deal with the arm that wasn't, which doubled most of her chores. So, in the middle of March, it was with great relief that she drove him to the clinic to have the plaster removed. Perhaps things would look up now, she thought as she drove back. Perhaps the central heating installation will be finished. Perhaps the tanker will arrive with the oil. Perhaps we'll be warm. Perhaps Damien and Liz will finally move on.

When they got back to Over and Above they found the engineers still there, the oil tanker hadn't yet been, and half the kitchen ceiling had collapsed.

CHAPTER 11

ESCAPE

'I couldn't stand it for another minute,' Tess informed Orla, as she drank her second glass of wine in the warmth of Orla's cosy flat.

'I'm not surprised,' said Orla. 'You must have the patience of a bloody saint to put up with that lot.'

'I'm not going back until that house is warm and the ceiling's back where it should be, and everything is cleared up.' Tess took a deep breath. 'That's if I go back at all!'

Orla's eyes widened. 'You're joking!'

'No, I'm not. I'm beginning to think I'm not cut out for rural living. Driving miles to get *anything*. No mains gas, no buses, frequent power cuts. And Simon's played that arm of his for all it's worth.'

'Well, that's men for you,' Orla retorted dismissively. 'You know what they're like: big babies.'

'Not stupid, though; gets him out of doing any work at all. Then there's Damien and his weird girlfriend loafing around the place, eating us out of house and home, wailing their bloody awful songs.' As Tess spoke she could see Orla suppressing laughter. 'It's *not* funny!'

'It is, you know,' said Orla, exploding into mirth. 'You couldn't make it up! They make sitcoms about this sort of thing!'

Tess, warm and relaxed, could feel her own mouth quivering into a grin.

'Shall I go back with you and sort them all out?' Orla went on, laughing.

At this Tess grinned some more. '*If* I go back.'

Orla rolled her eyes. 'Of course you'll go back! You're potty about that daft husband of yours and he's been phoning you about forty times a day ever since you arrived.'

That much was true, if exaggerated. Simon was very, very worried.

The ceiling had been the final straw. She'd painted every inch of that damned ceiling and the kitchen had looked great – the one room which was functioning normally and where she spent most of the day. It was all down to one of the central heating guys and the underfloor network of pipes. All Simon could say was, 'Well, looks like we'll be eating down the pub tonight!' And Damien, who'd ventured forth to see what all the noise was about, actually *sniggered*.

Tess had to get away, to distance herself from it all. While Simon was listening to the engineer's explanations and apologies, she packed a bag and loaded it into the back of the Land Rover. When Simon came out to see what she was doing she said, 'I'm leaving.'

His expression changed to complete bewilderment. 'What do you mean, you're leaving?'

'I've had enough, Simon. I've worked my socks off these last six weeks. I've watered the workmen, and I've fed and watered those two idle lumps, neither of whom have got off their arses or offered to help in any way. Not only that, they're smoking weed;

I can smell it. And you *know* what I said. Your arm's better now, so *you* sort it out!'

As she was getting into the driving seat Simon caught her arm and said, 'But *where* are you going?'

'Back to civilisation. I'll be in touch.'

'Tess, *don't*! We can sort this out! I'm sorry if—'

'No, Simon. I'm going.'

'And you're taking the Land Rover!' Simon looked close to tears.

'Well, it's a bit late in the day to start booking buses and trains.'

'But how am I going to get *around*?'

'Same way I did when you were up in London for a week.'

'But…'

'But nothing!' Tess slammed the door shut and roared down the driveway. It wasn't until she was at the top of the hill that she pulled into a layby and wept. She sobbed for almost ten minutes. Then, resolute, she dried her eyes, put her foot down and headed for the A30 and London.

Tess had forgotten what it felt like to be warm all day long. To be comfortable in one sweater instead of three. Orla's thermostat was set at a very cosy twenty-two degrees, which was around fifteen degrees more than she was accustomed to.

Amber had some time off mid-week so Tess spent a day with her at their austere minimalist flat where the temperature was too warm, if anything, with Amber swanning around in a T-shirt and jeans.

'So you fancied a little break?' asked Amber.

Tess hadn't filled Amber in on the details of her departure because she knew Amber would worry.

'Yes, just felt like a day or two away to catch up with you all, particularly as I hadn't seen you at Christmas.'

'That was a shame, Mum, but you know Peter booked that Thailand trip way back last summer. And, do you know, I think I'm rather partial to a bit of heat at Christmas.'

'Me, too,' said Tess with feeling.

Amber accompanied her to B&Q where Tess found bits and pieces she needed including yet more paint and enough trellis to screen off the oil tank. There was certainly some advantage in having a large, sturdy vehicle. Then over lunch Amber filled her in with all the local gossip, plus the goings-on between the two well-known stars of the film she was currently working on.

Tess stayed until the evening and, as she got up to leave, Amber said, 'Peter will be so sorry he's missed you.' Peter rarely got home before 8 p.m. and Tess wanted to be back in Orla's flat and on her third glass of wine by then.

The following day she spent with Lisa and the children. Matt was at work but – hearing that his mother was on a flying visit – he came home early.

'Is everything OK, Mum?' he asked anxiously.

'Everything's fine. Just needed a break.' And *how*, she thought.

As she prepared to leave little Ellie clung to her and said, 'I miss you, Nana. Please come back and live near us again!' And that was when she nearly gave way to tears.

Everyone wanted to know why Simon was phoning so often. 'He must be desperately missing you,' and 'Isn't he sweet?' they said.

All Simon wanted to know was *when* was she coming home? He was religiously doing the exercises he'd been given to strengthen his arm, and it was already feeling stronger. He could do *lots* more now. The ceiling had been repaired although it would need to be repainted. He'd had Gina come in to clear everything up. That woman, he said, was worth her weight in gold.

'And Liz has absconded!' Simon added dramatically.

'Absconded?'

'Gone. Had enough. Got a lift with one of the plumbers to Bodmin apparently, where she was going to get on the first train out of Cornwall, she said.'

'Well, no great loss,' said Tess. 'Does she know that you have to *pay* for a ticket on a train?'

'God knows. Now Damien says he wants to go back to London, too.' Simon sighed. 'I'll miss him.'

Tess knew better than to whoop with joy. Damien was, after all, his only son. She had to remind herself yet again how she'd feel if it were Matt or Amber with an erratic nomadic lifestyle and how she'd love them just the same and be thrilled if they came calling.

'I think they've both had enough of my cooking,' Simon said. 'And guess what? The oil's supposed to be delivered tomorrow.'

Tess decided it was probably time to head home. Frequently her husband drove her mad, but oh, how she missed him! Time to get things back on track.

CHAPTER 12

SPRING

Tess arrived home on 20 March. It was one of those days when the sun shone blindingly one minute and the heavens opened the next. Typical spring weather. All along the roadside as she headed towards the coast were daffodils – hosts and hosts of golden daffodils! And birdsong. Even those few days away had triggered a change in the seasons; late winter had given way to early spring. Perhaps it had been spring-like when she left, but she'd been too upset to notice. Or care. The sea was blue again too, and with impressive surf where half a dozen enthusiasts were out there riding the waves. As she came down the hill into Portmerryn she noticed a magnolia tree in full bloom, and primroses. She was nearly home.

Simon was beside himself with joy. 'I've missed you *so* much!' he said over and over again.

He led her into the kitchen. The collapsed ceiling hadn't damaged anything, he said, but had made a horrendous mess. He repeated that Gina was worth her weight in gold. Yes, the ceiling would need to be re-painted but the central heating guy had brought a plasterer in and they'd worked hard to make it all good again. And, look! The radiator was actually fitted. And yes, the oil had arrived but the plumbing wasn't quite finished upstairs and so it would be a few days yet before everything could be connected up and the heating turned on.

And Damien had gone. That very morning. He'd scrounged a lift with a delivery van to Plymouth and from there he'd find wheels of some sort to transport him back to London. He was ready to do some recording; the few weeks in Cornwall had inspired him.

Then Simon told her he'd paid a visit to the bank. Yes, he knew that they didn't want to be in debt but their funds were rapidly running out and they hadn't yet done anything about replacing those rotten wooden French doors on the two main rooms at the back. The wood was rotted through due to never having been properly maintained. Folding doors, like he'd had in the London house, would be terrific, but they were far from cheap. But just think, he said, about walking straight out on a summer's day as if there wasn't any wall there at all!

And something else; they really, *really* needed two cars. He realised that now. You couldn't live somewhere like this with only one set of wheels. *No way!* he said. Something small and economical to run was all that was needed. The bank had agreed with him that it would be most beneficial for them to take out a small mortgage to cover the cost of everything, and it could all be paid back *in no time at all!* After all, the guests would soon be arriving and Simon would hopefully be called to London for the occasional voice-over or small acting part.

Tess listened patiently. He was painting a very rosy picture but, as yet, there was no guarantee that they'd have regular guests and even less certainty that Simon would be offered work. The running costs of this house were likely to be astronomical.

'I've been thinking,' Simon continued, 'that we should up our prices and provide something really special.'

'We've already agreed that we're offering something special,' Tess said.

'Something on the lines of a retreat,' Simon said, 'for long-term guests who need to escape the rat race. Damien actually gave me this idea, because he seemed so inspired by the ambience. He was bursting to get back to London and his recording.'

'Long-term?' asked Tess. 'How long would "long-term" be?'

'Oh, I don't know. Months, perhaps? Put a microwave and a kettle in every room so they can do their own snacks. A tiny fridge, maybe? That sort of thing.'

'This is a guesthouse, not self-catering flats,' Tess said. 'Anyway, how much money are we supposed to be borrowing?'

Tess knew she'd be the one who would have to make the books balance one way or the other with Simon's grandiose ideas. Someone had to keep their feet squarely on the ground.

'One other thing,' she added, 'which won't cost anything. We need to change the name of this place. I really don't like Over and Above.'

'We could call it the Cliff House again,' suggested Simon. 'The Cliff House Boutique Retreat.'

'No,' Tess said. 'I had a much better idea while I was driving home. How about The Sparrows' Nest?'

Simon's face broke into a wide grin. 'Now, why didn't I think of that?'

*

Simon altered the website to read:

> Be free as a bird at The Sparrows' Nest, on the cliffside at Seagull Hill! Come to enjoy the ocean in all its moods, walk barefoot on the beach, relax amid the stunning coastal scenery, paint your pictures, write that book, find yourself again!

Tess researched folding doors and was not surprised to discover that the prices were, almost without exception, astronomical. The sitting room had a wall span of around fifteen feet and the new dining room had about twelve. Brickwork would have to be removed at the sides of the existing French doors, which were situated in the middle of each wall. And they'd have to be very careful with the wisteria. But she had to agree that they'd be sensational: a complete wall of folding doors, open all summer and leading directly onto the terrace overlooking the sea. Then Tess reminded herself that they still hadn't had either the plumbing bill or the central-heating installation bill. They'd estimated these, of course, but it went without saying that it would be more than they thought. *Over and above.*

The workmen would soon be gone. Next would be the hire of the machine to sand the upstairs floors, followed by sealing and polishing. And decorating. And having these rooms ready for May when the guests were due to arrive, which was less than six weeks away. At least their alcohol licence had been granted…

With some trepidation Tess ordered the folding doors. The company, Glide Easy, would come to measure and fit the things for the price quoted.

There was no time to waste.

*

There were a lot of panels involved, said Ivor, who'd been sent to measure up.

'Everything's metric now,' he sighed, 'except your door frames. You'll need new door frames and, if you don't take a bit off the top, the doors will have to be specially made.'

'We'll take a bit off the top,' said Simon.

'Perhaps we should just settle for sliding patio doors or something?' Tess asked as she saw their estimate escalating.

'That would be a shame,' said Ivor, calculator poised, 'with a view like this.'

'And this view,' Simon said, turning to Tess, 'is what will bowl our guests over, what they'll remember and recommend to other people.'

'Yes, but you can still see the view through patio doors or new French windows,' Tess said.

'They'd probably have to be made to measure, too,' Ivor sighed. 'But, just think of your guests coming down to breakfast in a room which would appear to have no wall at all! They can walk straight out onto the terrace; no doors opening out at right angles, no double panes of glass still blocking the view if you have patio doors. They'll fold right the way back. For the sake of just a few extra quid now...'

A few extra quid! Just as well the bank manager had liked Simon. But Tess knew that folding doors would look fantastic, no doubt about that.

'They'll never be cheaper than they are right now,' Ivor continued. 'This is the opportunity of a lifetime, Mrs Sparrow! We can offer you a special discount. And if you let us take some photos of the finished job, with your fabulous views, we can use them for advertising and knock a bit more off the price.'

He was a good salesman and Tess had no way of knowing if what he said was likely to be true but in any case, she was now sold on the idea. They ordered the doors.

Simon's agent did ring again. They were doing some drama for Channel 4, with a week's filming on Bodmin Moor. The week after next. They needed Roundheads and Cavaliers. He was to be a Roundhead. No lines to learn but he'd have to shout a lot. And be on site at 5 a.m. every morning for the week.

'Five o'clock!' Simon spluttered.

'Every morning,' confirmed the agent. 'I told them you'd be ideal because you lived right on the doorstep.'

'It's a half hour's drive,' protested Simon.

'The money's good.'

'Yeah, OK, then,' Simon agreed.

'How are you going to get there in the middle of the night?' Tess asked.

'Good question. You either do without transport all day or we go out to look for another car.'

The very next day they went to Plymouth and bought a second-hand white Fiat 500. It was a few years old but was in good condition ('one careful lady driver,' said the salesman), and cost twice as much as they'd intended to spend. Tess regarded it as a very useful run-around, and Simon said it was little more than a mobile shopping trolley, but it would do the job.

Things were looking up. Three days later the central heating installation was finally complete. One of the guys showed Tess how to press the button and the central heating bellowed into life. An hour later the house was *warm*! Everywhere!

Then Tess prepared for more dust as Simon was let loose with the floor sander upstairs. There followed a week of chaos. More dust, more cleaning. Carpets were delivered and fitted for their bedroom and for the stairs and landing. Furniture was arranged in the upstairs bedrooms. The ever-obliging Gideon was dispatched by his father to help move the new beds upstairs, and then Jed appeared, too. They couldn't risk Simon's newly healed arm coming to grief again, he said. And, he added, they'd unearthed an old, long bar from one of their sheds which, if painted up, would make a very acceptable reception desk in the hallway.

In the last week in April the folding doors were delivered, just prior to their first guest arriving. It did, of course, decide to rain that day but, never mind, it wasn't cold and it wasn't windy so at least the rain didn't blow straight into the rooms. While they worked Tess added the final touches upstairs. The floorboards looked beautiful, but each room had a large rug covering most of the floor in an attempt at warmth and also to deaden the sound of people walking around, particularly in high heels. She placed large fluffy colour-coordinated towels in each gleaming new bathroom.

She'd talked Simon out of his ideas for microwaves and the like. Apart from the expense, Tess didn't really want people to be cooking up here. They had to make money out of this venture and that meant providing lunches and dinners. She decided to do a set dinner each evening and, if they didn't like it, they could always walk down to the pub. But she'd certainly need help with all the cleaning. She'd ask Gina.

Hours before the first guest arrived the folding glass doors were finally in place. And they looked amazing, even when they were closed! Then, one flick of the switch, and back they folded. You could barely see them at each side as the wall completely disappeared.

Simon in the meantime had spent a week as a Roundhead and managed not to break anything. Things were finally looking up.

The Sparrows were now open for business.

PART TWO

CHAPTER 13

DOMINIC

Dominic Delamere hoped he was doing the right thing when he'd chosen to come to the South-West via the M4 and the M5, because everyone said that the A303 became very congested at this time of year. But my God, he thought, it's a bloody long way! County after county after county.

Still, it was a beautiful sunny day. As he drove onto the A30 at Exeter and slowed down a little, he began to notice for the first time the abundance of greenery on each side of the dual carriageway: the rough peaks and tors of Dartmoor on the left, the fresh sharp greenness of the spring leaves on the trees, the glimpse of lambs frolicking in a field and wild flowers on the banks. You wouldn't see frolicking lambs around Hampstead.

He did occasionally notice the seasons in London, apart from it being warm in summer and cold in winter, of course. He'd fleetingly observed blossom on the trees in the parks and on the heath. Pink usually, like cherry blossom, which always reminded him of Japan. And, later in the year, the dense carpets of gold and amber leaves which left the trees bare and vulnerable again. How often had he and Patrick crunched their way through those leaves! Patrick. He must learn to think of Patrick only in the past tense because Patrick wasn't coming back. As always he felt his eyes becoming a little misty and then he saw the sign by the side of the road: 'Welcome to Cornwall'.

Dominic's sat-nav instructed him to take the next turning off the A30. He blinked as he slowed down and chastised himself for being a silly old fool. He'd just turned seventy which was why it was entirely possible that Patrick, at fifty-two, had been tempted elsewhere. For someone called Finbar: another bloody Irishman, and the cause of the ensuing disaster.

Now he was most certainly on a B road, with just enough room for two vehicles to pass each other comfortably and for large juggernauts to inch past each other slowly and carefully. He was stuck behind one that did just that for a good part of the way. And then – for what seemed like hours – he got stuck behind a filthy tractor and trailer, doing about fifteen miles an hour and spewing out dirt – probably cow shit – all over his pristine silver Jaguar. Well, it had been pristine when he set out this morning but it certainly wouldn't be now. At last, the damned tractor turned into a field and Dominic continued on his way, navigating sharp bends, changing gear as he roared up and down hills. This was a different sort of driving from what he was used to and he was having to concentrate very hard. Then it struck him that he didn't *have* to drive at sixty miles an hour simply because that was the speed limit on this type of road, although he noticed that most of the other drivers were driving fast. In all probability they lived round here and knew where they were going. After a Fiat 500 overtook him on one of the only straight pieces of road he decided that he might as well slow down and enjoy the scenery.

He observed again the plethora of wild flowers lining the road: pinks and whites and blues. Campions, ox-eye daisies and bluebells. And fat brown cows grazing in a field and an occasional roadside cottage with scribbled signs up proclaiming 'Eggs for Sale' and 'Bags of Best Quality Horse Manure – Very Cheap'. How did you grade the quality of horse manure? Dominic wondered. Did you have to dissect it, smell it, or what? Or was it the horses that were best quality?

The road went on and on. Dominic began to wonder why on earth he'd chosen to come to this remote part of the world. There was still no sign of the sea either. Was he on the right road? You could never be sure; the sat-nav did make heroic boo-boos occasionally.

Patrick would laugh. He always called Dominic a 'hopeless townie' when Dominic shut his eyes and offered up prayers as Patrick roared round blind corners at heaven-only-knows-how-many-miles-per-hour on Ireland's country roads, not dissimilar to this. Well, Patrick *was* a country boy and Dominic, born and bred in Chiswick, was not.

He'd scoured the country looking for somewhere remote, by the sea, to write his book. And, because of the type of book and because of Patrick, it had to be Cornwall. This was certainly remote enough, but *where* was the sea? Dear Lord, how much *further*?

And then he passed the sign which proclaimed 'Portmerryn' and, from the top of the hill, the view literally took his breath away. Ahead of him was a panorama of blue Atlantic, cliffs descending dramatically into the sea, a scattering of houses, a beach. And now the road was bordered on each side by deep pink rhododendrons, growing wild. It was breathtakingly beautiful. It was the sort of stuff in some of the books that Dominic published that he classed as sugary and exaggerated. If his editors okayed it then that was fine, but it was not his sort of thing. He almost felt the urge to write a description of this himself! He should have come to paint and not to write!

He'd have liked to pull in to savour the view, but there was no lay-by, only houses lining the roadside, their gardens bursting with colour. And a little shop: 'Portmerryn Stores and Post Office'. Now the sea was right ahead of him and the road did a sharp turn to the left with only a line of cottages between him and the beach. They must back right onto the sand, he thought. And then a pub – good. He hoped it would be walkable to from where he was staying.

The sat-nav was now telling him to take the next left, which looked little more than a narrow lane. But the sign said 'Seagull Hill' and that was the address of the place, so it had to be right. It was very steep and he swore as he hit a succession of huge potholes. What a treacherous bloody place, he thought, my poor car! Then he saw the sign on the right: 'The Sparrows' Nest' and a driveway leading to it, although he could see no sign of a house through the trees.

When the house came into view it was exactly like the picture on the website: large and imposing with a steeply pitched roof, lots of chimneys, an open front door, a large parking area. But where was the *sea*? Just trees all around.

Dominic unfolded his lanky frame from the driving seat and stretched his aching muscles. He was getting to be too old for these marathon journeys. He stood for a moment gazing at the house. This, then, was where he'd opted to spend the next six weeks of his life.

And there certainly didn't appear to be much to distract him around here, so no excuses for not getting the book written, or at least started.

Then a lady appeared. Tall, quite attractive and a bit younger than himself, he reckoned.

She smiled broadly. 'You must be Mr Delamere?'

'Mrs Sparrow, I presume?' he replied as they shook hands.

'Call me Tess, please.'

'And I'm Dominic.'

'Come in, Dominic, and let me show you to your room. How was your journey? We're a long way from anywhere, aren't we?'

'You certainly are,' Dominic agreed, impressed with the spacious hallway and imposing central staircase. There was a strong smell of new paint.

Tess led the way upstairs, along the galleried landing and opened the door at the far end to Room 1.

'I do hope you'll be comfortable in here,' she said.

Dominic found himself in a large airy room, tastefully decorated. He crossed to the double windows and there was that view again – the perpendicular cliff he'd seen from the top of the hill, and a wide panorama of ocean, seagulls circling overhead. For a moment he was speechless.

'You said you were going to be writing,' Tess said, 'so I thought this might be useful.' She indicated a small oak desk in front of the window.

'Oh, how kind,' Dominic said, 'but I doubt I'd get much writing done as I'll be gazing out of the window so much!'

She laughed. 'You'll get used to it. Now, I'll go find my husband to help you to unload your stuff.'

'Oh, no need…' he said vaguely, still staring at the sea. Then he turned to inspect the room. A nice big double bed, a couple of easy chairs, a spacious antique-type wardrobe. Polished floorboards with a large pale-coloured rug covering most of it. He wandered into the bathroom. A shower and a bath – good. And lots of fluffy white towels and little bottles of soap and stuff. She'd certainly thought of everything, including a kettle and all the usual tea things including, glory of glories, a cafetière along with some ground coffee, so he could make his own brew. No fridge, but that didn't matter because he drank his tea and coffee black anyway. It was surely worth every mile and every pothole to get here. He supposed he'd better fetch his luggage.

When he got down to the front door there was a rather dapper, good-looking man standing there, smiling. Dominic had a vague feeling of having seen him before somewhere.

'Hi!' he said, holding out his hand. 'I'm Simon Sparrow. Simon.'

They shook hands. 'Dominic,' he said. 'And what a delightful place you have here.'

'Well, thank you,' said his host. 'We've only just finished doing it up, hence the smell of paint everywhere, for which I apologise. Hopefully it won't last long. And do let us know if you think we can improve anything because this is new territory for us. Now, let me help you carry some of these things.'

After they'd lugged everything upstairs Simon asked, 'How was your journey?'

'Well, the motorway bit was predictably busy and boring,' Dominic replied. 'But the last part of the journey just got better and better. It's such a glorious day.'

'It is,' Simon agreed. 'Now we were wondering if, after your long drive, you'd care to join Tess and I for a cup of tea or something out on the terrace?'

'That,' replied Dominic, 'would be delightful.'

Tess Sparrow led him out through a charming sitting room, the windows folded back completely – which gave the appearance of having no outside wall – onto the sunny terrace where there were chairs and sofas and things made of that material you can leave outside in all weathers and which they'd jazzed up with lots of colourful cushions.

'Do sit down, Dominic,' she said. 'You'll need a breather before you start unpacking. And would you like tea or coffee?'

'Tea would be wonderful,' he replied, positioning himself to best enjoy the view.

She reappeared shortly afterwards with a tray laden with tea things, including slices of lemon for Dominic's black tea. There was also a large plate of interesting-looking biscuits.

Simon joined them and, after a few minutes' general conversation, Dominic asked, 'Have I met you or seen you somewhere before?'

'I don't think we've met,' Simon replied, 'but I was, and occasionally still am, an actor so you may have seen me in something or other.'

'Ah, that'll be it.' Dominic looked around. 'So, have you given up acting now?'

'I'm afraid it's rather given *me* up,' Simon said sadly. 'But I do get an occasional call from my agent for bits of this and that, mainly voice-overs.'

'You have a very distinctive, attractive voice,' Dominic said.

'Well, thank you. And it comes in useful for earning some extra cash now and again but, to be honest, I'm really happy to be away from it all.'

Tess passed the plate of biscuits to Dominic. 'These are made by a lady who lives up the road,' she said, 'and they're delicious. Made with Cornish cream. Do try some.'

As Dominic helped himself, Simon said, 'I understand you're a writer?'

'Um, no, I don't think I'd call myself a writer just yet. I've been a publisher for the past forty years or so, handling other people's books, so thought it high time I tried writing one myself. At least I have a fair idea of what's likely to be acceptable, but I'll have to take my chance.'

'Good for you!' said Tess. 'You should always follow your dream.'

'And this will make quite a change for you after London,' Simon added. 'Will it help the creative juices to flow, do you think?'

'My God, I hope so!' Dominic laughed. He hoped fervently that they would flow. To have come all this way and booked this place for weeks and then have all your ideas dry up! He shuddered at the thought.

They were a nice couple and he liked the fact that they didn't quiz him about his private life, or what the book was about. These things could be mentioned in time if he chose to tell them. He'd never liked people who wanted to know all about you within minutes of meeting.

'Now, feel free to come out here any time you feel like it,' Tess said, waving her hand around at the terrace. 'And we'll do dinner at seven thirty in the dining room next door, if that's OK? And, as you're our very first guest, you're welcome to join us rather than sit on your own. Or we can bring it up to your room if you prefer? We're trying to cater for our guests' individual tastes.'

'And we're here if you need us, but we'll keep a low profile if you don't,' Simon added.

'That all seems ideal,' said Dominic.

CHAPTER 14

OPEN PLAN

'I rather like him,' Tess remarked after their one and only guest had retired to his room.

'Yes, I do, too,' Simon said. 'It would be awful if we didn't, though, wouldn't it? I mean he's here for six weeks.'

'No idea what sort of book he might be writing,' Tess said. 'And he didn't say anything about his personal life, did he? Do you think he was…'

'Gay?' Simon supplied. 'Yes, definitely. At least *you'll* be safe – not that you're going to have much time for any shenanigans, Mrs Sparrow! I'm keeping you chained up in the kitchen doing breakfasts, lunches and dinners and then collapsing gratefully into my arms at bedtime.'

Tess knew, of course, that Simon liked to show off his skills in the kitchen and that they'd share the cooking. Only this evening he'd cooked the very delicious chicken cacciatore.

'Well, if that's the case I'll be asleep in seconds, Mr Sparrow,' she said. 'Anyway, Dominic says he rarely eats cooked breakfasts, just likes a bowl of cereal and a piece of fruit. I don't expect we'll need to do many lunches if our guests are out during the day. Mind you, if Dominic's writing a book he probably *won't* be out during the day.'

'I suppose we should ask Gina to give you a hand with the cleaning. She's always looking for ways to earn extra money, and you get on well with her.'

Tess had been thinking very much along the same lines. She knew Gina was fed up working for Jed and Annie. 'They're a scruffy, untidy couple,' she'd confided to Tess, 'but I can guarantee that the kitchen is spotless because I damn well make sure that it is. And most of the meals are pre-prepared and just need microwaving, so there's a fair chance you and your guests can avoid salmonella.'

She'd like to have Gina help her but Tess wondered if they could afford it. Perhaps, when all their guests were settled in and looking for breakfast, lunch and dinner, she herself might not have much energy left for cleaning and laundry. Not for the first time she wondered if perhaps they had bitten off more than they could chew. It would be considerably easier if they were twenty years younger.

They'd decided to offer special rates for long-stay guests and then wondered if anyone, other than Dominic, would have a reason to stay on for weeks or perhaps even months. But there appeared to be a number of single people looking to get away from it all – for whatever reason. A single woman was due to arrive in five days' time, another single woman in a week's time, and a couple a few days later. Both of the women had booked for a month, possibly extending their stay, depending... depending on what, Tess was not sure.

Tess was relieved not to be busy straight away because Matt, Lisa and the children had rented one of the fisherman's cottages down on the beach for the weekend. She knew Matt was keen to see how the business was progressing and Tess was desperate to see her family.

'Wow!' exclaimed Matt, as Tess led them through the new sitting room and pressed the switch for the glass doors to do their folding. Except they only folded halfway along and then stopped. Matt and Lisa wandered out onto the terrace, apparently unaware that the bi-fold doors were not bi-folding. Tess felt disappointed that her 'Wow!' moment had unexpectedly failed. She pressed the switch again. Nothing. Perhaps there was a power failure? She tested a couple of lights. No problem there. Tess was relieved that no one was paying any attention to her as she shoved and struggled with the doors because Matt and Lisa were being entertained by Simon's rather exaggerated and entertaining account of the problems they'd encountered getting everything ship-shape in time for the first guest arriving.

'*What* a transformation since Christmas!' Matt exclaimed.

'Well,' Tess said, 'here's another problem for your repertoire, Simon! How about folding doors that are stuck halfway across and refuse to open or close? How about a room with no protection from the Atlantic wind and rain? And how about it being a Saturday so, naturally, nobody will be able to do anything until Monday?' And *why* was there always some damned problem?

Simon stopped mid-sentence. 'What do you mean, the doors aren't working?'

'I mean they're not working. Go and see for yourself.'

As she joined the others on the terrace she found Ellie skipping about excitedly while Lisa was retrieving Josh from trying to climb over the low wall that separated them from the sheer drop below and to certain oblivion. 'We are going to get something higher put up,' Tess said, 'but, since our guests are all adults and we've run out of cash, it has to go on the back burner for now.'

Simon came out again scratching his head. 'These mega-expensive folding doors have given up the ghost and are stuck halfway across,' he said. 'Probably a power failure. Why the hell didn't we choose the manual version? Anyway, I think there is some way to do it manually, isn't there?'

'There had better be,' Tess replied, 'because they are well and truly stuck. And there's no power failure.'

'Don't worry about it now,' Simon said airily. 'I'll have a look at it later.'

Tess sighed. She'd so looked forward to Matt's visit and now all she was doing was panicking about doors that refused to move in any direction.

Dominic had gone to visit Truro. Was there a Marks & Spencer there? he'd wanted to know. On being told that there was a large one at Lemon Quay, he said he'd forgotten to bring his chinos and he wanted to buy a couple of pairs. And so, now that their one and only guest had gone out, Simon was able to give them a tour of all the renovations, pointing out all the work that had been done since Christmas.

Matt was impressed. 'My God,' he said, 'you two have worked hard. But this place is beautiful and the view is phenomenal.'

'Why can't we stay here often, Nana?' Ellie asked.

'Well, sometimes you'll be able to but mainly in the winter probably. But, hey! I've got just the place where you could stay *anytime*. Do you remember Windsor Castle?'

'Where the Queen lives?'

'Not quite. The place where Grandpa Simon and I were sleeping at Christmas.'

Tess took Ellie's hand and led her out of the front door, across the parking area and along the path through the trees.

'Oh, it's your little *house!*' Ellie clapped her hands with delight. 'Oh, I'd *love* to stay here! Can I show Mummy?'

Tess was none too sure Mummy would approve. She didn't think Lisa was a caravan holiday type of person. She'd already grumbled about having to walk through the kitchen to get to the bathroom in the fisherman's cottage, but at least that was a full-sized proper bathroom.

Lisa refrained from commenting other than to say that the children would probably love it and, when they were a little older, perhaps they could come down by themselves during the school holidays. Tess could decipher the relief in Lisa's voice at the prospect of saving weeks of child-minding and au pair fees, not to mention the endless ferrying them around. Lisa was first and foremost a career woman in an executive job with a hotel chain. She'd bowed to convention by marrying Matt (although Tess knew that she did love him) and having two children. And she didn't doubt that Lisa loved her children dearly, too, but she'd freely admitted there was absolutely no way that she could stay at home all day cooking and cleaning and wiping snotty noses or whatever it was stay-at-home mothers were supposed to do. It was all *so* different from her own life when Matt and Amber were small! But that was nearly forty years ago and times and attitudes change. The main thing was that Matt was happy, and Tess had two lovely grandchildren.

As they emerged out from the trees towards the front door Tess saw Matt stroking the cat.

'Dylan's still alive, then?' he said.

'Yes, he seems to like it here. Mind you he's slowing up; he's only managed to catch one mouse in the seven months we've been here but he spends a lot of time looking out of the window at the birds, his whiskers twitching.' Tess looked fondly at the cat. 'Simon keeps on about getting a Labrador or something, but it wouldn't be fair on poor old Dylan.'

Tess had prepared a selection of salads for lunch on the dining room table but didn't dare attempt to open up the doors in here in case they stuck, too. She and Simon and Matt had all had a go at trying to move the ones in the sitting room, both physically and electronically, to no avail.

Although it was Saturday afternoon Simon decided to ring the company on the off chance that somebody might be taking emergency calls at the weekend. But there was only a recorded message thanking him for calling Glide Easy windows and could he please phone during office hours, nine to five, Monday to Friday – and thank you very much. Simon was furious.

The idea was that they would all meet up for a meal at The Portmerryn Arms in the evening.

'We can't go out without being able to lock the doors,' Tess pointed out. 'We're missing half a wall.'

'Probably safe enough in this neck of the woods,' said Simon, who was hankering after a pint of Doom Bar.

'Come on, Simon, *anybody* could walk in and clear the place!'

'Well, we could ask Dominic to keep an eye on the place, couldn't we?'

'There's no guarantee Dominic is going to be in this evening. He said he wouldn't have dinner because he'd eat while he was out, and he may well decide to make an evening of it.' Tess was irritated by Simon's flippant attitude. 'And, even if he is in, we can hardly ask a paying guest to look after our house.'

'What if it rains?' Matt asked. 'Shall I google the weather forecast for this evening?'

Without waiting for a reply he dug out his phone and, after a minute, reported, 'Wind and rain approaching from the west.'

'Oh bugger!' said Tess.

'Don't worry,' Simon said. 'We'll fix up a tarpaulin over the opening. Perhaps you'd give me a hand, Matt?'

'With pleasure,' said Matt, and the two of them set out to find a tarpaulin which Simon reckoned might just be somewhere in the garage.

At this point little Josh decided he'd had enough of socialising and wanted a nap. Tess tried to settle him down in their bed but he wasn't having any of it.

'I'll have to take him back to the cottage,' Lisa sighed. 'If he doesn't get a nap now there'll be hell to pay later when we're trying to eat dinner.'

While Simon and Matt battled to get the tarpaulin into position, Tess drove Lisa and the children down to the cottage, which was next door to the one she and Simon had stayed in on their first visit. She got back at exactly the same time as Dominic, who informed her that he was going to have a quick shower and then take himself off to the cinema in Wadebridge where they were showing a film that he'd missed seeing in London. Well, thought Tess, he wouldn't have been able to do any house-sitting even if I'd agreed to ask him. She wandered into the sitting room and found it in semi-darkness with the tarpaulin blocking out half the light and her husband and son still struggling to get it to stay in place. A few minutes later they came walking round the house and in the front door.

'That should do it,' said Simon airily.

'It won't exactly keep the burglars out,' Tess snapped.

'You're obsessed with bloody burglars,' said Simon. 'This is Cornwall! People do *not* get burgled round here!'

'Yes, they do! Gina told me that somebody tried to get into Pearly's shop one night not so long ago, but Pearly's alarm sounded full volume and off he scarpered with only a big box of Rose's chocolates.'

'Big-time criminals round here,' Simon muttered jokingly to Matt.

Matt gave his mother a hug. 'I'd better go see what the family are up to,' he said. 'See you later.'

'We cannot go out this evening,' Tess said when they were alone.

'Of course we can,' replied Simon.

'Well, that's up to you. I'm staying right here.'

'Don't be silly,' he said.

They'd arranged to meet up in the pub at around seven o'clock, and at six thirty Simon began to get himself ready to go.

'You mean you're actually planning to *go*?' Tess asked as he emerged from the bedroom.

'Well, of course I'm going! And so are you, aren't you?'

'*Someone's* got to stay in the house,' Tess insisted.

'Well, it isn't going to be me,' snapped Simon, 'because it's completely unnecessary.'

'In that case it'll have to be me.'

'Don't be ridiculous! We're only going to be out for an hour or so because they're going to want to get the kids to bed,' Simon said.

'I'm not leaving this house with half a wall missing!'

'Oh, for God's sake!'

Tess was becoming angrier and angrier. How dare he treat their security so lightly! And how dare he ridicule her for worrying about it! She sat at the kitchen table and waited for him to come in and say, 'OK, you go. It's *your* son after all, and I'll stay here.' She waited and waited and then – at five minutes to seven – he put his head round the door and said cheerfully, 'Well, I'm off! You know where we are if you decide to join us, or if you need help to confront the gang of robbers on your own.'

The inconsiderate bastard! Tess felt her eyes well up with tears of self-pity and rage. She picked up the glass of water she'd been drinking from and hurled it at him, but he'd already closed the door and so it smashed into smithereens all over the floor.

Weeping openly, she realised she should have had everyone to dinner here. Why hadn't she asked them? Had she been secretly hoping that Simon would be gallant enough to insist on staying? And now what would she do if someone *did* break in? For sure she should never have married this selfish man who rated a pint of Doom Bar more highly than the safety of his wife.

She needed a drink. She was halfway through her second large glass of a very nice Malbec when she heard footsteps outside. Now she was probably about to be murdered and she wouldn't even be able to say 'I told you so'.

As she stood up shakily to investigate the door burst open and in they all came, brandishing parcels wrapped in newspaper.

'Did you know that a fish and chip van comes and parks outside the cottages every Saturday night?' Simon asked breezily, as they all deposited their packages onto the table.

'We got you haddock and chips, Mum. Is that OK?' Matt placed a package in front of his mother. 'Can you find us some salt and vinegar?'

'I'll open some more wine,' Simon said, 'because there doesn't seem to be much left in this bottle.' He raised an eyebrow at Tess.

'Have you been crying, Nana?' Ellie asked climbing onto a chair next to Tess.

Tess put an arm round her. 'Of course not,' she said, 'I'm just a bit tired.'

She supposed she should be pleased at this obvious solution to the problem. But all she wanted to do was wring Simon's neck.

CHAPTER 15

CELIA

Celia Winsgrove had never driven such a long way in her entire life, which was sixty-seven years and three months. Her old Vauxhall, which had replaced the ancient Morris Minor some fifteen years back, had rarely gone further than Sainsbury's and the once or twice she'd driven down to Bath to see her cousin, Elinor. She liked Bath. Now she was free she might consider moving to Bath eventually, but not now.

This BMW sport was something else! She'd only taken her eyes off the road for a couple of seconds to look at some lambs in a field and when she looked back at the speedometer she realised she was doing *eighty* miles an hour! That was way over the speed limit and she could get arrested! Eighty miles an hour! She'd never driven at more than forty or fifty miles per hour in her whole life but this machine accelerated like a bullet so she'd have to be careful.

Celia hadn't gone out with the intention of buying a BMW, of course, and certainly not a sports model, but the salesman – when he realised how much money she was prepared to spend – was very persuasive. And she liked its colour – red, which was very racy.

She realised that she wouldn't be able to make it from Dudley to Cornwall in one go, so she'd stopped overnight at one of these chain hotels just outside Bristol. It was a motel, really, a place for drivers to stay when they needed a break from hour after hour of driving. It was a bit drab, but clean and comfortable, and it had an en suite bathroom! With a bath *and* a shower and lots of little bottles of shampoo and the like. It was quite nice really, but not nearly so luxurious as the place she was heading for now.

Celia did not like motorway driving, but it had to be the only sensible way to get to the South-West, otherwise she'd have to find a load of A and B roads, and look out for signs, get stuck in traffic jams and probably get lost to boot. There were no traffic jams on the M5, just cars whizzing by her all the time. She rarely ventured out into the middle lane and she couldn't even contemplate getting into that fast overtaking lane. What was their hurry anyway? She liked to enjoy the countryside, not that she could see much stuck between enormous trucks and caravans.

It was a little easier on the A30, which was dual carriageway and marginally less manic. Even so, when she'd ventured out to overtake a caravan doing about twenty miles an hour, some car behind had tooted at her and flashed their lights. Why? She'd signalled, hadn't she, and she certainly wasn't breaking the speed limit? He was plainly going far too fast. She'd overtaken the caravan and got back into the inside lane.

It was cloudy but warm, and she decided to open the window. It was difficult to open it a little because, the moment she touched the button, the window shot down all the way with the speed of light. It was so much easier in the Vauxhall when you could just wind it down to where you wanted. She'd get used to this, she supposed. Like she'd get used to the remote control that locked and unlocked the doors. This was all fine as long as there wasn't some electronic failure and then she'd need to be able to unlock the door with a proper key and have a handle with which to wind down the window.

Now, she was to look out for some exit or other so she slowed down to be able to read the signs more clearly. The next one she saw said 'Welcome to Cornwall', which was nice. She'd never been to Cornwall before. Mummy hadn't cared for long journeys and she couldn't very well have gone off on her own. Particularly not during those past few years when Mummy was more or less bedridden.

'What do you want to be painting for?' she'd asked when Celia bought the big box of watercolours.

'I've always fancied it,' Celia had said, remembering that she'd been good at art in school. But Mummy had tut-tutted and said something about her getting above herself, and what was wrong with reading a nice book or knitting another jumper?

Now, here she was, heading for some magical seaside place where she'd be able to paint all day long if she liked. So what if she'd got above herself? It was the first time in her life that she'd had any freedom or any money. Here she was, in her Jaeger jumper and trousers, driving a red BMW, and going on a painting sabbatical! She was calling it a sabbatical because it was going to be longer than a normal holiday. She planned to stay a month at least, unless of course she had to move on quickly. But she didn't think anyone was likely to find her where she was going.

Then she espied the sign which heralded an exit to a load of places she'd never heard of but there – at the foot of the list – was

Portmerryn. Take the third exit at the roundabout, her printed-out instructions informed her. She'd positioned them on the passenger seat so she could glance at them quickly from time to time. Now she was on the last leg of this epic trip.

The road went on and on, but Celia didn't mind. There was no need to go above forty most of the time, and there were lots of bends and hills which necessitated slowing down to thirty or less. At one point she could see a line of eight cars behind her in the rear-view mirror, but most of them roared past her when she got to one of the few straight stretches of road. Everyone was in such a hurry these days! She'd come miles and miles without needing to hurry, so goodness only knew where all these people were rushing to.

It was a lovely day now, the cloud clearing and the sun finally emerging. And these wild flowers all along the side of the road in pinks and blues and yellows! She wished she could stop right now and paint some of them. May had always been her favourite month with everything so fresh and green, even in Dudley.

She'd been driving for a good half hour before she got to the top of Portmerryn Hill and the view which took her breath away. Such dramatic scenery and such an expanse of sea! Again she felt she'd like to get her paints out this very minute, but there was nowhere to stop. As she descended to the coast she saw the rhododendrons – masses of them, lining the roadside and all in full bloom. And what a quaint little shop, with a post office, too! Not that she'd be expecting any mail and she certainly wouldn't be sending any postcards, although there was a time when she might have done. Now she was driving along the coastal road with the sea pounding away on her right and some surfers wobbling around in the water.

It must be cold in there which was why they'd be clad in these black things from head to toe – wetsuits, were they called?

She was to look out for the pub and then to turn left shortly afterwards. There it was: Seagull Hill! Celia navigated her way up very carefully around some large potholes and almost missed the sign on the right: 'The Sparrows' Nest – Guesthouse'. And then she was *there*, parking in front of this beautiful big house, alongside a Land Rover and a smart Jaguar. Just as well she hadn't rolled up in the old noisy Vauxhall.

Celia rang the bell and the lady who answered it said, 'You must be Miss Winsgrove? Do come in!' She'd asked for a room with a sea view but all she could see at the front of the house were trees. But when the lady opened the door to the bedroom Celia could see that she certainly did have a sea view, and a stunning one at that! Then she said, 'Call me Tess, and I'll go find my husband to help you up with your things.'

'Thank you,' said Celia, looking round at her new abode. This Tess seemed very pleasant and efficient, and the room was most acceptable. This was to be her home for an indefinite period and she'd rather hoped it might be pretty and chintzy. But the colours in this room were plain and muted and rather austere for her taste. Nonetheless, as she looked around at the twin beds, the easy chairs, the pretty wardrobe and then at the view again, Celia felt she'd made a good choice.

And no one was likely to find her here.

CHAPTER 16

GLIDE EASY

The Glide Easy people finally arrived on the Tuesday morning, which was none too soon, as that was the day when Miss Celia Winsgrove was to arrive in the late afternoon. Glide Easy had the doors folding and unfolding in a very short time, accompanied by a long explanation for what had happened, none of which Tess understood. She only wanted to be assured that this 'blip', as they called it, would not happen again. It wouldn't, they told her; it was a one in a million chance. Tess knew that every time she put her finger on that damned switch her heart would be in her mouth. No charge, they assured her, all covered by the guarantee. What wasn't covered by the guarantee was the row she and Simon had had over it.

They had all enjoyed their fish and chips last Saturday night, but Tess discovered that had been Matt's idea. Her dear husband would have been perfectly happy eating in the pub without a thought for her, alone, guarding their property and their possessions. At times Simon could be incredibly selfish, no doubt due to being pampered in his acting heyday and, not least, being the baby in a family of three girls and the much-wanted son. His older sisters had adored him, cuddled him and pandered to his every whim. It was, admitted his sister Shirley, a miracle that he turned out as well as he did. Probably due to getting more than his quota of looks and charm as well.

By the time Matt and the family headed back to London Tess could contain her wrath no longer.

'They must have thought you were very selfish and uncaring to leave me here while you just went off to the pub like that,' she said, as she stacked the lunchtime things in the dishwasher.

'Of course not,' said Simon, 'they probably only thought you were being obsessive. Anyway, we all came back here, didn't we?'

'And whose idea was that? Not yours. That was Matt's.'

'A very good idea it was, too,' said Simon airily.

'It wouldn't have occurred to *you*. You'd have spent the whole damned evening in The Portmerryn Arms with *my* family and thought nothing of it.'

'Tess, for God's sake, will you let it rest?'

'No, I bloody well will not let it rest! It's the principle of the thing; that you'd risk your wife's feelings and safety for the sake of a pint of bloody beer and a less-than-gourmet meal.'

And so it had gone on and on until Simon made some excuse about having to go out, and Tess continued to fume and wonder if she should consider a divorce.

As she was preparing dinner Simon returned, bursting through the kitchen door with an armful of red roses. Dozens and dozens of them.

'I'm sorry,' he said.

'Yes, well…' She adjusted the oven temperature, then said, 'Where on earth did you find all these?'

'I did have to drive quite a distance,' Simon said, laying the roses on the kitchen table, 'but you're worth it. Come here!'

Tess reluctantly let herself be embraced.

'Relax!' he said. 'I *said* I was sorry. I'm sorry for being a thoughtless, selfish, stubborn pig. Will that do?'

'Just about,' Tess said, grinning. 'Just add "arrogant".'

'I'm a thoughtless, selfish, stubborn, arrogant pig,' he agreed, before they both dissolved into laughter.

No, her husband wasn't as perfect as she'd first imagined! But she still loved him to bits and only prayed that these wretched windows would give them no further trouble.

As Tess awaited the arrival of her second guest she thought how lucky she was to have Dominic. He was so easy: didn't want a cooked breakfast, was out most of the day, and kept his room tidy. It couldn't last, of course, not with three more lots about to arrive. She was curious about this Celia Winsgrove, not quite knowing what to expect. She was coming to paint watercolours, she said. Her email had been brief and to the point; she'd much prefer to communicate by letter, she said. And, when the letter arrived to confirm her booking, it was beautifully written in an almost calligraphic script. She'd signed it: 'Yours faithfully, C.A.H. Winsgrove'. She had to be old and she had to be fussy.

So, when the red BMW appeared outside Tess wondered if she might have guessed wrongly.

An elderly bespectacled lady emerged from the driving seat. She had a slight stoop, and short grey hair. At close quarters Tess could see watery blue eyes behind the spectacles, no make-up of any kind, and her clothes were of good quality, neat but dull.

She hadn't raved about the view from her room as Dominic had done. And she hadn't said, 'Call me Celia' either. She would, she said, like dinner at seven thirty and she wasn't keen on anything too spicy or too foreign. And she'd like some tea, in her room, as soon as convenient, with milk, please. Tess hadn't bothered to point out the tea tray in her room. Anyway, the poor woman was probably exhausted from her journey and wanted to be waited on.

'Simon,' she said when she got downstairs, 'could you please help Miss Winsgrove carry her things upstairs?' She wondered what Simon would make of their latest guest.

When he came back he said, 'Well, she didn't make a pass at me or anything. I think you're safe!'

'Seriously, Simon, what did you make of her?'

'Typical old spinster, I'd say. Quite a flashy car, though, and I think she's probably got some money. Leave it to me, I'll win her round in due course and find out the nitty-gritty.'

Dominic liked a couple of vodka and tonics in the sitting room before he had his dinner. As Tess served him she asked, 'Where did you go today?'

'Oh, just along the coast,' he replied. 'I'm still looking for inspiration and the sea is very important.'

'Will your book be about the sea, then?'

'Well yes,' he said, 'I'm planning to write something about the smuggling that used to go on around this coast. They were my favourite stories when I was young.'

'Lots of shipwrecks out there, I'm told,' Tess said.

'I'm really just at the research stage at the moment,' he said. 'Looking for information.'

'I know who might be able to help you,' Tess said as she poured the tonic into his vodka, 'Jed down at the pub. Have you been in there yet?'

'Not yet.'

'Probably worth a visit. Apparently, they have great beer, too. Anyway, Jed comes from an old Cornish family and a long line of innkeepers. He's also got pictures of old sailing vessels all round the walls. Jed's a bit of a rough diamond but good-hearted and he knows a lot about local history.'

'I might have a wander down there after dinner,' Dominic said.

Tess cleared her throat. 'The thing is, we've had another guest arrive today. She wants to eat at seven thirty as well, and I wondered if we should put you both at the same table, or give you a little table each?'

Dominic took a sip of his drink and smiled. 'Wouldn't it be a bit peculiar us sitting in solitary splendour at separate tables?'

'Well, yes, I suppose it would. But what if you don't get on? I mean, she seems very nice but you can never tell, can you?'

'Let's see what happens this evening and, if she's absolutely awful, then I'll eat in my room or change my time, if that would suit you.'

'We'll play it by ear,' Tess agreed.

*

Celia Winsgrove appeared on the dot of seven thirty. She'd changed into a cream blouse and tweed skirt, which she wore with sturdy-heeled court shoes.

'Would you like a drink before dinner, Miss Winsgrove?' Simon asked.

'No, thank you. Some water with my meal would be nice. Tap water, that is. I don't agree with all these silly-sounding and expensive so-called spring waters in bottles.'

'Quite so,' said Simon.

Tess busied herself behind the open door into the kitchen so she could hear their conversation, keen to know how Miss Winsgrove would fare with Dominic.

Dominic, pink-faced after two large vodkas, emerged from the sitting room and sat down opposite. He held out his hand. 'Dominic Delamere,' he said.

'Celia Winsgrove,' she said, shaking his hand. 'It would appear we're the only two guests.'

'For the moment, yes,' agreed Dominic. 'But I do believe others will be coming in the next week or two. Have you come far?'

'I've come from Dudley,' she said. 'Except I stayed overnight near Bristol.'

'Oh,' he said.

Simon came back into the kitchen and grabbed a bottle of wine.

'Dominic,' he said, 'will you be having your usual claret?'

'Oh, most definitely,' said Dominic. 'Would you like a glass, Miss Winsgrove? This is a very nice wine.'

'I don't actually drink alcohol very much,' she replied. 'Except at Christmas, when I generally partake of a sherry or two.' She giggled.

'Well, this is also an occasion for celebration, is it not? I understand you've come to paint? I think that calls for a glass of wine, don't you?'

'Well, just a *very* small one, then, Mr Delamere.'

'Please call me Dominic.'

'Are you here on business, Mr Dela… Dominic?'

'No, I'm also hoping to be creative. I'm planning to write a book.'

'How interesting. I say, these mushrooms are rather nice.'

'Tess and Simon are excellent cooks and very good hosts. I'm looking forward to the goulash.'

Celia took a small sip of wine. 'Goulash? I don't think I've had that before. I'm afraid I have rather conservative tastes.'

'Well, there's no time like the present for trying something new. Aren't artists supposed to have eclectic tastes?'

'I've not actually painted before,' Celia said, taking another sip. 'This is just something I've always wanted to do.'

Tess was pressed up against the edge of the door hoping to find out something more about each of her guests. Aware that they'd finished their first course, she ventured into the dining room to remove the plates.

'That was delicious, Tess,' Dominic said. 'I was just about to ask Miss Winsgrove here why she had left it so late to start her new hobby.'

'Oh, is this a recent interest, then?' Tess asked.

'Well, I've always been interested but I couldn't give it much time before.'

'Oh, why is that?'

'My mother died recently and she was an invalid for many years, so I didn't have the freedom to get out and about. I was working as well, until a couple of weeks ago.' Celia sipped her wine again.

'Oh, I'm sorry about your mother,' Tess said.

'Well, she was ninety-seven and very cranky,' said Celia matter-of-factly. 'That starter was delicious.'

'Thank you,' said Tess.

As she headed back into the kitchen she found Simon dishing up the goulash. 'Did you hear that?' she whispered. And they both dissolved into giggles. They really did have an eclectic mix of guests!

CHAPTER 17

TITANIA

Titania Terry swore continually as she did eighty miles an hour down the M5 in her sporty old Toyota. She couldn't abide these dreadful drivers tootling along at less than seventy in the middle lane and holding everyone up. The motorway was busy today, being Friday. She wished she'd set off a day earlier. Then she got stuck in the middle lane because of so much overtaking traffic and ended up behind an enormous great truck trying to overtake another enormous great truck. The one in the slow lane was probably doing fifty miles an hour, and the one overtaking it doing fifty-one, so the whole operation took about five minutes, and why the hell would they bother? Titania wondered. God, it was a long way to Cornwall. But she'd get there in another couple of hours hopefully.

She was wearing her purple kaftan with the silver embroidery, along with her black leggings. She wasn't sure about the silver boots; they weren't particularly summery or comfortable, but they looked just right with this outfit. And she was wearing her chains and her bracelets which jangled each time she changed gear.

The A30 was busy, too, and so was the B-road that supposedly led to Portmerryn. It went on and on and on. Titania sang along to Radio 2 and shouted at some silly old fool in front who – as well as holding everyone up doing thirty miles per hour – had suddenly decided to turn left without any warning. He shouldn't have a driving licence, Titania decided. Probably some sort of country yokel. When she got to the top of the hill she got stuck behind a bus, which partly blocked her view. But she could see a lot of ocean out there, so this must be Portmerryn. And, boy, didn't it look like a one-horse town! What on earth had possessed her to book a room in this godforsaken hole? She was missing London already. She drove past the pub and saw the sign for Seagull Hill. The bus carried on to goodness-knows-where.

Didn't anyone ever fill in potholes round here? God, they were horrendous!

The guesthouse was easy to find and there was plenty room to park. That was the thing with London: parking was a complete nightmare. She checked the mirror before she got out of the car to see if the kohl had smudged round her eyes, but it was fine. What sort of people would live in a place like this? she wondered. Well, here was the first of them: a tall woman in jeans and a shirt.

'You must be Titania Terry?' the woman said.

'And you must be Tess?' Titania said, trying to ignore the arthritic protestations of her bones as she heaved herself out of the car, and wondering if she'd overdone it with the silver boots.

'Yes,' the woman said. Titania could see her looking at the boots. 'How was your journey?'

'Bloody awful,' said Titania. 'Heavy traffic most of the way.'

'Oh dear. Well, never mind, you're here now. Can I help you take some things up to your room? My husband will bring the heavy stuff.'

At that moment a rather attractive man, presumably the husband, appeared. 'Simon Sparrow,' he said.

Titania had seen him somewhere before, no doubt about it. 'Titania Terry,' she said, smiling and hoping there wasn't lipstick on her teeth.

'Ah,' he said, 'the famous Titania Terry! Didn't you do the Old Vic back in the—'

'Yes, it was a few years ago,' she interrupted. 'I've done most of the West End theatres, darling, and lately just touring. You know how it is.' She hesitated. 'I feel sure I've seen you somewhere along the line.'

'You might have done,' he said. 'I was an actor. Still am occasionally.'

'Oh, how *wonderful!*' Titania beamed. 'How wonderful to find someone from show business in this remote place!'

'We must have a chat later. In the meantime, let me carry your luggage upstairs. I say, I love your number plate! T1 TER!'

'Well, obviously, darling, I would have *preferred* "Titania Terry", but these stupid DVLA people have no imagination!'

The stairs were tricky in the silver boots and she wobbled a little. Simon showed her into a very nice big room with a very nice big bed. There appeared to be plenty of storage for her things, and the en suite was a proper bathroom, and not those little cupboards you used to get in boarding-houses on the road. She'd hated touring. Often she'd actually had to share a bathroom with a couple of the others. At one time, when she was the star, that would have been unthinkable.

'This room doesn't have a sea view,' Simon said. 'But the view is very pleasant.'

Titania glanced out of the window and all she could see was the cars parked below and a dense collection of trees and the hill above.

'But the lounge and dining room downstairs do have great views of the sea,' Simon continued. 'So do feel free to come down any time you fancy. When the weather's warm we sit out on the terrace. Now, can we get you anything? Shall I leave you to unpack?'

Titania knew exactly what she wanted. 'Yes, I'll unpack first,' she said.

She waited until he was safely out of the door before she unearthed the bottle of gin from one of her bags. Somewhere there was probably a lukewarm tonic. She searched some more and found two of them. Pity there wasn't a fridge in the room but never mind.

She was a little concerned about Simon Sparrow having been an actor. Would he have known about her long-running relationship with Henry Houseman? Most people in the business knew about Titania Terry and Henry Houseman. Not as famous as Elizabeth Taylor and Richard Burton perhaps, but their names were linked together for years, too. Like Marks & Spencer. And Morecambe and Wise. Until that bitch came along, of course. No point in dwelling on it, she thought. It's in the past and I'm going to get my revenge. And, at eighty-five, I haven't got any time to waste.

She poured herself a hefty measure of gin and topped it up with tonic before looking in the mirror, raising her glass and saying, 'Here's to you, Titania Terry, and every success in your mission!'

CHAPTER 18

AN ECLECTIC MIX

'My God!' said Tess. 'She was like a walking Christmas tree! I've never seen so many baubles on one person in my life! Did you see the layers of make-up, Simon? How old do you suppose she is?'

'She's ancient,' Simon agreed. 'Must be well into her eighties. She was treading the boards long before I started in the business. She never quite made it to the top, though.'

'At least she says she'll eat anything,' Tess went on, 'so that's a relief. And she likes a cooked breakfast, as does Celia – can you imagine them sitting down together?'

'Should be interesting. I feel sorry for Dominic, though, with those two for company at mealtimes. I hope he doesn't regret coming.'

'I hope not. Did Titania Terry say what she was going to be doing here?'

Simon shook his head. 'Nope, just coming to relax, she said.'

'Hmm,' said Tess. 'I wonder…'

'Don't let your imagination run away with you! She's just a dotty old has-been although I do seem to remember some bloke she was tied up with. But it really all happened before my time.'

*

Dominic had almost finished his second vodka when Celia appeared.

What a strange old girl she was, Tess thought as she removed the empty tonic can. Celia was dressed as always in some boring beige ensemble and Tess couldn't work her out at all. She didn't think elderly, prim, teetotal spinsters existed these days, except in Agatha Christie novels, perhaps. What was she doing here? She said she'd always wanted to paint, which she supposed was fair enough, but somehow she suspected there was more to it than that. And then there was all this 'Mr Delamere' and 'Miss Winsgrove' business.

'Good evening, Miss Winsgrove,' Dominic said, standing up politely while she sat down on the sofa opposite. 'How are you this evening?'

'Very well, thank you, Mr Delamere,' she replied. 'Hasn't the weather been glorious?'

'It has,' Dominic agreed. 'But I *do* wish you'd call me Dominic. After all, we do look like being under the same roof for some weeks to come and I think it's perhaps time we relaxed a little.'

She didn't speak for a moment and Tess wondered if he'd over-stepped her buttoned-up mark.

Then she said, 'Yes, indeed. After all, we've known each other for a few days now. I'm Celia.'

'Have you had a good day, Celia?' Dominic asked.

'Oh, it's been very enjoyable,' she replied, 'if a little frustrating. I don't know why I thought watercolour painting would be easy, but I don't seem to be getting the effects I'd hoped for.'

'I should think it takes time, Celia.'

'Would you like a drink, Miss Winsgrove?' Tess asked.

'A lemonade, please.'

'Fine,' Tess said. 'By the way, we have another guest now. She'll probably be down in a minute.'

Celia had been sitting out on the terrace for most of the afternoon with her watercolours, and she was telling Dominic how difficult it was to depict the wild Atlantic rollers and the spray as they pounded against the cliff.

'I've been gazing at the sea today, too, trying to fire my imagination,' Dominic said. 'I think I must pay a visit to the pub this evening.'

Seven thirty came and went, dinner was almost ready and there was still no sign of Titania.

'Who's going to go up and knock on her door?' Simon asked.

'You are,' said Tess.

When he came back some minutes later, Simon was wiping his brow.

'You'll never guess,' he said, 'she was fast asleep, on top of the bed. And there was a half empty gin bottle on the table.'

'Oh God,' said Tess, 'that doesn't bode well, does it?'

Simon laughed. 'We might need to keep an eye on this one. She said she'd be down in a minute.'

'I suppose we should really give her the benefit of the doubt. After all she's an old lady and she's driven a long way.'

'True,' said Simon. 'Anyway, we can shortly start serving dinner to the other two. She shouldn't be long.'

Tess went into the sitting room and placed Celia's lemonade on the table.

'Thank you. We've decided,' Dominic said, 'to dispense with the formalities and have agreed to use first names. Have we not, Celia?'

Celia smiled primly. 'Oh, indeed.'

'Good,' said Tess, 'and I forgot to ask, would you like ice in your lemonade, Celia?'

'That won't be necessary, Mrs Sp—'

'Tess, please!'

'That won't be necessary, er, Tess.'

Dominic suppressed a yawn, shook his paper and tucked it down the side of his chair, focusing his attention on Celia.

'So you're retired now, Celia?' he asked.

'Oh yes,' she said, 'but only a few weeks ago.'

'Really? What line of business were you in?'

'I was a book-keeper, Mr... er, Dominic.'

'And for whom did you keep the books?'

She hesitated, went a little pink, and was plainly considering her reply. 'He was a garage owner.'

Not for a moment could Tess imagine her in the world of car sales, either new or second-hand. Then again she did have a smart BMW.

'I assume you're interested in cars?' Dominic asked.

'Not in the slightest,' Celia replied. 'It was purely a convenient place for me to work.'

'Oh,' Dominic said, looking baffled.

Then she must have felt some sort of explanation was called for because she added, 'I had to be close to home, you understand, because Mummy was an invalid for so long. I needed to be able to nip home. Always in my lunch break, and sometimes in my tea breaks, too.'

'I see,' said Dominic, who plainly didn't. 'Were you there for some time?'

'Oh yes,' Celia replied. 'More than thirty years.'

'You must have enjoyed it, then?'

'No, I didn't,' she said, 'I told you, it was convenient.'

Tess reappeared. 'There's no sign yet of our newest guest,' she said, 'so I thought we might as well start serving dinner.'

The large table in the dining room next door seated twelve people, and Dominic and Celia had taken to sitting opposite each other at the far end, closest to the view. A third place had been set next to Celia.

They'd almost finished their Cornish crab starter when Tess saw Titania walking in: a tiny old woman with badly dyed red hair, a low-cut pink mini-dress which displayed an off-putting amount of crepey cleavage and wrinkly knees, and short, silver, high-heeled boots.

Celia almost dropped her fork and sank back in her chair, while Titania plonked herself down.

'Hi!' she said. 'I'm Titania.'

'Nice to meet you, Titania,' Dominic said. 'I'm Dominic, and this is Celia.'

'Oh, right,' said Titania, picking up her napkin. 'Have you two been married a long time?'

Celia choked noisily on her roll.

'No, no,' he explained hastily. 'We're quite separate. I'm here to write, and Celia's here to paint.'

'Oh,' said Titania, 'I suppose that's the sort of things people do down here.'

'Why are you here?' Celia asked, openly staring at the newcomer.

'Resting, darling,' Titania replied. 'I do have one little matter to settle, but basically I'm here to get away from it all. Show business tours are *so* bloody exhausting.'

'So you're an actress,' Dominic said, 'aren't you? I *thought* I might have seen you somewhere before.'

Titania seemed pleased. 'Oh, you've no idea how *tired* I am! The matinees, the late nights, the parties! Do you write plays by any chance, darling?'

'No, I'm hoping to write a novel about smuggling and shipwrecks on this coast. It's a subject that's always fascinated me.'

Titania sighed. 'You only need to watch a few episodes of *Poldark*,' she said. Then, taking a sideways glance at Celia, said, 'What sort of painting do *you* do?'

'Oh, watercolours,' Celia replied. 'I love the soft muted colours, the seascapes and the glorious English countryside. I was just telling Dominic how difficult I'm finding it to get the paint flowing the way I want it to.'

'Not my type of thing,' Titania said dismissively. She was gazing longingly at Dominic's wine bottle. 'I wouldn't mind a glass of that.'

'Then you must ask Tess to bring you a bottle,' Dominic said. 'The idea is that you have a glass or two and then it'll be stored away for you until dinner tomorrow.'

'You must tell me what wine you like,' Tess said as she cleared the plates.

Titania turned to Celia. 'What's that you're drinking? Doesn't look very interesting. Aren't you having any wine?'

'No,' Celia replied primly. 'I rarely drink.'

'How dull!' Titania was examining her closely. 'You know what, Celia? I reckon a couple of glasses of wine are just what you need to get your creative juices flowing. You'd have your paint flowing in no time at all.'

'That's as may be,' Celia said.

'I don't think Dominic knows what's hit him with these two!' Tess exclaimed as she leaned against the kitchen table.

'He'll cope!' Simon said.

'He's such a gentleman,' Tess went on. 'Unfailingly polite and charming, although I can see him suppressing yawns where Celia's concerned. But I can't imagine how he's going to cope with Titania.'

'He'll probably need an extra vodka,' Simon said, bending down to load the dishwasher and chuckling to himself. 'But you never know, they might all be firm friends before the week is out!'

CHAPTER 19

AMBER

Tess was finding it exhausting coping with cooking, cleaning, laundry, shopping and attending to the vagaries of her very disparate guests. Although Simon often helped with the cooking, he was kept busy with general maintenance and, in particular, erecting an expanse of glass panels on top of the low wall that was all that separated their guests from a certain demise.

They'd had the inevitable visits and inspections from Health and Safety. Their kitchen was declared to be hygienic, their fire precautions adequate, but the terrace wall might not be there at all, they said, for as much good as it was doing. You could easily trip over the thing, they said, and that would be the end of you. Something must be done about it quickly and, until such time as it was, a notice must be placed in the middle of the terrace warning guests to keep their distance. Furthermore, the inspector said, he'd be back shortly to check that the work had been done.

'Does he think we're driving our guests to suicide or something?' Simon had joked. 'Should we call it "Lemmings' Leap"?'

Tess had been worrying about the wall for some time, particularly when the children visited. How did you make the terrace secure without blocking the view from downstairs? Hence the glass panels. Tess now lived in fear that Simon might be called up to London for more voice-overs or something and leave the job half done. They couldn't afford to turn down the opportunity of any further money. But in spite of all the extra expense Tess finally accepted that she needed help in the house, and phoned Gina.

'Yes, of course,' Gina said. 'How about I do a couple of hours every morning after I've finished in the pub? I'd get all the cleaning done easy and, if there was time left, I could do some of your ironing or something.'

Tess sighed with relief. Gina began work at The Portmerryn Arms at about seven thirty, clearing up from the night before, and she could be with Tess by half past nine to start cleaning upstairs while the guests were breakfasting. Well, two of the guests would probably be breakfasting at a normal time but Titania Terry was a law unto herself, rarely emerging before the breakfast deadline of ten o'clock.

'Does she have late nights, then?' Gina asked Tess as she sat down for a coffee, having done Dominic's and Celia's bedrooms and bathrooms. 'Not that there's exactly a surplus of nightclubs round here.'

'No, she doesn't go out,' Tess replied. 'She says she likes to watch old movies in her room, but I suspect she has a supply of gin hidden somewhere.'

'Never a dull moment!' Gina said cheerfully. 'I'll check for empty bottles.'

Tess grinned. 'I think she's probably thought of that because I notice she brings down a carrier bag in the morning and puts it in her car before breakfast.'

'Ah, concealing the evidence!'

'Exactly!'

Tess was concerned mainly about Celia. Dominic was amenable to everyone, did his writing, read his newspaper and drank his vodka tonics before dinner, when he had a glass or two of claret.

Titania took herself off during the day to goodness-knows-where and generally got back in the late afternoon and probably started on the gin. She then prattled on non-stop all through dinner – always clad in something outlandish – about her theatrical experiences, who she knew, who she didn't know.

Celia, for all her painting aspirations, rarely ventured far. Tess reckoned she had a haunted look about her and it was patently obvious that she and Titania were not getting on. This was hardly surprising if you considered they were two completely opposite and extreme specimens of elderly womanhood.

They breakfasted separately, none of them bothered about lunch, but it was in the evening that the three of them came together for drinks and dinner. This was the problem with having three single guests, and perhaps it would be easier when the fourth bedroom was let out in a week's time to a couple from Essex who were 'hoping to rejuvenate their marriage', whatever that meant. In the meantime, Bedroom 4 was still vacant.

Tess telephoned her daughter. 'Have you any time off in the coming week, Amber?'

'Let me check,' Amber said. Then, a minute later, 'Hey, I could do Sunday and Monday, Mum. I've got to be on set for a Thomas Hardy thing they're filming for TV on Tuesday morning. Let's see if I can get a flight down on Saturday night and one back Monday night. Peter would love to come but he's off to Dubai on Sunday; you *know* how it is!'

Tess did indeed know how it was. Although Amber and Peter had only married a couple of years ago, they'd been living together for a very long time – Peter on his worldwide business trips and Amber, a senior make-up artist who was much in demand, and frequently on location somewhere or other. Tess didn't know how they survived as a couple because their paths so rarely coincided in that large state-of-the-art Wimbledon apartment. Perhaps that was exactly why their relationship *did* survive.

Now Tess was excited at the prospect of Amber's visit. She got on well with her only daughter and missed their lunches together when Amber related the latest juicy show business gossip, who was sleeping with whom, and all sorts of celebrity secrets.

It was a pity Room 4 didn't have a sea view but that couldn't be helped. Anyway, Amber was quite capable of enjoying the scenery from the terrace without toppling over the wall.

Amber arrived on a late flight at Newquay and it was almost dark when Tess drove her up the drive to The Sparrows' Nest.

'Hey, Mum, this looks impressive!' she said as she got out the car, shaking her auburn hair and straightening out her long limbs. She yawned and stretched. 'This looks like a lot of house!'

As Tess led the way in, Simon emerged from the kitchen to hug his stepdaughter. 'Hi, Amber! Good flight?'

'Not bad,' Amber replied, heading into the kitchen. '*This* is very nice.'

'You should have seen it when we first arrived!' Tess exclaimed. 'There was a sink, two electric points and not much else. When you've had a look round I'll bore you with the before and after photos of this place.'

'Our guests have all gone upstairs,' Simon said, 'so why don't you two go through to the lounge and I'll bring you drinks. I've even floodlit the terrace in your honour!'

Amber smiled. 'I see you've got him fully trained, Mum.'

Later, as they sat together with a bottle of wine, Tess regaled Amber with descriptions of their somewhat odd guests.

'I remember Titania Terry,' Amber said. 'She had a small part in a war epic I was on some years ago. It took me longer to scrape off all her own make-up than it did to do her up for the film. She had a big thing with Henry Houseman for years. Remember him?'

'Only vaguely,' Tess replied, sipping her wine.

'Well, he was known to be a bit of a lothario and I think most of the passion was on her side. Then he scarpered off with some other old bird, Clarice Somebody-or-Other, and he was dead within weeks. Come to think of it, I seem to remember that Clarice lived down here somewhere in Cornwall – the Lizard, I think.'

'Perhaps Titania plans to visit her?' Tess suggested.

'I doubt it. I shouldn't think there was much love lost between these two. After all, she stole Titania's bloke.'

'I wonder why she's come down here then? Perhaps Henry's buried in Cornwall and she's come to visit the grave?'

'Who knows?'

'Anyway, you'll like Dominic. He's nice, easy to get on with. And he's writing a book. Don't know what you'll make of Celia. She's very prim and proper, no make-up at all, looked after an ailing mother for years. Real stereotypical spinster but there's *something* about her… can't quite make her out. She's trying to paint. They're all here for weeks but at least they're paying well, and we have lots of bookings for later in the year.'

'That's great, Mum, and not too many for you to cope with; just the four rooms.'

'When you vacate your room we have a couple from Essex coming for a month. Don't quite know what they're planning to be doing.'

As Amber headed upstairs she told her mother that she wouldn't be eating a cooked breakfast but had decided she'd like to join the guests out of curiosity. She'd appear for a continental breakfast when she knew they'd be sitting down.

She made her entrance into the dining room just as Dominic was spreading marmalade on his toast and Celia was pouring herself another cup of tea.

Tess made the introductions. 'Amber's just come down for a couple of days to see the place before our next guests arrive.'

Dominic stood up to shake her hand and Celia, seated, did the same.

'Have you come far?' Dominic asked.

'From London,' Amber replied. 'Flew down last night and Mum picked me up from Newquay. So it was dark when I got here and I wasn't able to see the view. Isn't it amazing?' She wandered across to gaze out the window before sitting down next to Dominic.

'It's stunning,' said Celia, dabbing her lips daintily with the napkin. 'I'm trying very hard to do justice to it with my painting but I fear the effect I'm striving to create completely eludes me.'

At that moment Titania appeared, clad in an emerald green kaftan heavily embroidered with silver and gold sequins on the front, silver high-heeled sandals, half a dozen jangling bracelets and her dyed hair tied up in a messy knot adorned with some sparkly clips. Although Amber had vaguely remembered seeing her before, Tess noticed her daughter still did a double take. And she knew exactly what Amber was thinking – this woman really did look just like a walking Christmas tree!

Amber shook Titania's bony be-ringed hand. 'I think we may have met some years ago,' she said, 'when I did your make-up for *They Shall Not Win*, remember? I think it was at Elstree Studios.'

'Oh probably, darling,' Titania replied dismissively. 'I was kept so busy at that time it's hard to remember everyone. Was Henry with me?'

'Not that I recall,' Amber replied.

'How nice to meet someone from the world of show business!' Titania exclaimed, sipping her orange juice. She looked with distaste at Celia, who was rising from the table with a polite 'excuse me' and heading hastily out the door, closely followed by Dominic, who said it was time for his morning walk.

Amber turned her attention back to Titania. 'Well, it must be nice to get away from it all. I understand you're here for some time?'

'Oh, just a few weeks, darling, to recharge the batteries.'

'What do you plan to be doing? Reading? Writing? Painting? Walking?'

'Oh, just one or two things that need attending to,' Titania said vaguely.

At that moment Tess came back in with Titania's cooked breakfast and Amber made her escape. Tess followed Amber into the kitchen and began to load up the dishwasher.

'Leave that for a moment, Mum,' Amber said. 'I'd like you to show me round outside.' Tess linked arms with her daughter as they wandered past the line of parked cars and then headed through the trees to the famous Windsor Castle. Amber grinned at her mother. 'I can see your handiwork in here, all these colourful cushions and curtains. Very cosy. Peter and I could happily ensconce ourselves in this quirky little retreat. Mind you, I can understand how nervous you must have been here alone during the long dark nights when Simon was in London. I can well imagine how scary it was.'

When they wandered round to the rear of the house to admire the view they found Simon struggling to erect the final few glass panels on the wall.

'Can't wait to get this job finished and take that damned sign down,' he said. He indicated the expanse of glass that formed the dining room window. 'I'm sick of being gawped at by that old bat.'

Tess turned round to see Titania gazing out admiringly, watching Simon's every move.

He sighed. 'It's disconcerting, I can tell you.'

Tess was highly amused by Titania's obvious adoration of Simon.

'Oh yes,' she said to Amber as they sipped coffee in the kitchen. 'She never takes her eyes off him and it's driving him mad! What do you think of her, anyway?'

Amber thought for a moment. 'I know she's slightly batty but I get the definite impression that she's down here for a reason. Keep me posted on what she gets up to!'

'I will,' Tess said.

'I assume that flashy red BMW is Titania's?'

'Believe it or not,' Tess replied, 'that is *Celia's* car.'

'*Celia's*? I imagined her driving around in an old Morris Minor or something. Well, that's a surprise! I had a good look through the windows and there's less than a thousand miles on the clock so she's not had it long. And have you noticed her watch?'

'Not really, no.'

'Well, from where I was sitting it was almost certainly a Rolex. It was expensive, anyway. Did you say she was retired?'

'Yes, apparently she is,' Tess said.

'She must have a good pension, then.'

Tess looked thoughtful. 'I wouldn't have thought it was excessive. From what I gather she worked in the office of some garage or other for years and years. Mind you her mother died recently so possibly she inherited a fair bit.'

'Probably invested it wisely so she could have a nice long holiday. With a nice flashy car. And a nice flashy watch.'

'Probably,' Tess agreed.

*

Tess enjoyed Amber's visit. She took Amber down to The Portmerryn Arms for lunchtime drinks and sandwiches as the guests had all gone out for the day. There was the usual quartet of ancient locals rattling away with their dominoes in the corner, and several groups of walkers with their sturdy boots and backpacks, all ordering one of Jed's famous lunchtime fry-ups. More surprisingly, Dominic was sitting in the corner with a pint of beer and reading his *Daily Telegraph*. He looked up and waved as they came in, but then continued reading his paper.

Tess introduced Amber to Jed and to Gideon, who was drying glasses in the background.

'Well, this is all as it should be,' Amber remarked as they sat down by the window. 'Proper spit 'n' sawdust pub! I bet it's cosy in the winter.'

'It is,' Tess agreed, 'and Jed and Annie have been very helpful to us. And Gideon, too.'

'Nice looking chap,' Amber observed.

'Gideon? Bit of an enigma,' Tess said, 'and still living at home with Mum and Dad. He must be well in his forties. Nice guy, though.'

Afterwards they strolled along the beach to watch the surfers and Tess pointed out the rear of the cottage which she and Simon had rented nearly a year ago.

'You're not sorry you came, are you, Mum?'

'No, not at all,' Tess replied truthfully. 'It's been a struggle at times to get everything up and running, but worth it in the end. Do you think you could climb up the cliff? There's a not-too-steep path that winds its way up, and the view from the top is spectacular.'

'Just as well I brought my trainers then.'

As they made their way carefully up the stony coastal path they met several groups of serious walkers, complete with poles.

'Lots of people walk the South-West Coast Path,' Tess explained. 'Very few walk it all in one go but you get a lot of others who walk so many miles each time, and then come back the following year to continue from where they left off. The pub does a brisk trade all summer.'

The path was steep in places and they stopped halfway up for a rest.

'We must look like real wimps,' Amber said as groups of walkers overtook them with cheerful remarks like, 'Steep, isn't it?' and 'Lovely day!'

When they got to the top Amber was overcome by the view up and down the coast from Hartland Point to Trevose Head, while the surf crashed onto the rocks beneath. On the horizon a couple of enormous container ships were heading up to Bristol and – closer to shore – a couple of fishing boats were bobbing up and down on the waves.

'It's stunning,' Amber observed as she took countless panoramic shots on her phone. 'I almost expect Ross Poldark to come riding along any minute!'

'Well, they do film it on this coast,' Tess said, 'but not at the moment.'

They spent almost an hour sitting on the old wooden seat amidst the thrift and the gorse and the wild thyme at the top of the cliff, gazing out to sea. When they got back to The Sparrows' Nest they found Simon had finished erecting the glass panels and had removed the offending sign.

*

Amber's visit was all too short and, early the next evening while Simon was starting to prepare dinner, Tess drove her to Newquay Airport to get the flight back to London. Amber enthused about her visit, about the house and about the stunning scenery. She promised to return, with Peter, and that they'd be more than happy to be accommodated in Windsor Castle.

'Don't forget, Mum,' she said, 'I want you to keep me updated with all the nitty-gritty on your crazy guests!'

'Don't worry, I will,' Tess said. 'You're not the only one who's dying to know what they're planning to do next.'

CHAPTER 20

THE MERRYWEATHERS

Joe Merryweather swore as he got stuck in his Mercedes behind a tractor for mile after mile with no opportunity to overtake.

'Wouldn't you think he'd pull in somewhere and let us pass?' he ranted.

'Well, he's only doing his job and we're in no great hurry,' Jackie reasoned.

'Oh, I get it, the tractor driver's right and I'm wrong, as usual,' Joe snapped.

'Pretty much,' said Jackie, adjusting her hair in the mirror.

'You've done nothing but criticise my driving the whole bloody way down here!'

'No, I haven't. I just get fed up of you shouting abuse at other road users and then driving up the backside of whatever car's in front.'

At this point the tractor turned into a farm gateway.

'Not before time!' Joe snarled as he accelerated wildly, only to find himself behind a very slow-moving tanker. 'Bloody *hell*.'

Jackie sniggered. 'Serves you right!'

'I don't know why you chose this hell-hole of a place anyway; we could have gone to Southend or Margate or – if you really wanted to get further away – Blackpool! That's a great place, Blackpool!'

'We wanted to get away somewhere completely different, if you remember? We wanted peace and quiet so we could sort ourselves out, and that's what we're going to have, Joe.'

Joe pulled a face and continued at a steady thirty behind the tanker. 'What's *he* doing in the middle of nowhere, anyway?'

'Probably heading for Portmerryn, same as us.'

'Bloody hell, we've miles to go yet!'

Jackie sighed. This did not bode well for what was supposed to be an idyllic break to repair their ailing marriage – although at times like this she was none too sure if she really wanted it repaired. The kids were off their hands years ago, they'd both retired, the mortgage was paid and freedom beckoned. Perhaps what she needed was freedom from this bully of a man she'd been married to for the past thirty-seven years. This holiday had been her idea. Jackie hoped that, away from everyone and everything, they might recapture something of those early days before he got so stressed and bad-tempered with business. One last try and, if it didn't work, she was off. People didn't stick in dodgy marriages these days. And she was only just beginning to realise that she didn't have to put up with Joe's behaviour any more.

The tanker slowed right down.

'*Now* what?' Joe yelled, and they crawled along for at least a couple of hundred yards before they saw a young deer jump up from in front of the tanker and hurl itself through the hedge.

'Oh, how lovely!' Jackie exclaimed. 'I think it was a young one.'

'Damned nuisance!' Joe growled. 'The tanker driver should have had it – nice bit of roadkill venison.'

'Is there no end to your nastiness?' Jackie sighed. 'Such lovely creatures!'

She realised nothing was going to please him. He didn't want to be here in the first place and he seemed to be becoming more and more aggressive. She was already regretting her decision to make this trip.

'Just *look* at that view!' exclaimed Jackie when they rounded the top of the hill and Portmerryn came into view.

'Yeah, very nice, what I can see of it round this bleeding tanker.' Joe's temper was not improving.

'And look at that cliff! It's practically vertical! And all that sea – the Atlantic Ocean!'

'I did do geography at school so I know it's the Atlantic bleedin' ocean. Blackpool's on the Atlantic, just in case you hadn't noticed.'

'I suppose it is in a *way*, but it's really the Irish Sea,' Jackie sighed, 'and it's not the same as the proper ocean. Just look at all that surf!'

Her husband snorted but said nothing. As they came down into the village Jackie said, 'What a sweet little shop!'

'Fine if you need to buy a bucket and spade but shouldn't think they sell much else.'

'Do you *always* have to be such a pessimist?'

'I'm just bloody realistic, that's all. It's you who's in cloud cuckoo land. Anyway, shouldn't think there's much call for your sushi stuff round here.'

'I've not come to Cornwall for sushi, I've come for peace and quiet and a cream tea or two!'

As they passed the row of fisherman's cottages Joe espied The Portmerryn Arms. 'At least there's a pub!'

'Next left,' said Jackie.

'What? *Where?*'

'Slow down, Joe! Damn, you've missed it – it was that narrow turning back there. You'll have to reverse a bit but there's no one behind.'

Joe swore under his breath as he reversed back and then accelerated up the hill, hitting one of the larger potholes as he did so. 'Bloody hell! There's even craters in the road!'

'Well, if you didn't drive like a maniac you'd be able to see them and avoid them. Now, we're looking for a turning on the right but slow down or we'll miss that, too.'

'Godforsaken place!' muttered Joe as he swerved up the drive to The Sparrows' Nest. 'What sort of a name is that, anyway? Shouldn't think the sparrows would bother to fly up here.'

'It's because it's a Mr and Mrs Sparrow who own it. I think it's a brilliant name.'

Joe parked alongside a smart red BMW. 'Looks like they might have some decent guests here,' he conceded as he stood admiring it. 'That's the latest sports model, must have cost a bob or two,' he added approvingly.

As they entered through the open front door Jackie headed towards the attractive lady behind the desk in the large hallway.

'Hello!' said the lady. 'You must be Mr and Mrs Merryweather? How was your journey?'

'Bloody awful,' said Joe, 'holiday traffic everywhere, crawling along…'

'It wasn't *that* bad,' Jackie said, glaring at her husband. 'Anyway, it's what you'd expect this time of year. I'm Jackie, and this is Joe.'

'I'm Tess. Let me get your key and I'll show you to your room.'

Tess picked up the key and led the way upstairs to Room 4.

'Oh, what a lovely room!' said Jackie, looking around.

'Where's the sea view?' asked Joe.

'I *told* you we didn't have a sea view,' snapped Jackie.

'I'm sorry but the two rooms with sea views are booked for several weeks,' Tess said, 'I did explain that. But we have a glass-walled sitting room and dining room and a large terrace from where you're most welcome to enjoy the sea view.'

'Lovely!' exclaimed Jackie, looking through the door into the bathroom. 'Look, Joe, a lovely big en suite with a bath and all!'

'A shower's good enough for me,' said Joe.

He was determined not to like anything, approve of anything or even be moderately pleasant. Jackie was feeling ashamed and embarrassed and wondered again if she could stand his undiluted company for even a few days, far less a few weeks. This looked like having been a dreadful, dreadful mistake.

'I'll get my husband to help you up with your luggage,' Tess said.

'No need,' said Joe, 'I can manage a couple of cases. We ain't here for months.'

'Well then, I'll leave you to it,' Tess said. 'Dinner is at seven thirty but I could do you a cream tea, if you liked, in the meantime?'

'Have you any beer?' Joe asked.

'Yes, we have cans of beer but the pub down the road has lots of different beers on tap.'

'That's where I'll be going,' he said.

'You'll be going on your own then,' said Jackie under her breath.

CHAPTER 21

PORT ISAAC

Tess wandered round to where Simon was erecting a trellis around their large oil tank.

'So many rules and regulations,' he sighed. 'Got to leave a foot clear all the way round, got to do this, got to do that. Where would we be without Health and Safety ruling our lives, eh? Was that the new people I heard arriving?'

'It certainly was. Not a happy couple, and he's really quite objectionable, bordering on rude.'

'Probably just had a bad journey?'

'Think it's more likely they've got a bad marriage,' Tess said. 'He's off to the pub already and she's making tea for herself in the room while she unpacks.'

'All sounds very jolly,' Simon said as he hammered the final nail of a section of the trellis into the post. 'Dinner should be fun; I wonder what Dominic will make of them.' He laid down his hammer and glanced at his watch. 'It's only one o'clock so why don't we go out for a couple of hours on our own? How about Port Isaac? We could have a drink and a snack.'

'What a lovely idea!' Tess said.

Ten minutes later they were heading down the road that hugged the coast, admiring the stunning view of the harbour at Boscastle and the sheer ruggedness of the cliffs as they headed towards Tintagel. Tiny clouds were drifting across the sky and dappling the aquamarine and turquoise of the sea with patches of mauve where they cast their shadows, all topped by the white horses as the wind whipped the top of the waves.

On arrival at Port Isaac Simon said, 'I'm parking at the top of the town because I've no intention of squeezing through those narrow alleys they call streets round here.'

They walked down as far as the Golden Lion which, they were relieved to see, was relatively quiet, practically empty, in fact. As Simon ordered the drinks he commented on this to the barman who said, 'It's 'cos everyone's down at The Platt watching the filming. It's a *Doc Martin* day today.'

Tess was tempted to go down and have a look, but Simon wouldn't hear of it. 'I was an extra on the first episode of *Doc Martin*, and that was enough for me, thank you very much! The poor runners, running hither and yon to stop folks walking down the back lanes and coming into shot. Then you have the locals waiting to drive through and beeping their horns so the footage is unusable, and they have to refilm. Believe me – it's chaos. Besides, you can get a wonderful view from the balcony out there and be above it all.'

Tess was in need of sustenance and the prospect of a cool shandy and a crab sandwich won the day, while Simon opted for a pint of prawns.

As Tess sipped her drink, she said, 'Aren't we lucky to live here!'

Simon placed his hand over hers. 'So you've no regrets then, my love?'

'None at all,' Tess heard herself say and realised how much she meant it. 'I know we've been here less than a year but already I feel part of the place and can't imagine living in the South-East again.'

'The noise, the traffic, the aircraft screaming overhead,' Simon prompted.

'Having to wash my hair every day,' Tess added, 'whereas down here it still feels and looks clean after three or four days.'

'Everything's at such a slow pace, though,' Simon said. 'Nobody rushes to do anything. It'll all get done *dreckly*!'

'I'm finally beginning to understand that the world won't end if we don't get something done like *yesterday*,' Tess said.

'And what about our guests?'

Tess thought for a moment. 'Well, they might be a tad eccentric, but I really like that. Although they hail from upcountry we'd never have met them there, would we? I mean we'd probably have written them off as a bit weird and forgotten them. But you can't write off people who're living under your roof, can you?'

'No, you certainly can't. And you don't miss the family too much, do you, Tess?'

'Just sometimes,' she replied, 'particularly the little ones. When you only see them every few months you realise how quickly they're growing and you worry they might forget you.'

Simon grinned. 'They aren't going to forget *you*! And, like you said, when they're a little older they can come down on their own.'

'What about Damien?' Tess asked hesitantly.

'What about him? He's a free spirit. He's made his lifestyle choice, Tess, and I have to accept that. Of course I'd like him to be a family man and come visiting with wife and kids, but that's not Damien's style.'

'There's still time,' Tess said.

Simon shook his head. 'I doubt he'll ever lead a conventional life. Now, in spite of what I said, I'm beginning to wonder if they want anyone for a speaking part for *Doc Martin*?'

'Surely your agent would have been in touch if they needed you? You don't miss acting too much, do you, Simon?'

'I miss it much less than I thought I would,' he replied. 'But you must admit the money would be useful.'

'You're much more useful to me charming the guests and cooking an occasional dinner!' Tess said. 'Between us we'll make it OK. I love it so much now I couldn't bear for it to fail. We're attracting the type of people who are seeking peace and seclusion for whatever reason, and the bookings for next year are rolling in. We're going to be OK.'

'Yes, we are,' Simon agreed. 'Now, when we've finished here, shall we wander a little further down and get ourselves one of the huge ice creams I see everyone clutching as they pass by, trying to devour them before they melt!'

'I wonder how many flavours we can squeeze into one cone?' Tess pushed away her plate and drained her glass. 'Shall we go find out?'

'Yeah, let's,' Simon confirmed, as they stood up.

CHAPTER 22

UNWANTED COMPANY

Celia decided to have an early night. She'd hoped to have a couple of hours reading her book in comfortable, companionable silence in the lounge, as she had on previous evenings with Dominic. But no such luck, with that dreadful Titania going on nonstop about the plays she'd appeared in, the actors she knew, the awful goings-on these people indulged in. Dominic probably had some idea what she was talking about, but she certainly didn't.

At times like this Celia questioned her wisdom at coming to this place, and who might be coming next. Lucifer himself, probably. She'd chosen The Sparrows' Nest mainly because it was well off the beaten track. People did not pass here on their way to somewhere else because Portmerryn – if you came down into the village – was pretty well at the end of the line. And Celia did not wish to be found. She intended to stay here until she decided what to do and where to go on a permanent basis. She could afford to stay here as long as she liked, to drink wine every night if she so desired. She'd opened a bank account with a new bank after years and years of being with Barclays. Mummy would have been horrified, of course, but Mummy had finally passed away, and Celia intended to have *her* time before it was too late.

She couldn't help but wonder how Dick Sampson was reacting. Tricky Dicky, as he was known in the trade. Nasty little man in his camel hair coat, selling second-hand cars. He'd even been dragged to court a couple of times for selling unroadworthy vehicles, but mostly he got away with it.

Several times over the years she'd asked for a pay rise.

'Listen, darling,' he'd say, 'times are hard at the moment. Ask me again in a month or two.' And, in the thirty-two years she'd worked in that poky little office, he'd only upped her wages a couple of times, and then purely because, by law, he had to comply with paying the lowest living wage. But the garage was a five-minute walk from home, so no commuting costs, and she could pop back for coffee, for lunch, for any problem. And Mummy had plenty of problems.

She was good at her job. Apart from doing his bookwork, VAT, tea-making and phone answering, she cleaned the office and the tiny toilet, and she even bought the loo rolls. He knew when he was on to a good thing. None of these young girls he drooled over would do half of what she did, and he was well aware of it. By the same token Celia could have found a much better paid job just about anywhere, but it would have meant a minimum of half an hour on the bus or train each way, and would have left Mummy with only a ten-minute visit from the poor old overstretched social services in her absence. How would she have got to the bathroom? It didn't bear thinking about. No, the arrangement worked well for both Celia and Dick. And Dicky was never one for checking the bookwork.

Now here she was in Portmerryn, which was about as far away as you could get from Dudley and the industrial Midlands where she'd always lived, without going abroad. She didn't want to get involved with passports. She didn't mind Dominic because he kept himself to himself, he was polite and he didn't ask questions. But now this awful woman had arrived, with her painted face and ridiculous clothes and, Celia suspected, an alcohol problem. Yak, yak, yak, and asking questions all the time. Celia intended to give her a wide berth.

The next day, Celia found a nice little ledge halfway up the coastal path among the gorse bushes where she could set up her easel in comparative privacy. It afforded her not only a great view of the ocean but also of the surrounding countryside. And she discovered that she was much better at coping with the greens and golds of the trees and fields than she was at trying to depict the raging moods of the sea. At least the countryside stood still.

It was late afternoon and she thought that shortly she should be packing up and going back to have a shower. She loved her little spot and each day was terrified that someone might encroach on her hideaway or, worse, decide to paint alongside her.

Just then she heard a female voice call out, 'Coo-ee! Aren't you *clever*! What a lovely picture!'

Celia bristled. She smiled politely at the short blonde woman who was probably in her mid-sixties.

'I've always wanted to have a go at painting,' said the woman. 'Now I'm retired maybe I will.'

'Good idea,' said Celia shortly. *Now go away!*

'You live round here?' the woman persisted.

'No. I'm on holiday.' Celia leaned forward and accidentally dropped some water on her blue sky which gave her a rather splendid cloud effect.

'Ooh, lovely, so am I!' There was no getting rid of the woman. 'We've just arrived. Isn't this a beautiful place?'

'It is.'

'Well, I'd better get back to the Sparrows or my husband will be wondering where I've got to. Mind you, he's probably still in the pub.'

'The Sparrows?' Celia asked, carefully washing her paintbrush.

'Yeah, over there, up that hill. That's where we're staying.'

'Oh, indeed. Well, I'd better introduce myself then because it would appear we're staying in the same place. Celia Winsgrove.'

'Well, fancy that, Celia! What a coincidence! I'm Jackie Merryweather. What have you done with *your* other half?'

Celia cleared her throat. 'My other half? I don't have an other half.'

Jackie appeared unperturbed. 'Ah, so you're here on your own then, Celia. Lucky old you! I'm beginning to wish I was. Still, we can be friends, can't we?'

'I'm afraid I'm rather a solitary person,' Celia said.

'Well, never mind! You needn't be any more! I'd best be off – see you at dinner!'

With that she was gone, stepping carefully down the slope in her T-shirt, tight jeans and expensive-looking trainers, leaving a distinct trace of some musky perfume in her wake.

Celia sighed. So much for the peace and quiet she had been looking for.

CHAPTER 23

TITANIA REMEMBERS

Titania decided on the fuchsia pink and green patterned silk palazzo pants, teamed with her strappy pink top. She'd already acquired a little bit of a suntan and she knew she'd easily outshine the other women around here. Which wouldn't be difficult. Tess was quite stylish but Titania intended to open Simon's eyes as to how a woman could *really* look: exciting, colourful, flamboyant.

He was such an impressive lovely man, that Simon Sparrow. OK, so she was considerably older than him, but that was all the fashion these days. Look at Vivienne Westwood! Look at Brigitte Macron! *They'd* got the right idea!

Titania had gone shopping yesterday and stocked up with gin and cans of tonic, which she kept hidden in her locked suitcase in the bottom of the wardrobe. She wondered if she should join the other two for a drink before dinner this evening but then decided against it. Simon did a lot of the cooking apparently so, as a result, didn't usually appear until after they'd eaten to ask if they'd enjoyed the meal and to offer liqueurs. No point in wasting her lovely outfit on those other two.

Never in her life had Titania met such a dull woman as that Celia with her buttoned-up blouse (and personality), her floral skirt and awful clumpy sandals. Not a scrap of make-up! And boy, did she need some adornment! Had no one ever injected any fun or colour into her life?

Dominic was OK. Titania had seen straight away that he was gay, but that was fine by her. She'd got loads of gay friends in show business and at least he wouldn't be coming on to her, like lots of men did, being as she'd never lost her sex appeal.

Titania rather hoped Simon Sparrow might be coming on to her because, my God, he was *so* fanciable. Titania liked her men younger these days. Who would want some old guy in his eighties, for goodness' sake? All they wanted was a cook/housekeeper/nursemaid for their dotage and she wasn't going to be having any of that, thank you very much.

Anyway, no one would ever match up to Henry, the love of her life. 'Titania Terry and Henry Houseman' used to be uttered in the same breath, until the time that evil, scheming bitch, Clarice D'Arcy, got her claws into him. At least Clarice hadn't had Henry for very long because his poor heart couldn't keep up with her infamous voracious sexual appetite. She had killed Henry as sure as if she'd stabbed him through the heart. Then, all that wailing to the press about how much she'd *adored* him, how much he'd *adored* her, and how very *special* their short time together had been. When one reporter had asked, 'Don't you think Titania Terry might be grief-stricken, too, after all the years *they* were together?' she'd had the gall to reply, 'Titania Terry? She's *history!*'

And so will you be shortly, madam, Titania Terry avowed. And that was the reason she was really staying at The Sparrows' Nest.

Tomorrow she intended to make her first expedition to the Lizard to find Black Rock Cove which – so far as she could discern from her map – was very close to Land's End. She'd need to suss the area, make some calculations. She could ask Simon tonight the best way to get there and achieve the opportunity of a few precious moments in his company.

Titania was, as always, a little late in getting to the dining room. Dominic, Celia, a blonde woman and a loutish-looking man were already tucking into their starters. Celia was wearing a very boring blue-and-white-striped shirtdress this evening, plus clumpy sandals and her grey hair tucked behind her ears. The blonde was wearing a tight-fitting sundress, huge hoop earrings and a lot of make-up. She looked as if she might pop out of the dress at any minute.

Titania looked from one to the other of the new couple. 'Titania Terry,' she announced. They showed no sign of recognition. Such *ignorant* people. The man grunted something inaudible, and the woman stood up, pumped her hand and said, 'Jackie and Joe Merryweather! And *I'm* the Jackie!' She giggled, then looked at her husband with some distaste.

'You may have seen me on stage,' Titania said grandly. 'I used to do a fair bit of touring. Where do you come from?'

'We're from Colchester; that's in Essex,' said the blonde called Jackie. 'But we don't go to the theatre that much.'

'We'd certainly remember *you* if we did,' said the loutish husband with a smirk.

'I don't think,' said Titania, sitting down, 'that we ever performed in Colchester. We went to the big cities like Manchester and Birmingham – and Edinburgh, of course. But mainly I acted in the West End.' She poured herself a generous measure of wine, glad that she hadn't decided to have pre-dinner drinks with this lot. Dominic was OK but Celia was dull and boring, and these two were positively *common*.

'So, are you going to be acting around here somewhere, Titania?' asked the blonde Jackie.

'Dear me, no!' Titania exclaimed dramatically. 'I've come here to get away from it all, darling. My agent has advised me to relax until a nice juicy part comes along.'

'Well,' said Jackie, beaming at everyone, 'haven't we got a clever bunch here! There's Dominic the author, Celia the painter, and now Titania the actress! Makes us feel ever so dull, doesn't it, Joe?'

'No,' said Joe.

Jackie ignored him. 'But we ran a very successful company, didn't we, Joe? We shouldn't tell you *really!*' She paused, plainly waiting for everyone to say, 'Go on! Do tell us!' which nobody did, so she giggled and went on anyway. 'We made ladies' undergarments – you know, stuff to hold you in, firm you up, like Spandex. It might sound funny but you'd be surprised at how many ladies are tightly controlled by us!' She laughed at her own wit. 'But we've sold up now, and we're free to get on with the rest of our lives, aren't we, Joe?'

'Aren't we *just*,' he growled, filling up his wine glass.

'Well, we're certainly an interesting lot,' Dominic said. 'And at least retirement offers us choices. I used to be a publisher and now I can only hope that some publisher might like my literary efforts. Gamekeeper turned poacher, you might say. A complete reversal of roles.'

'Well, I have no intention of retiring,' said Titania, brightening up as Simon himself came in with the main course. 'But lovely Simon here was an actor, too, and look at him now! Mine host!'

Simon smiled. 'And Tess was a skilled dressmaker,' he said, 'and she's had to turn her hand to cooking and baking and bed-making.'

'Ooh!' said Jackie. 'Now I know where I've seen you! You've been on the telly, haven't you?'

Simon smiled modestly. 'Now and again.'

'Oh Joe,' she prattled on, 'do you remember that serial we watched on the telly last year? What was it called?'

Joe shrugged. There followed a detailed discussion about every TV programme and film that Simon might have appeared in and who he'd starred with. It was all about Simon. What about *her*? She'd been treading the boards while he was still in diapers, and no one was asking her *anything*!

Titania hitched up the strap of her pink top which had slid over her shoulder and down her arm and, if she wasn't careful, her right boob would be on show for all to see. At least that might make them sit up and pay attention!

She might fancy Simon but no way was he better known than she had been in her heyday. It was time to remind them of that.

'I remember playing Desdemona in Bristol once,' she said dreamily, 'and dear Henry was Othello. They were *wonderful* days!'

There was a polite silence before Jackie said, 'We don't go in much for Shakespeare, do we, Joe?'

Joe snorted.

'Henry was *so* brilliant as Othello,' Titania added.

'Who was Henry?' asked Jackie.

Titania looked at her with disdain. *Who was Henry!* 'Henry Houseman, of course! My partner, my mentor!' She paused for effect.

'Can't say I've ever heard of him,' Jackie said, heaping potatoes onto her plate. No wonder that dress was bulging.

Then dear Simon came to the rescue. 'I remember him, Titania.'

'He was *so* handsome!' Titania closed her eyes, the better to recall his dark eyes, chiselled features, that sensitive mouth.

'I bet you fancied him, then?' asked the stupid, inane, asinine Jackie.

'We were together for *years*!' Titania snapped. 'He was my lover, my soulmate, my *life*!'

She noticed Celia looking distinctly uncomfortable. Good. The old prune probably never had any man in *her* life.

'We made love in every major city in the UK and Europe,' she added for good measure.

'Is he dead, then?' asked Jackie.

Titania sighed. 'If he were alive, my dear, he'd be *here*.' That wasn't strictly true but she felt confident that none of this lot knew anything about *that woman*, whose name would not sully her lips. Well, Simon might, of course. And Dominic, who was no spring chicken.

Dominic cleared his throat. 'Quite so. Now, just to change the subject for a minute, Simon, how ever did you cook this pork? It is absolutely delicious.'

Simon then launched into a long monologue about marinades and herbs and things, and the moment was lost.

Titania dabbled with her pork for a few minutes and wondered when would be the best time to get Simon on his own. She didn't want it to be public knowledge that she was planning a trip down to the Lizard, because the less people who knew of her whereabouts the better. She declined pudding and followed Simon into the kitchen where, fortunately, there was no sign of Tess.

'Simon,' she said, helping him to unload some plates, 'I hope you don't mind me following you in here but I just wanted to pick your brain.' And lots more besides, she thought to herself. 'You must know this area pretty well by now and I just wondered what might be the most direct route across Cornwall to the Lizard? I fancy doing some sightseeing.'

'I'm afraid I'm no expert,' he said. What a modest man he was! 'I've never actually been down to the Lizard myself – just never had the time. But we've got some good maps which I can lend you. I'm assuming you haven't got a sat-nav, then?'

Titania shook her head.

'Well, Tess has. I'm sure she wouldn't mind you borrowing it.'

'Oh, no, no,' Titania said hastily. 'Maps will be fine. Even better if there's someone to read out the directions!' She looked to see if he was likely to respond. 'You'd be most welcome to come along for the ride if you fancied a day away from here.'

'Oh, that's a kind thought, Titania,' he said, heading towards the dishwasher, 'but there's so much to do here. If you wait in the lounge I'll bring in some maps with your coffee, as soon as I've finished serving the desserts.'

'So where's your lovely wife?' Titania asked.

'She's having a nice long bath. She's the one who did the pork that everyone's raving about. Did you want the recipe, too?'

'No, thank you,' snapped Titania. 'I'd like my coffee on the terrace, please.'

Provided, she thought, that tiresome Jackie woman isn't out there.

CHAPTER 24

NO PEACE FOR CELIA

Jackie Merryweather was becoming a nuisance; Celia didn't wish to be rude to her, but *really*! Celia had carefully chosen this secluded little spot among the gorse so she could enjoy the morning on her own. But Jackie seemed to be everywhere, minus the husband. Not that Celia blamed her for that; how had she ever come to marry such an unsociable oaf in the first place? Now she kept appearing whenever Celia set up her easel, and she was nosy. Why had Celia chosen Portmerryn? Why had she waited so long to start painting? Why had she chosen such a flashy car?

A flashy car! It wasn't flashy; it was just red and, she supposed, fast. Not that she'd ever had it above fifty. And she'd wanted to know all about Mummy, too. Had Celia never considered putting her in a home? Why had Celia spent the best years of her life looking after a doddering and demented mother?

'She wasn't doddering and demented,' Celia had snapped. 'She was just an invalid.'

'Call it what you like,' Jackie said, 'but you'd have had to sell the house, of course, to fund her care, wouldn't you?'

'No,' Celia replied, 'we wouldn't. The house was rented.' Then she cursed herself for having told her.

'Rented?' Jackie spent a few moments digesting this. 'Well,' she said, 'perhaps she kept her money under the mattress!' Then she laughed inanely.

How rude! Celia knew now for sure she should not have told her the house was rented and she was not about to inform her either that her mother had been virtually penniless. *I've had to rely on myself, and myself alone, to acquire this money.*

'Can we change the subject?' Celia asked. 'Why did *you* choose Portmerryn?'

''Cos it's just so different from where we normally go,' Jackie replied. 'It's quiet and peaceful and I thought maybe we might be able to recapture how we felt about each other forty years ago.'

Celia added some water to the blue. 'And are you?' she asked. 'Are you recapturing how you felt forty years ago?'

Jackie shook her head. 'Not yet, but it's early days, of course. Joe doesn't like it here. He's either in the pub or he sprawled out in the lounge reading his whodunnits.'

'Perhaps you should go to the pub with him then,' Celia suggested. *Instead of poking your nose into my business.*

'Who wants to sit in a gloomy old pub when there's all this lovely scenery?' Jackie asked, waving her arm about.

'Well, your husband obviously does,' Celia said.

'Yeah, to be honest I'm beginning to fancy the idea of being free like you, Celia. I envy you, you know. You can please yourself, do what you want, go where you like. Didn't you ever fancy getting married?'

'It never happened,' Celia said shortly.

'Funny, that. Ah well. So, do you think I should leave him, Celia?' Jackie asked as she plonked herself down on the grass beside where Celia was trying in vain to add froth to the waves in her painting. It wasn't going well. She wondered if she should scrap this painting and start all over again. Perhaps she should have chosen to work in oils and then she could slap one lot of colour on top of another. Maybe she just wasn't a very good artist. And it didn't help that she was constantly distracted by this wearisome woman.

'I've no idea,' Celia replied.

'I mean, it's not *too* bad being on your own, is it?'

'I'm quite content.'

'It's just that Joe keeps saying he's bored and wants to go home.'

'Well, tell him to go then,' Celia said wearily.

'But *I* don't want to go. Anyway, we've booked for another three weeks.'

Celia gave up on the froth and laid down her paintbrush. She'd been about to say, 'Well, *you* stay then,' but thought better of it. Another three weeks of this woman would drive her demented.

'I suppose I could stay on by myself, couldn't I?' Jackie appeared to be deep in thought.

Celia didn't reply.

'Right! I've decided! I'll tell him I'm staying right here and he can sod off home if he wants to. It's all paid for, anyway.'

Celia dipped her paintbrush in clean water. She might as well pack up.

'It'll either make the heart grow fonder, Celia, or bugger up our marriage altogether. At least I'd *know*, wouldn't I?'

'There's no point asking me,' Celia said. 'I'm no authority on the subject.'

'Oh, but you've helped, Celia. You're such a good listener! I'm going to talk to Joe tonight.'

Celia began to dismantle her easel and pack everything away.

'Can I help?' Jackie asked, scrambling to her feet. 'That's a beautiful picture, Celia.'

'No, it isn't,' Celia said. 'It's rubbish. I'm going to scrap this and start again.'

'Oh, you can't do that – it's *lovely*!'

'Well, you can have it then,' Celia said in the hope that Jackie and her horrible husband and the disastrous seascape would all leave together this very evening.

'Oh, I *couldn't*! I'll pay you for it, Celia.'

'No, you won't. If you don't take it I'll tear it up right now in front of you.'

'Don't do that! I'll take it! That's so kind of you! I'll find a way to repay you, Celia. I've never had an original watercolour before. Do you suppose there's somewhere round here where I could have it framed? Or maybe I'll wait and get it done in Colchester. Oh, thank you so much! Hey, I *love* your watch!'

Celia said nothing.

'It's a Rolex, isn't it? What does it do?'

'It tells the time. Now, if you don't mind, I really need to concentrate on what I'm doing.'

'Oops! Joe always says I talk too much. See you later, then!'

Celia sighed with relief as she watched Jackie descend the coastal path. She was going to have to find another spot to do her painting where, hopefully, she'd be difficult to track down. She pondered their conversation and her purchases. Considering she didn't wish to draw attention to herself, why on earth had she been persuaded to buy that red car? She'd bought it because she liked red, because it represented her new freedom and, perhaps, adventure, and because the suave salesman had assured her that it would retain its value if and when the time came to sell it. That would only be when she decided to relocate permanently. And the watch was pure indulgence. Who could blame her after years of never having anything nice, of making do with cheap clothes, cheap furniture – cheap *everything*. She'd loved the look of that watch, its white mother-of-pearl face and the stainless-steel bracelet, and she liked knowing the date. And she liked it being waterproof.

She hadn't gone mad. She'd bought the car, the watch, a few items of clothing and a few weeks at Sparrows'. The rest was to fund her new life, when she decided where that should be. Somewhere remote: the Outer Hebrides? Shetland? She'd buy a cottage there and paint all winter, selling the pictures to the tourists all summer. That was the dream. For now all she needed was a little time, some peace, some quiet. Perhaps she'd made the wrong decision in coming to The Sparrows' Nest?

CHAPTER 25

DOMINIC'S DATE

Dominic lowered his newspaper to get a better view of Gideon. He really was a most attractive man, probably in his forties. Would a thirty-year difference in ages matter? Well, certainly not to me, thought Dominic. He'd caught Dominic's eye a couple of times and smiled. There must be a way to get to know him better; he hadn't felt such stirrings since the early days with Patrick, so perhaps he was finally recovering. Of course he'd come here mainly because of Patrick and the one thing he had to do before the matter could be laid to rest. But he could clearly hear Jed talking to his son.

'No point in goin' on about it, lad,' Jed was saying, 'you'll have to go on the bus 'cos I'm goin' to be needin' the van.'

Gideon groaned. 'You know it can take nearly all day to get to Penzance, and I only got a couple of days off!'

Dominic picked up his empty glass and headed towards the bar.

'Excuse me,' he said, 'but I couldn't help overhearing your conversation, and I have to make a trip to Penzance in the next few days, so perhaps I could offer your son a lift?'

Gideon turned, met Dominic's eye, and noticeably brightened up.

'Well, now,' said Jed, 'that be right kind of you, sir, but we wouldn't want to put you to any trouble.'

'It wouldn't be any trouble at all,' said Dominic. 'I've been meaning to ask you for some time about the history of this coast, the shipwrecks, the smuggling, that sort of thing. Tess tells me you're something of an expert.'

Jed puffed himself out and beamed. 'Well, now you come to mention it…'

'So I'd be returning the favour, if you see what I mean?'

'Well, that's one way of lookin' at it, I suppose.' At this point Annie emerged from the kitchen, her grey hair askew, wiping her hands on her apron. 'This kind gentleman's offerin' our Gideon a lift to his brother's.'

'That's very kind,' confirmed Annie.

Gideon smiled and nodded. 'That would be great, sir. It's my brother's birthday on Tuesday, see.'

'Please call me Dominic.'

'Thanking you, Dominic, and what would you be wantin' to know about the pirates an' that?' Jed asked.

'Anything you can tell me, Jed. I'm writing a book, you see, all about smuggling, and I'm going to need some accurate information.'

'A *book*, eh?' Jed was clearly impressed. 'Didn't know you was an author, like. Fetch 'im another pint of Doom Bar, Gideon – and this one's on the 'ouse, Dominic.'

'Thank you,' Dominic said, not really wanting another pint but not wishing to offend. It was now more likely he'd be sleeping rather than writing this afternoon. He was about to ask Gideon when he planned to return when Jed said, 'If you was to come back Wednesday afternoon I could come to fetch you. Haven't seen Michael and the kids for a month or so, 'ave we, Annie?'

'No we 'aven't,' Annie agreed.

Jed turned back to Dominic. 'That's Michael, our other son, an' 'e runs a nice little bar in Penzance. ''E does food too and 'e'd give you a nice little lunch when you drop Gideon off.'

'That's a very kind thought,' said Dominic, 'but I have some business to attend to so I'll be moving on. Some other time perhaps.'

Arrangements were made. Dominic would pick Gideon up at 10 a.m. on Tuesday morning.

'You sure that's OK?' Jed asked anxiously,

'Oh, I'm quite sure,' Dominic replied.

Dominic turned onto the A30, heading westbound. His passenger, in T-shirt and jeans, seemed completely unaware of how very attractive he was. That in itself was a novelty; most of the good-looking men he'd encountered in the past had been only too aware of their looks.

'So,' Dominic said, 'you've never fancied leaving your parents and perhaps having your own little business somewhere? Like your brother's done?' He felt a little sorry for Gideon, who seemed to be permanently at his father's beck and call with little life of his own.

'No,' Gideon replied. 'Perhaps I'd feel different if I was married like him, though.'

'And have you never been tempted to marry?'

'Nope, never.'

'There must be pretty girls around?' Dominic persisted.

Gideon shrugged but said nothing.

'Wouldn't you like to have children, Gideon?'

'My brother's got three of them and that's enough for me! How about you, then?'

'Me?'

'Yeah, how come you're not married either?'

'Ah well, just never found the right person,' Dominic replied. And that, he thought, is such a lie. I did find the right person but he found someone else. And that's why I'm here and that's why I'll be heading for St Ives the moment I've dropped you off.

'Oh well,' sighed Gideon, 'I guess that makes two of us.'

You don't know how right you are, Dominic thought.

They arrived in Penzance about midday, Gideon giving directions to his brother's pub.

'You'd be ever so welcome to lunch,' Gideon said as he got out of the car.

'Thank you but no thanks, Gideon. I have some business to attend to. Enjoy your visit.'

'I feel I should be paying you something,' Gideon said.

'Of course not! I was coming here anyway. It's been a pleasure. Let me give you my number just in case your dad isn't able to pick you up tomorrow. I'd be happy to help.'

'That's real nice of you,' Gideon said, pocketing Dominic's card. 'But Dad *will* be here tomorrow.'

'Don't forget, if there's any problem…'

'I won't. Thanks.'

As Dominic drove off he wondered again if he might be recovering from Patrick at last.

Now he needed to find a florist. He had no idea where to begin looking but, as he drove out of the town, he spotted a supermarket and decided that would have to do. As he walked through the floristry section he caught sight of a collection of hydrangeas in pots: perfect. Patrick loved hydrangeas, particularly the blue ones and, as luck would have it, there was one little blue one sandwiched between several pinks. Dominic wandered round the supermarket with the blue hydrangea in his basket and added a few further purchases including toothpaste and shaving cream.

It was a short drive from Penzance on the south coast to St Ives on the north coast across the narrowest part of the Cornish peninsula. He'd never been to St Ives; St Ives, with its exceptional light and its colony of artists and sculptors. If he had time, he'd go on there today after he'd carried out his task.

After he'd bypassed Hayle and Lelant he tried to drive slowly, studying every bend on the road, which proved to be difficult since he was part of a steady stream of holiday traffic. And so it was with some relief that he came across a layby where he was able to park. He got out of the car and looked around.

The traffic was relentless. He should have known not to come at this time of year; he should have come in winter. Now he realised there was nothing for it but to walk because what he was looking for was round here somewhere and he was pretty sure he hadn't passed it, so it must be ahead. The walk would do him good provided he wasn't annihilated in his quest to find the gate to Lemerton Farm which was where it had happened.

Dominic set off walking, keeping as tightly into the roadside as possible as car after car roared past. It would surely be a cruel twist of fate if he were to come to grief here, too. And then, after about five minutes, he saw the gate with the sign. The road was a little wider here and he dashed across it, dodging the traffic in both directions, to where there was a ditch. Would there still be tyre tread marks? he wondered. Probably not, bearing in mind the rate at which everything grew down here.

He began to examine the ditch closely through the dense growth of cow parsley and campion and through which the water was barely visible. A few yards further on Dominic found a deep rut, now partly grown over but still indented. It must be the right place. He clambered over the ditch and sat on the bank. Oh, Patrick, he thought. How often did I lecture you about driving like a bloody maniac? It could have been me with you. But no, it was Finbar. Could I have done anything to prevent this? Could I have persuaded you to stay with me a little longer? Would you still have drunk too much on that night in June last year? Now I'm still here, but you and Finbar are gone.

Dominic had bought a little trowel in the supermarket which he now withdrew from the bag and tried to find a spot where the ground might be soft enough to dig. It wasn't going to be easy because the earth was dry and hard, but perhaps he could moisten a small area. He removed his canvas deck shoes and lowered himself into the ditch to scoop up water, with his trowel, to the chosen spot. It was going to be a slow process.

Then he saw some shards of glass shining in the water not far from where he was standing. It confirmed not only that he was in exactly the right place, but that he was also in imminent danger of lacerating his feet. It was lucky that he hadn't already stood on some. He mustn't move his feet while he completed his task.

Cars continued to whizz by, their occupants no doubt curious as to what an elderly man was doing pottering around in a ditch. What if a police car came along? Dominic continued with his labours for a good five minutes before he felt the earth relent a little and he was able to dig in a few centimetres with his trowel, before repeating the process again and again.

It took almost half an hour to excavate a hole large enough to accommodate the blue hydrangea. Then Dominic sat on the bank and looked at it while the sun beat down on him and his feet dried off. He hadn't thought to use any sun protection so he'd probably suffer later. Never mind. He stroked the large papery pompoms and hoped it would grow into a sturdy shrub. Patrick would have been pleased.

Dominic put his shoes on again, vaulted over the ditch, and headed back to where he'd parked his car.

CHAPTER 26

TITANIA EXPLORES

Titania had done some research on Clarice D'Arcy. She'd googled her, read all the showbiz articles about her, and knew that Clarice had a pied-à-terre in London but that her main residence was here in Cornwall. There had even been a five-page spread in *Hello!* magazine about Clarice's amazing cliff-top residence. *Another* cliff-top residence! The house was called The Hideaway but Titania wondered how it could possibly be a hideaway when you allowed photographs of the place, inside and out, to be plastered across pages of a magazine which most people browsed through in the doctor's or the dentist's waiting room. Titania had pulled the article out of the magazine as surreptitiously as possible while waiting for the hygienist and while the waiting room was empty except for a gum-chewing adolescent who didn't glance in her direction. She'd memorised every detail of the pictures, even the one of the bedroom with the ornate antique four-poster which Clarice had described as 'the love-nest I shared with my darling Henry'.

Clarice was, of course, a little younger than she was. Not much, though. And men liked younger women, a lot younger than Clarice was. Titania liked younger men, come to think of it, but that didn't mean she'd have deserted Henry for the first toyboy that cast an eye in her direction. Not that any of them did, unfortunately. And she wasn't making a great deal of headway with Simon Sparrow.

The article had given no clue as to where The Hideaway was, only that it was somewhere on the Lizard peninsula, on a cliff at Black Rock Cove. Why was everyone so obsessed with looking at the sea? Titania wondered. She was sure she'd get fed up of staring at water all the time, particularly as, for most of the year, it was grey and boring. She thought she'd prefer to be looking at the countryside: fields, trees, grazing cattle. No, she wouldn't. She'd prefer to be looking out over Regent's Park and red double decker buses.

Simon had provided her with a map she didn't really need because she'd already worked out how to get to the Lizard. Finding The Hideaway would be the main problem, since *Hello!* gave no indication as to where on the Lizard Black Rock Cove might be and it didn't feature on any map. It was a huge area with miles of coastline so this could well be a search for the proverbial needle in the haystack. But find it she would, although she would probably have to make several trips and do a lot of asking around.

Titania had reckoned it would take her at least an hour to drive from the north-east of the county to the south-west, but she was in no hurry and it gave her time to think and to strengthen her resolve.

Because she'd never forget the day Henry told her he felt 'compelled to leave'. Titania had suspected he might have been unfaithful occasionally because, after all, he was still a very handsome man and he worked in a world full of young aspiring starlets. It was inevitable that some pretty, empty-headed little trollop might try to seduce him but it would mean nothing to him. She had to accept that. But *Clarice D'Arcy*! Clarice had had a well-publicised succession of lovers – usually other people's – and then she wanted Titania's Henry. 'I feel I've been hypnotised,' he told her that fateful June afternoon two years ago. Hypnotised indeed! The evil bitch had set out to get him ever since they did that six-week stint of *Antony and Cleopatra* at The Globe that previous year. That gave Clarice ample time to cast her net and slowly, slowly bring in her haul.

It had broken Titania's heart. She'd become aware of the pitying glances, she was offered fewer and fewer parts, and it signified the beginning of the end for her career and her love life.

Titania stopped for lunch at a roadside café: Di's Diner. She was on the Lizard now, heading down the one and only main road and making forays to the east coast. It was all very scenic: tiny thatched cottages clinging together in coves, small fleets of fishing boats, jagged black rocks jutting out to sea.

Surely Black Rock Cove must be around here somewhere? She hadn't passed a pub for some time and she was hungry, having only had a continental breakfast at Sparrows' because she'd wanted to get away early. She ordered cottage pie and a pot of tea and looked around. The little café was busy and appeared to be run by a cheery, very overweight middle-aged couple, who Titania took to be Di and her other half.

When the other half delivered her pot of tea, he asked, 'Going far?'

Titania hesitated for a moment. 'I don't suppose you know of a Black Rock Cove somewhere round here? I've very stupidly lost my friend's address.'

'No, never heard of it,' he said and then, turning towards the counter, he yelled, 'Ever heard of somewhere round here called Black Rock Cove, Di?'

'Can't say as I have,' Di yelled back.

'Must be further on down,' he said.

Titania planned to do as much of the east side of the peninsula as possible today, stopping at every village and hamlet. She'd ask in shops, pubs, post offices. Particularly post offices, although there weren't many of them left these days. She'd look for red mail vans; the postmen would know.

She bought newspapers and peppermints she didn't particularly want and queued up for stamps she didn't particularly need at the one and only post office she found, all in an attempt to ask the vital question. No one knew anything about Black Rock Cove. She got as far as Cadgwith and realised suddenly that it was half past four and she should be making her way back. She'd want a shower and several gins before dinner. There was still the Lizard itself and the other coast to explore. She'd continue her search in a few days' time.

CHAPTER 27

JACKIE

'What the hell are you talking about?' Joe Merryweather asked as he emerged, naked, from the bathroom after his shower. 'And where did you put my pants?'

Jackie indicated a drawer and tried to remember the speech she'd spent half the afternoon concocting.

'Like I said, Joe, I know you're bored here, but I'm not. I like the peace and quiet and I've become quite friendly with Celia.'

'What – that old prune?'

'Don't be so rude! Anyway, I was thinking that, as you and I seem to be leading separate lives down here, maybe you'd like to go back?'

Joe donned a pair of black-and-white striped pants. 'Good idea. We can leave any time you like provided I get my money back.'

Jackie sighed. She'd obviously not got her point across. 'What I mean is, *you* go if you want to, but I'd like to stay on for a bit.'

'Why the hell would you want to stay in this godforsaken hole? I'll have a word with the Sparrows about getting my money back and then we can get out of here. With a bit of luck I could be home in time for Norwich's game with Ipswich.'

'I'm staying here,' Jackie said.

'Like hell you are! What would people think? You're my wife and you're coming with me.'

'No, I'm not.' And, as she spoke Jackie realised that she had never defied him before. Never. 'I'm staying on for the three weeks we've paid for.'

He stopped in the middle of buttoning up his shirt. 'In that case, don't bother to come back at all!'

'All right, I won't!'

'Stay here with your new friend, then!'

Jackie could see the purple rising in his face which indicated fury and – one of these days – a heart attack. 'She's a nice person! And she's given me one of her lovely paintings.'

Joe looked around the room until he finally noticed Celia's rejected seascape propped up against the wall on the bedside table.

'What a load of crap!' he bellowed as he thundered across the room, grabbed the watercolour and began to tear it in two.

'No, no, please don't!' Jackie was weeping now and grabbing him by the arm in an attempt to stop him. It was too late; he'd torn it into several pieces. 'How *dare* you, Joe!'

He dropped the pieces of paper on the floor and advanced towards her.

'You bastard!' she shouted, just as he struck her across the face, his signet ring hitting the side of her cheek, close to her eye. Sobbing and holding her head, Jackie sank to the floor, while he pulled a suitcase out of the wardrobe and began to pack, chucking in unfolded shirts, trousers and pants. Then he grabbed some toiletries from the bathroom and slammed them on top.

'You can stay here and rot as far as I'm concerned,' he snapped, picking up his case and his car keys, before heading out of the door and slamming it behind him. With tears streaming down her face Jackie watched from the window as he flung his case into the back seat of the Merc, then got into the car, revved up noisily and roared down the drive.

She sat down, her head in her hands, and wondered how she'd be able to face everyone. Their row and Joe's departure had been noisy so probably everyone in the house had heard. Jackie felt a mixture of emotions: fear, sadness, confusion. Relief? Should she hide away in her room? She'd have to explain the situation to the Sparrows because they'd expect her, and Joe, for dinner as usual.

Jackie dried her eyes, brushed her hair, took a big breath and headed downstairs. Tess, at the desk in the hallway, looked up as she approached. 'Are you all right, Jackie?' she asked.

Jackie burst into tears all over again. Without waiting for an answer Tess said, 'Come into the kitchen and I'll get you something to drink. Simon's working outside, so it's only you and me.' As Jackie let herself be led into the kitchen Tess added, 'I think you need a brandy.'

With a brandy in front of her at the kitchen table, Jackie took a sip and felt the warmth creep across her body. She dried her eyes again and said, 'I'm so sorry, you must have heard us rowing upstairs.'

Tess didn't reply but knelt down to examine Jackie's face. 'Did *he* do that? He's just missed your eye, thank goodness.'

'Does it show very much?'

'You're going to have a bit of a shiner over the next few days. The bruise is coming out now so you need to put some ice on it, to reduce the swelling.' Tess took some ice cubes from the freezer, wrapped them in clingfilm and instructed Jackie to hold it to her face.

'I'm so sorry to be such a bother,' Jackie said, trying not to cry again.

'You're not a bother.'

'Can I stay here for the three weeks, please?'

'Of course you can. But I'd prefer it if that husband of yours doesn't set foot in here again.'

'He won't,' Jackie said.

'Good. Now, do you want to have dinner with the others tonight, or would you prefer to be on your own?'

'I don't know,' Jackie replied.

'Well, have a think about it. Has this happened before, Jackie? I can easily call the police if you'd like me to.'

'No, no, really! Honestly, it's fine.'

Jackie was used to his tantrums and the last thing she wanted was any kind of fuss. Then she tried to work out what she'd like least: to be all alone in her room with dinner on a tray, or to be with the others who would probably remark on her swollen face and ask where Joe was. Without a doubt Titania would have something to say. She thought for a minute. If she didn't face them tonight she'd have to face them tomorrow, so she might as well get it over with.

'I'll eat in the dining room with the others,' she said.

The ice had helped but the area round her eye was noticeably swollen and already badly discoloured. Jackie thought she might be able to disguise the discolouration with make-up, but she could do very little about the swelling. They'd guess what had happened anyway, particularly as she would be on her own. She decided to go down early to have a pre-dinner drink and get their reactions out of the way.

Jackie chose her outfit with care, deciding that the blue would look good against the beginnings of her tan. She was on her own now, and she'd better get used to it. She'd email her sons tomorrow, but neither was likely to be very surprised. They'd never got on well with their father and rarely visited these days; maybe things would change now.

She took some deep breaths before she walked into the lounge, and was surprised to find only Celia there, reading her book and drinking something clear and fizzy. Water? Tonic? Lemonade? Jackie knew from the way Celia refused wine at dinner that she hardly ever touched alcohol. Celia looked up and lowered her book. 'I heard you,' she said, 'and I think you're well rid of him.'

Fancy Celia saying that!

'Thank you, Celia,' Jackie said.

'Did *he* do that?' Celia asked, pointing at her eye.

Jackie nodded. 'He's always had a terrible temper.' Then she remembered. 'Oh Celia, I'm so, so sorry – he tore up your beautiful watercolour!' She could feel her eyes welling up again.

At that moment Tess came in and asked, 'What would you like to drink, Jackie? How about a brandy and ginger, so you don't have to mix your drinks too much?'

'Yes, please,' Jackie replied. She turned back to Celia. 'I tried to stop him but…'

'It was a terrible picture anyway, so no loss. I'll paint you another one.'

'Oh, Celia, that's so sweet of you! But no, you don't have to do that!'

Celia didn't reply.

Jackie's brandy arrived at the same time as Dominic, who sat down with his vodka tonic, said, 'Good evening' but made no comment on her appearance.

'Did you go to Penzance today?' Celia asked him.

'Oh yes,' Dominic said. 'And I had a look at St Ives, too. What a charming place! Pity there's so many tourists, though. Have you ever been there?'

'No,' Celia replied.

'Well, you should go. It's a mecca for artists, something to do with the light down there.'

'I'll think about it,' Celia said.

They chatted about the lovely weather, the tourists and the traffic, the ridiculous cost of fuel.

As usual there was no sign of Titania as they wandered through to the dining room. She was always late and Jackie noticed that she always smelled of gin, so she obviously had a bottle in her room. They'd almost finished their starters when Titania swanned in, clad in a full-length orange kaftan.

'Have you had a good day, Titania?' Dominic asked politely.

'Quite interesting,' Titania replied, 'did a bit of exploring.' Her eye alighted on Jackie. 'You been in the boxing ring? Hope you knocked him out. Where is he anyway?'

Jackie smiled but didn't reply.

'Her husband's had to go back,' Celia said, glaring at Titania. 'So, where did *you* go today?'

'Oh, just decided to have a look at some of the south coast,' Titania said. 'And I have to say it's quite exhausted me. I think I shall be having an early night.'

The meal continued without any further reference to Jackie or the missing husband. And, as Jackie headed upstairs afterwards, it struck her that she'd hardly ever slept on her own in the thirty-seven years she'd been married to Joe. She wondered if she'd be able to sleep. Would she lie awake and worry all night? Would she regret not leaving with him?

She watched an old episode of *Morse* on television for a while, then began to feel her eyelids becoming heavy, switched off the light and was fast asleep within minutes.

Eight blissful hours, and she didn't wake up once.

CHAPTER 28

ORLA

Tess felt utterly exhausted. She shouldn't complain, she told herself, because their guests were all really easy-going. They went out a lot, they rarely wanted lunch, they complimented her on her cooking, they didn't have parties or make a noise. Apart from Joe Merryweather there had been no upsets of any kind. And Gina helped with the cleaning upstairs five days a week. No, she had nothing whatsoever to complain about.

It was just that she and Simon didn't actually ever *go* anywhere. They didn't go for an evening to the cinema, mainly because it was some distance away, and the only theatres were in Plymouth, which was even further. There were few restaurants nearby and their only escape was to go for a drink down to the pub, which had a limited appeal. This was not how she imagined spending her retirement years.

And then Orla rang to say Ricky was delivering something-or-other to Redruth and Truro, and he could drop her off nearby, so could she come to stay for a few days? 'I know you're busy,' she said, 'but I could give you a hand. And I'm very happy to sleep in Buckingham Palace.'

'Windsor Castle,' Tess corrected her, 'and I'd love it if you came!'

Orla! How she missed Orla's company, her banter, her humour! And she couldn't wait to get Orla's reaction, after the chaotic Christmas visit, now that the work was completed. She couldn't wait either to get Orla's reaction to their guests, either. Knowing Orla, she'd have plenty to say.

The plan was that Ricky would drop Orla off at Bodmin before driving on south and, because he'd be returning overnight or early the next day, Orla would need to make her own way home. Anyway, Orla was coming and Tess cheered up.

Ricky was due in Bodmin about noon and Orla would keep in touch by phone to let Tess know if they were running late. Fortunately, it was a day when everyone was out, no one wanted lunch and Tess got her chores done early before setting off in the Land Rover for Bodmin, where Ricky arrived, bang on schedule, with several hundred television sets and Orla.

'If you get fed up of her,' Ricky said, 'I'll be heading back upcountry in the early hours!'

'I'll bear it in mind,' Tess said as she embraced her friend.

'Here's me thinking you'd be all bronzed and beautiful,' Orla said as she clambered into the Land Rover, 'and you're white as a sheet!'

'That,' said Tess, 'is because I spend most of the day working, not lying around in the sun like some people I know.'

'Ah well, I'm here to top up my tan, and it's time we got started on yours. You look tired, Tess.'

'I shouldn't be,' Tess said. 'We've only been open a few weeks and it isn't really hard work, particularly as I've got Gina doing upstairs five days a week. But you just have to *be* there most of the time. And we had such a manic winter and spring trying to get everything finished off so we could open at the beginning of May.'

'You should have had a holiday before your guests arrived,' Orla remarked.

'Well, that would have been nice but there was neither the time nor the money.'

'Never mind, we'll get out and about now I'm here.'

'I told everyone I'm off to stay at Buckingham Palace,' Orla said as she carried her case across to the caravan. 'And you should have seen their faces!'

'You're not, it's Windsor Castle,' Tess said. 'I'm sorry the facilities are a tad limited, but the toilet's fine for a pee, there's hot water, and you can come across to our shower room for everything else. I'll give you a key to the house, and don't forget there's a loo in the laundry room, too.'

'I'll be fine,' said Orla, 'and I can't wait to meet your zany guests.'

Tess laughed. 'Simon keeps saying, if you were casting a play with four completely diverse and eccentric characters, you couldn't do better than our lot!'

'I need to see what you've done to the house now your guests are out,' Orla said.

Half an hour later Tess gave her the guided tour.

'My God!' Orla exclaimed as Tess showed her upstairs, with Simon on the lookout in case any of their guests returned unexpectedly. 'Now, whatever happened to that bathroom we were all queueing for? With the rope from the cistern?'

'It's been divided into two en suites,' Tess explained, showing Orla the two gleaming bathrooms attached to the front bedrooms. 'We sacrificed the two small bedrooms to make bathrooms for the two rooms at the rear.'

'Unbelievable! You've had some work done up here. And what about all the painting and curtains and everything? Did you do that?'

'Most of it,' Tess admitted.

'Well, no wonder you're knackered.'

'You haven't seen downstairs yet,' Tess said as she re-locked all the bedroom doors.

Orla loved it all. 'You've got a proper kitchen! And radiators everywhere!' She looked in amazement at Tess and Simon's bedroom. 'Wasn't this our lounge at Christmas?'

Tess then led her into the two public rooms at the back and, as she pressed the switches, offered up a swift prayer that they'd open fully without any problems. And they did.

'Oh, my word,' said Orla, 'I'm running out of adjectives!' She looked longingly at the terrace bathed in sunshine. 'Can we sit out here?'

'Of course we can,' Tess replied. 'Stretch yourself out on a sun bed and I'll get us some sandwiches. You must be starving.'

Simon had already thought of that and appeared with a platter of sandwiches, a bottle of Pinot Grigio and two glasses. 'Sit down!' he ordered Tess. 'Don't move!'

As they lunched Tess gave Orla the lowdown on their guests.

'They're all nice enough; the only horrible one left a week ago,' Tess said, 'and left his wife, Jackie, behind. Or rather, I think she sent him packing. They had a rip-roaring row and he landed her one near her left eye, so she's now all bruised. She's wandering around like a lost soul because she hasn't got a car or anything. Then there's Celia, who must be about seventy, never married and very prim and proper. Then, our only remaining male, Dominic, who's gay. He's lovely and no trouble at all although Simon reckons he's got the hots for Gideon, who's the son of the publican down the road. Apparently, Dominic sits in there most evenings, gazing at Gideon, who's not very worldly and probably has no idea whether he's gay himself or not. And, last but not least, there's Titania. *What* can I say about Titania? She was an actress back in the days of yore and she's a walking, talking Norma Desmond, if you've seen *Sunset Boulevard*? You can't miss her, she's done up to the nines.'

'I can hardly wait.'

'The best way to meet them is for you to eat with them one evening. But not tonight! Tonight we'll catch up with the gossip!'

The next day Tess and Orla had a stroll along the beach and climbed up Penhennon Cliff. Tess pointed out Celia sitting amidst the gorse bushes where she probably hoped no one would see her.

'We won't disturb her,' Tess said, 'and you'll be meeting her later anyway.'

Then Orla insisted on treating her to lunch at any pub other than The Portmerryn Arms.

'Somewhere where we can sit outside and relax,' Orla insisted.

Only Jackie had wanted some sandwiches for lunch and Simon had said he was quite capable of putting some slices of bread together and that Tess should escape for a few hours while she had the chance.

The pub they found near Boscastle had a pretty garden and tables beside the river. Tess drank a white wine spritzer because she was driving, and Orla had a couple of glasses of Cabernet Sauvignon. They chatted about family and friends, and the general state of the world, and the country, and the dreaded Brexit. If it were left to Tess and Orla to sort things out the world would, of course, be a much better place. With the sun on her limbs and listening to her friend's banter, Tess was already beginning to feel better.

'Tonight,' said Orla, 'I'm going to be eating with your guests. I can hardly wait!'

'Well, Titania will be late because she knocks back gin in her room before she ventures downstairs. Dominic will have his vodka tonic and *Daily Telegraph* in the lounge, Celia will be reading a book and sipping an orange juice or something, and Jackie will be sunbathing all afternoon and ready to hit the wine. That's it in a nutshell.'

CHAPTER 29

COURSE WORK

Jed was scratching his head. 'No,' he said to Gideon, who was with him behind the bar, 'there's no way I can pick you up every night at five o'clock for a whole bloody week! Can't leave your mother 'ere on 'er own when it's busy like this, can I?'

Gideon looked crestfallen. Dominic couldn't bear it; he'd have to say something.

'You got transport problems then, Jed?' he asked as casually as he could. He'd taken to sitting on a stool at the bar while Jed regaled him with swashbuckling tales of the region in between dishing out pints.

'Oh, it's just Gideon's wantin' to go on some fancy course next week in Bodmin, all about wine and cocktails and stuff. 'E's got all them ideas about stockin' more wines and makin' them fancy drinks now we're gettin' all them furriners in 'ere.'

'Well, that would seem to be very sensible,' Dominic said.

'Thing is,' Jed went on, ''E could get a bus to Bodmin first thing, but there ain't no bus comin' back near that time. And I can't be doin' without me van all day, and I can't be leavin' Annie 'ere on her own in the evenin'.'

Dominic didn't want to appear too eager, but this was an opportunity not to be missed.

'It's not that far to Bodmin,' he said, 'so perhaps I could help?' He avoided looking at Gideon. 'I normally stop writing around four o'clock and I've time to kill until around half six to seven. And, Jed, I'm so grateful to you for all the detail you've given me for my book and this is the only way I can reciprocate.'

'You've already given 'im a lift to Penzance.'

'I was going there anyway, Jed.'

'Well, that would be more than generous of you, Dominic. But *five days*?'

'No problem.' Dominic thought that Gideon might be blushing, or was it the light?

'That would be great, wouldn't it, Dad?' he said, without meeting Dominic's eye.

Jed shrugged. 'S'pose so.' He turned to his son. 'Don't know why you're so keen on doin' this fancy stuff. We already got plenty of wine 'ere.'

Gideon rolled his eyes. 'You've got to get into the twenty-first century, Dad. We need a bigger selection of wine and we need to know how to make cocktails that people actually want to drink.'

'Wot do our regulars want with bloomin' cocktails?' Jed snorted. He turned to Dominic. ''E gets all them ideas, does Gideon.'

Dominic sighed. 'Yes, but times change, Jed, don't they? I mean, you get visitors all the year round now and there's not many pubs round here specialising in cocktails, is there? It could become a destination pub and you'd have customers coming from all over the place once you get a reputation.'

'That's what I've been telling him,' Gideon said, meeting Dominic's eye at last and smiling.

Dominic felt his heart give a little lurch. 'Well, Gideon, if you tell me where the course is and what time it finishes, I can be outside waiting.'

'Five o'clock each evening, at the Tregallen Hotel, starting on Monday. I'll just go and register online. Thank you, Dominic.'

'It's a pleasure.' Dominic felt his spirits soaring. He was tempted to offer to deliver Gideon to Bodmin each morning as well, but thought better of it. That would be overdoing it.

Dominic parked the Jaguar in the car park of the Tregallen Hotel at ten minutes to five on Monday. He checked his teeth, his hair and his fingernails as he waited. All seemed satisfactory. He hoped he hadn't overdone the aftershave. He'd already had the car valeted inside and out.

And then he saw Gideon appear with several others and once again felt a little shiver of anticipation.

'This is very luxurious,' Gideon said as he slid into the passenger seat. 'Makes a change from Dad's old van.'

'Have you never considered having a car of your own?' Dominic asked as he pulled out into the traffic.

'I've had a couple in the past,' Gideon said, 'but they gave up the ghost. Haven't really thought about replacing them, to be honest. I don't go away that much.'

'That's a shame,' Dominic said.

'Anyhow, I'd never be able to have a posh car like this.'

'Well, I'm nearly thirty years older than you, Gideon. And my work used to involve some travelling around.'

'Up in London?'

'Yes, up in London. Do you get up there much?'

Gideon shook his head. 'Only been a couple of times. Don't like the noise, the traffic, everyone hurrying everywhere as if their lives depended on it.'

'Good point. But where I live in Hampstead it's very pleasant. Have you heard of Hampstead Heath?'

'Yeah, I've heard of it. Sounds nice.'

Dominic wanted to tell him he could come to stay any time he wanted. Perhaps he'd suggest it later in the week. Instead he asked, 'How was the course?'

'Really good,' said Gideon. 'In the morning we had a talk from a winegrower from the south of France, Long-something.'

'The Languedoc region?'

'Yes, that was it! You're very knowledgeable! We had some of their wine with our lunch. And this afternoon we learned how to make two American cocktails, an Old Fashioned and a Manhattan. Don't suppose there'll be much call for them in Portmerryn, though.'

'You never know, Gideon. Visitors come here from all over the world.'

'I've made notes.' Gideon withdrew a large notebook from the depths of his bag. 'I'll forget otherwise.'

'And you've never fancied having your own little pub or bar somewhere, like your brother?'

'Never thought much about it, truth be known. Anyway, Mum and Dad are both in their seventies, you know, and need a bit of help. Moving around barrels and that sort of thing.'

'I suppose so.' Dominic gave him a sideways glance. Here was an attractive man in his forties, still living with his parents, and yet worldly enough to be interested in expanding his knowledge of wines and making cocktails. He'd admitted previously to not having had a girlfriend. Didn't he feel the need for love, for having a family of his own? For sex? I have a week to find out, Dominic thought.

As they arrived back at The Portmerryn Arms Gideon said, 'Thanks so much, Dominic. Hope you'll be down for your nightcap later? It's on me!' And he gave Dominic a cheeky wink.

'Oh, I definitely will,' Dominic replied.

Dominic found it difficult to concentrate on Tuesday. He sat, gazing out of the window, the laptop open and idle in front of him. He seemed unable to compose a coherent sentence. Whatever was the matter with him? It was almost as if, having planted that hydrangea in memory of Patrick, he felt a sense of release, his heart free to love again at last. But, as he knew to his cost, allowing someone into his heart always risked hurt. It had happened before; it would happen again.

At five o'clock he was back outside the Tregallen Hotel again. It had begun to rain and when Gideon emerged he made a dash for the car and leaped into the passenger seat, brushing against Dominic's arm as he did so and causing him ripples of pleasure.

'What did you learn today?' Dominic asked as he switched on the ignition.

'Oh, all about Chilean wines, and this afternoon we made piña coladas, and mine was the best!'

'Congratulations!' Dominic resisted the temptation to pat his knee.

'I've been buying the ingredients, see?' Gideon indicated his bag. 'I could make you one tonight.'

'That would be lovely, but I usually just have a brandy or something for a nightcap after dinner.'

'So why don't you come *before* dinner?'

Dominic's heart was lurching all over the place again. 'I could, I suppose,' he said, 'but it's just that I've got into the habit of having a pre-dinner vodka tonic at the Sparrows'.'

'I could do you vodka tonics,' Gideon said.

'Shall I come before dinner then?'

'Why not?'

'I'm giving Gideon a lift back from his cocktail-making course each evening,' Dominic explained to Simon, 'and he's keen to show me his expertise. I hope you wouldn't mind if I had my aperitif down there tonight?'

'Of course we wouldn't mind!' Simon said, patting his shoulder. 'You go and enjoy Gideon's cocktails.'

Dominic was always fastidious about his appearance but spent even more time than usual on it this evening. Did it mean what he hoped it meant, Gideon asking him down like that?

The pub was already filling up when Dominic arrived just after half past six, and he had to grab his usual stool at the bar when he saw two large ladies with rucksacks heading towards it. There was no sign of Gideon.

'Nice to see you down 'ere early,' said Jed. 'Wot can I get you?'

'Well,' said Dominic, 'Gideon has threatened to make me one of his cocktails so I'll wait until he comes.'

'Rather you than me,' Jed said with a grin, before turning to serve the two large ladies.

And then Gideon appeared. Gideon, who was normally clad in T-shirts and blue jeans, was tonight wearing knee-length white shorts and a navy blue short-sleeved shirt. He'd also combed his dark hair, complete with a dead straight parting. He was carrying the cocktail shaker he'd presumably bought in Bodmin.

'Would you like a drink, Dominic?' asked this new super-trendy Gideon.

Dominic's mouth had gone dry. He ran his tongue along his teeth. 'I'll have a piña colada, please.'

'Sure you wouldn't prefer your vodka?'

Dominic definitely would have preferred his vodka. 'No, I'll have a piña colada please, Gideon.'

'Bloody 'ell,' said Jed as he caught sight of his son. 'Why're you all done up like a dog's dinner?'

Gideon ignored him, and continued pouring the ingredients into the shaker. 'Got to look the part if you're making cocktails,' he said, winking at Dominic.

Dominic's insides were in turmoil. Gideon had never winked at him before. Surely this meant the feeling was mutual? There was silence in the bar as Gideon began to rattle the cocktail shaker with great style and, when he finally poured the creamy, frothy mixture into a glass which he presented with a flourish to Dominic, there was a round of applause. Dominic knew he was blushing furiously, but could do nothing about it. 'Thank you,' he said, not daring to meet Gideon's eye, and took a tentative sip. It was far too sweet for his taste.

'Delicious!' he proclaimed to one and all, then finally looking Gideon in the eye. 'I feel transported to a Caribbean island, under a palm tree, on the beach.'

'Can I come, too?' asked Gideon, smiling at him. There was a definite twinkle in his eye.

'Most definitely,' Dominic replied.

And he *knew*.

CHAPTER 30

ORLA'S BULL'S EYE

'This,' said Tess, later that evening, 'is my friend, Orla, who's here for a few days and she'll be joining you for dinner.'

Dominic folded his newspaper, stood up and shook Orla's hand. 'I'm Dominic, delighted to meet you,' he said.

Celia nodded politely. 'I'm Miss Wi… er, Celia.'

Jackie, bright pink with the sun, said, 'And I'm Jackie. I expect you've heard all about me!'

'No,' Orla lied blithely. 'I know nothing about anyone, but I'm all ears.'

'You're Irish!' Jackie exclaimed. 'I *love* that accent!'

Dominic cleared his throat. 'I'm trying to write a book, and the scenery and the ambience here is very inspiring. I took a little time to get started but it's flowing quite well now.'

'And what's your book about, Dominic?' Orla asked.

'Oh, smuggling, shipwrecks, that sort of thing. Don't suppose that's your choice of reading?'

'Well, I did read all the *Poldark* novels years ago and should think this is just the place to dream up a good smuggle,' said Orla. She turned to Celia. 'Now, I'm seeing you as someone who's interested in rocks and stones, or archaeology perhaps?'

Tess saw Celia look at her in astonishment. 'I have no interest in rocks, stones or archaeology,' she said tersely. 'I'm here on a painting holiday.'

'Oh really? I'd love to see some of your work,' said Orla.

'She does lovely seascapes,' Jackie piped up. 'You're doing one for me, aren't you, Celia?'

Celia gave a brief nod but didn't expand on the subject.

'Isn't that kind of you now?' Orla said. 'Have you been painting long?'

'Only since retirement.'

'You should be joining one of the local artists' groups, Celia. There must be loads of them in Cornwall; the place is swarming with arty-crafty looking folk and you'd meet like-minded people.'

'I don't wish to join any groups,' Celia said firmly, sipping her orange juice.

'Oh well, never mind.' Orla met Tess's eye for a brief moment.

'*I'm* not doing anything creative,' Jackie said, 'I'm just enjoying doing nothing after years and years of being involved in the manufacture of ladies' knickers and things; the kind that pulls you in, if you know what I mean?'

'Oh, I do indeed!' Orla turned to Tess. 'Tess and I know all about women holding themselves in, don't we, Tess? We used to have a boutique specialising in outfits for large ladies. She's a very talented lady, is Tess. Any time you want an outfit that'll knock pounds off you—'

'That's in the past,' Tess interrupted, 'all I make these days is curtains. Now, dinner's ready so do please come through to the dining room.'

As they sat down Celia stared at the bowl placed in front of her and asked, 'What's this?'

'It's vichyssoise,' Tess explained, 'which is basically chilled potato and leek soup.'

'I've never had cold potato soup before,' Celia said, continuing to look suspiciously at her bowl.

'It's delicious!' proclaimed Dominic.

Celia took a mouthful. 'Hmm,' she said, but then she took another spoonful, and another.

Tess retreated into the kitchen where Simon was removing sea bass from the oven.

'Looks good, doesn't it?' he said.

'Yes, it does,' agreed Tess. She sighed. 'I'm wondering how wise it was to let Orla loose with the guests; you know how outspoken she can be. And heaven help us when she meets Titania!'

Titania appeared just as Tess was clearing all the empty soup bowls away. This evening Titania was wearing a black chiffon tunic adorned with sequins, pink silk trousers and jewelled sandals, all set off with glittery earrings which dangled to her shoulders. She'd obviously been colouring her hair because the white roots had gone and it was now a uniform dark magenta.

'I won't have a starter, thank you,' she said to Tess as she pulled out her chair and then, as she spotted Orla, said, 'And *who* are you?'

'I'm Orla, a friend of Tess's, and *you* must be Titania Terry! How wonderful to meet you at last! I've been so interested in your acting career!' She made it sound as if this was the fulfilment of a lifetime's ambition.

Titania visibly brightened, straightened up and said, 'How very sweet of you!'

She held her hand out to Orla, who, shaking it, said, 'And here you are, as glamorous as ever!'

Tess groaned inwardly. Orla was overdoing it to the point of farce.

But Titania was loving it. 'I just *adore* your charming Irish friend!' she said to Tess. 'We're going to have such lovely chats.'

Tess looked out of the windows from time to time to see Titania holding court out on the terrace, with Orla listening intently and Jackie pretending to read a magazine. Dominic had made his evening pilgrimage to the pub and Celia had retired to her room.

It was ten o'clock before they disbanded. Simon was watching television in the bedroom and Tess was emptying the dishwasher when Orla swanned into the kitchen.

'God, Orla, you've been out there for over an hour. Is she so very intriguing then, Titania Terry?'

Orla shook her head. 'No, but she had a few fascinating tales to tell and once she gets going there's no stopping her. And *what* an interesting bunch your guests are!'

'Well, I gave you the lowdown on all of them,' Tess said. 'Have you discovered anything new?'

'Titania is now my friend for life, because I don't think anyone's bothered to listen to the poor old girl for years, so she was making up for it tonight. I can't tell you how much she hates that Clarice What's-Her-Name – the one who stole her precious Henry. And I remember reading somewhere that Clarice lives down here in Cornwall so I have a hunch that that's why Titania is here. That woman is an urbanite; she's not interested in the sea and the scenery and all that stuff. But she is interested in your dear husband! It's Simon this and Simon that!'

'So what would be the reason for her visit, then?'

'Could be perhaps to visit Clarice? To tell her what she thinks of her? Or maybe to visit Henry's grave? Would he be buried down here?'

'No idea,' said Tess.

'I'd put money on the fact she's got something in mind because she was deliberately vague when I asked her why she was here. I think Simon's right about Dominic because he had a real gleam in his eye when he said he was going to the pub. Then there's Jackie, who's not got a lot between her ears but she's nice enough and, you'll be interested to know, she is *not* going back to that husband of hers, but is going to take him for every penny they made out of all that knicker elastic.'

'You *have* been busy,' Tess said drily, 'but you haven't mentioned Celia.'

'Ah now, Celia's the *real* dark horse! She doesn't tell you a bloody thing but there's a lot more to Celia than meets the eye. She's going to surprise you.'

'You're joking!'

'She may look as dull as ditchwater, and she sure doesn't want to stand out. Yet she's got that stylish car and everything, so it doesn't add up at all.'

'Well, they're all here for a little longer, so I'll keep you informed,' Tess said.

*

Orla stayed for five days during which time she took Tess to the cinema in Wadebridge and insisted on holding the fort for a day while Tess and Simon escaped to Padstow to lunch at Rick Stein's. On the second last night of Orla's stay they decided to pay a visit to The Portmerryn Arms, only to find the pub crowded due to the annual darts competition between Portmerryn and a neighbouring village, Polcarrow.

'Shall we go home?' Simon asked as they pushed their way through the crowd in an attempt to find a table.

'No, no, I like a busy pub,' said Orla, 'and there's two people leaving over there – quick!'

They grabbed the newly vacated seats and, while Simon went to order drinks, Orla said, 'Look, there's Dominic sitting at the bar.'

'Yes, he's here most nights,' Tess said.

'I think Simon's right, he has got the hots for Gideon,' Orla said, 'and do you know what? Gideon likes it!'

'For God's sake, Orla, you've only been in here five minutes – you and your overactive imagination!'

'I'm telling you, Gideon is responding, even if he doesn't know it!'

Then again, Tess thought, Gideon is in his forties and, from what she'd gathered, never had a steady girlfriend.

'So, you must let me know if Dominic manages to seduce him,' Orla went on. 'My word, you *do* have a funny old crowd under your roof! Don't know about it being a sparrows' nest, a hornets' nest more like!'

The darts players were preparing to pair up: one man, one woman, the names to be drawn out of two beer mugs. There was a rush to the bar to stock up with drinks before the draw. Both Jed and Gideon were working flat out.

As the names were drawn out of the ladies' mug and paired with the next one drawn from the men's mug, there was much raucous laughter at the couplings. Then, as they got to the last pair, one man declared loudly, 'Where's *my* partner, then?'

'We must be a lady short,' said the man in charge of the draw. He looked round at everyone. 'Reckon one of our ladies hasn't shown up.' There followed a general discussion as to who hadn't shown up. Then the partnerless man looked around and called out, 'I need a lady! Any lady here care to partner me?'

There was a lull in the conversation for a moment before Orla stood up. 'I will!' she shouted. There was a resounding cheer.

'God, Orla, I didn't know you could play darts,' Tess said.

'It's been a while,' Orla admitted. 'But isn't he a looker!'

A looker! Tess studied the man now advancing towards Orla, hand outstretched. He was probably in his sixties, tall, dark-eyed, a good thatch of close-cut greying hair, and a friendly smile.

'Danny Cobbledick,' he said.

'Orla Regan,' she said.

And then Orla was swallowed up in the crowd as they prepared to begin the competition.

'I didn't know Orla played darts,' Simon said, sipping his beer.

'Neither did I,' said Tess, 'and I only hope she doesn't make an idiot of herself. I think the man was the main attraction, so I only hope she manages to hit the dartboard occasionally.'

It was when the competition reached the final stages that Tess and Simon stood up to watch. Orla was excelling herself and her partner was beaming. How, Tess wondered, had she ever learned to play so well?

There was more cheering as the scorer chalked up the figures. And, lo and behold, Orla Regan and Danny Cobbledick were the winners and duly presented with the £100 prize money! More cheering.

Orla pushed her way back through the crowd with her new friend in tow.

'This is Danny. Danny, meet Tess and Simon.'

They shook hands and Tess could see why Orla might find him attractive after years of Ricky, who was short, chunky and balding. This Danny was tall, slim and had these very attractive dark brown eyes.

'Where on earth did you learn to play darts like that, Orla?' Simon asked.

'Ah, my misspent youth!' said Orla. Then, turning to Danny, she asked, 'Did we really win a hundred quid?'

'Yes,' Danny replied. 'There were twenty of us, and everyone put in a fiver.'

'But *I* didn't put in a fiver,' Orla said.

Danny winked. 'I put your fiver in,' he said.

Orla beamed, plainly very pleased with her partner.

'So at least we can buy you folks a drink,' Danny said, just as Tess was about to say, 'Well, we really should be going now.'

'That would be great,' said Orla.

So, over two pints and two gin and tonics, they discovered that Danny Cobbledick was a retired farmer from Polcarrow, a village about five miles away. He was a widower, one of his sons had taken over the farm, and he was in the process of converting a barn for himself. Immediately Tess could see that Orla was smitten.

'Now,' said Danny as he drained his pint, 'I'm going to have to leave you because we all hired a minibus to get us here and I can see everyone's preparing to go. As regards our winnings, Orla, how about we go out to dinner one night?'

Orla's eyes were shining. 'Oh,' she said, 'but I'm leaving the day after tomorrow.'

'We'd better make it tomorrow night, then,' he said.

The final day of Orla's visit she spent in a state of high excitement. Should she wear this, or that? Why hadn't she brought a nice dress with her?

'Because you weren't planning on snaring a local farmer,' Tess said.

Orla sniffed. 'I've no plans to *snare* him, and anyway I'm going home tomorrow.'

'Windsor Castle is at your disposal any time you want to visit,' Tess said, 'if you can cope with sleeping out there.'

'Oh, I can cope fine.' She stared into space for a moment. 'But I don't suppose I'll ever see him again after tonight. And anyway it's too late to cancel my train booking now.'

'What about poor old Ricky?'

Orla sighed dramatically. 'He's away half the time, Tess. And, to be honest, the relationship's becoming a bit dreary. It's not like I've ever wanted to *marry* him or anything.'

'Well, I can't imagine you would consider marrying a Cornish farmer either. Get real, Orla!'

Orla said nothing but continued to fuss around. Did her hair need trimming? Should she wear the green eyeshadow? Or the blue? On and on it went until Tess was relieved to see her disappear out of the door when the divine Danny arrived, in a muddy BMW, at seven o'clock.

*

There was no sign of Orla when Tess and Simon went to bed around ten thirty.

'I hope she's all right,' Tess said. 'After all, we know nothing about him.'

'For God's sake,' said Simon, who was trying to get to sleep, 'she's a grown woman! We know his name and where he comes from and, if you're out on a date and you're single, this isn't exactly late. Now, go to sleep!'

An hour later Tess was still awake. Then she heard a car drive up, some voices, a car door closing and then it drove away. She sighed with relief and finally got to sleep.

In the morning Orla appeared at nine o'clock. 'Just some coffee and a slice of toast,' she said.

'So?' said Tess.

'So what?'

'Don't make out you don't know what I'm talking about! How did the date go? Are you seeing him again?'

Orla sipped her coffee and smiled. 'It went fine.'

'And...?'

'And, yes, I'm seeing him again. He said he might even come up to London, but he's hoping I'll come back soon. Thing is, he's converting this barn and living in a bloody *caravan*! What is it with caravans in this place? I told him about Buckingham Palace.'

'Windsor Castle.'

'Whatever. Anyway, can I come down and stay in the royal residence again in a couple of weeks' time?'

'Of course you can,' Tess replied. 'But you may find that his caravan is superior, it might even be plumbed in to mains drainage! Now, we're going to have to leave shortly if you ever have a hope of getting that train.'

'Aw, don't worry, Tess. Danny'll be here in around twenty minutes to take me to the station. We'll have a good chat on the phone when I get home.'

CHAPTER 31

A LATE AWAKENING

Celia hadn't taken the time or the care with this painting as she had with the first one. She'd rushed to get it finished and done with, and given to Jackie as she'd very stupidly promised. She'd felt sorry for the silly woman and the gesture had been spontaneous, if misguided. But the strange thing was that this painting was a great improvement on its predecessor, even though she'd dashed it off quickly. That was possibly why; perhaps she should spend less time fiddling around with details and just let the colours flow. She might even do another one for herself, although she was becoming a little tired of this particular spot where Jackie came to disturb her half a dozen times a day. If she heard Jackie's sing-song voice saying, 'Ooh, isn't that coming on lovely!' one more time, she'd scream.

She didn't dislike Jackie. You couldn't really dislike Jackie, because she was like an eager puppy, desperate for everyone's approval and affection. Whatever kind of a marriage had the poor woman endured? If only she dressed more appropriately for her age instead of forcing those chunky thighs of hers into ridiculously short shorts, and exposing most of her bosoms. 'Common', Mummy would have called her. Celia wondered for a moment what Mummy would have made of Titania. Words would probably have failed her and words didn't fail Mummy very often. She smiled to herself.

Celia liked it here, though. She liked The Sparrows' Nest and the fact that Tess and Simon were always around if you wanted them but they never interfered or asked questions. And, apart from Jackie, she only saw the other two guests in the evenings, neither of whom were very interested in her. Hopefully Jackie would be gone in another week or two. Who would be the next guest in Room 4?

Celia wondered if she should be thinking of moving on, too. But where? She'd developed a mild passion for the sea, perhaps as an antidote to a lifetime in the Midlands. She'd rather like to spend her final years looking at it and enjoying all its moods.

She was sitting back studying her painting when she heard the shout close by. This was followed by some groaning. What on earth…? Celia stood up and edged round the gorse and there, just above her on the path, was a man on his bottom, rubbing his ankle.

'Oh, shit!' he said, staring at his phone.

She walked up to where he was sitting. 'There's no need for that sort of language round here!' she snapped.

He glared back at her and said, 'I'm sorry but I think I may have broken my ankle.' He waved his phone in the air. 'And my phone needs recharging.'

'How very irresponsible,' Celia said. 'And, since I don't have a phone with me, I'm afraid I can't help.'

As she turned to walk away she heard his groans and gasps of breath, and he said, 'I don't think I'm going to be able to walk. Would you be able to get in touch with *someone* for me? The ambulance service? Do you suppose they'd be able to find me here?'

He was a big man, balding, with piercing blue eyes and wearing the usual walking kit of T-shirt, shorts, sturdy walking boots and a waterproof jacket tied round his waist. And, on the ground beside him, a large backpack. Celia reckoned he was probably around her own age.

'Unlikely,' she replied, a little disconcerted by his stare. She'd never seen such intense eyes.

He was trying to stand up on one leg without much success. 'Perhaps I can slide down the hill on my bottom.'

Celia sighed. Her peaceful afternoon appeared to be at an end. If it wasn't one thing – Jackie – it was another, this wretched man with the blue eyes. 'I'll pack up my things,' she sighed, 'and go to find help. What did you do anyway – trip over your own feet?'

'I got my foot caught in a bramble,' he replied. 'And I'm really sorry to be such a nuisance.'

His smile disarmed her for a moment and the sensation surprised her. And then Jackie appeared. 'Oh, Celia! *There* you are! I was worried for a minute when I saw your stuff but no sign of you.'

'No need to worry,' Celia said shortly. 'I was just interrupted by this man who appears to have injured his ankle.'

'Oh, you poor man!' Jackie said looking at Celia's intruder. 'Can you put any weight on it at all?'

'I'm afraid not,' he replied. 'I was just wondering if I could slide down on my bottom.'

'It's very steep,' Jackie said. 'But look, Celia and I can help you down to the beach and then we can phone for an ambulance.'

'You're very kind,' he said, looking from one to the other. 'My name's Arthur Mitchell, but everyone calls me Mitch.'

'Well, I'm Jackie and this here's Celia. Now, if we can get you up, and you put an arm round each of our shoulders, we can get you down, can't we, Celia?'

Mitch was looking at Celia. 'What a charming name! You remind me of someone but I can't think who that might be.' Then he groaned again as he got awkwardly to his feet.

'Get your painting things, Celia,' Jackie ordered, 'and I'll carry half of them for you.'

Celia said nothing but went round the corner to pack up her paints and checked that her masterpiece was dry before she packed it away, along with her folded-up easel.

'If you put an arm round each of our shoulders, Mitch, we should get you down in no time,' said Jackie, picking up Celia's box of paints.

Celia grabbed the rest herself, leaving one side clear to support this man down the slope. She stiffened for a moment as a hairy masculine arm found its way round her shoulders. With Jackie supporting his other side the three took some tentative steps forward. It was a steep and narrow path and Celia was afraid of slipping. With care she managed to keep her footing, but her emotions were in turmoil. She had never been in such proximity to a man in all her adult life. Never. It was not altogether an unpleasant experience. She'd thought he might be sweaty, but he smelled quite fragrant.

When they finally got down to the beach Jackie said brightly, 'I'm sure Celia wouldn't mind taking you to the local hospital for an X-ray, would you, Celia?'

How could she refuse? There was a moment's silence before Mitch said, 'That would be great but I wouldn't want to put you to any trouble.'

What could she say? She could ask Jackie to phone for an ambulance but that could take hours to arrive, particularly as his injury wasn't life-threatening. And they couldn't very well leave him sitting here by the roadside. With a sigh Celia said, 'OK, wait here and I'll go get the car. Can you look after my painting stuff for me?'

'You're an angel,' the man named Mitch called after her. No one had ever called Celia an angel before – at this particular moment, she wasn't feeling at all angelic.

Twenty minutes later, having trudged up Seagull Hill and found her car keys, she was back down at the roadside in her car, and Jackie was helping the man into the passenger seat.

'There you are!' she said, patting his shoulder, 'Celia will look after you now!' And, with a wave, she was gone.

Celia turned reluctantly to face her passenger, avoiding the eyes which so disconcerted her, and concentrated on his nose instead.

'Hey,' he said, 'this is a great car! But I hope the hospital's not too far away because I know I've wrecked your afternoon.'

You certainly have, thought Celia. 'No, it's not far,' she said. 'There's a cottage hospital just about ten miles away.'

They drove along in silence for a few minutes, and then she felt she needed to break the silence.

'Do you do a lot of walking?' she asked.

'It's an annual indulgence,' he replied. 'I aim to do a certain stretch of the coastal path each year, but I can see I'm not going to be doing much more this time, although I have a couple of days left.'

'That's a shame. Do you always walk alone?'

'Yes,' he replied. 'I've become a bit of a loner ever since my wife died eight years ago. Are you married, Celia?'

'No,' she said shortly, 'never have been.' She stared straight ahead as she accelerated up the hill.

'Ah,' he said. Then, a few seconds later, 'I assume you're retired?'

'Yes,' she said.

'Me, too. I was in the police, made it to Detective Inspector. Birmingham.'

Celia's blood ran cold. She had to get rid of this man as soon as possible.

'What did *you* do?' he asked.

'Oh, I worked in an office,' she said.

'And now you're a painter?'

'Well, I try; it's only a hobby. Here we are!' Celia managed to park close to the door by waiting for another car to pull out. She had no idea how she was going to get him into the accident and emergency department.

'I may have to put my arm round you again, Celia,' he said, and she could hear the tease in his voice, 'while I hobble to the door.'

At the exact time when Celia could feel a blush coming on, she saw a wheelchair near the entrance. 'Just a minute!' she said, making a dash out of the car door. She could see a large woman heading towards her goal and so she ran, for the first time in years, and grabbed it just in time.

'I was going to have that,' the woman barked at her.

'Well, you aren't now,' said Celia, surprised at her own boldness. The woman said something derogatory, but Celia didn't wait to determine what it was as she dashed back to the car.

'You can certainly move,' said the man called Mitch as he climbed into the chair.

'Needs must,' she said shortly, pushing him towards the entrance.

As expected the department was busy. Someone would be with him as soon as possible.

Celia sighed. She could be here for hours, but she couldn't very well abandon him now. 'Where will you be staying?' she asked him.

'In my tent, I expect,' he replied. 'Occasionally I treat myself to a B&B, but mostly I just erect my tent somewhere near a half-decent pub where I can get a drink and something to eat.'

'How very uncomfortable.'

'Not at all. I sleep very well under canvas; probably comes a result of having been a Boy Scout.'

Just then a nurse appeared and called out, 'Arthur Mitchell?'

As he got up and hobbled towards her, the nurse added, 'Would your wife like to come in, too?'

His wife! Celia was mortified and felt the most fearsome blush coming on.

'I am not his wife!' she snapped. 'I just rescued him from the coastal path, and I shall wait right here!' She could see the nurse looking embarrassed and this Mitch character suppressing laughter. What was so funny? She wished she could drive off and leave him to it. She yawned and leafed through some dreadful women's magazine, wondering who on earth would read this stuff. 'My husband has run off with my sister!' was highlighted on the cover. 'Read all about it inside!' Celia wished she'd brought her book. She'd just got to an article about a fifty-five-year-old woman who'd given birth to triplets when Mitch came limping towards her with his foot bandaged.

'Good news!' he proclaimed. 'My ankle's not broken, just badly sprained. They've bandaged it up really firmly and dosed me with some painkillers. Now I'm supposed to keep my foot up as much as possible, and rest it.'

'And how are you going to be able to do that?'

'I don't know. Is there a little B&B round here?'

Celia shrugged. 'The Portmerryn Arms let out a few rooms, I think. We could try them.' She prayed they had a vacancy so she could leave him there.

They didn't. Jed shook his head sadly. 'Both rooms gone 'alf an hour ago, family of four.'

Mitch looked crestfallen. 'Where are you staying, Celia?'

'Oh, it's a guesthouse, just up the hill, but I know that all the rooms are currently occupied.'

'Are you *sure* they haven't an extra room somewhere?' He looked so worried that she began to feel a little sorry for him. Not only that, her heart gave an unexpected flutter.

'Well, OK,' she said. 'I'll take you there although I don't think they do. But they're sure to know of somewhere in the area.' This man was disturbing her for some reason and she was now ready to drive him anywhere just to see the back of him.

'This really is a great car,' he said again, as they turned up Seagull Hill. 'What's its top speed?'

'No idea,' Celia said, glancing at the speedometer. 'A hundred and something. But I never take it above fifty, sixty sometimes on the motorway.' She decided not to mention the occasion when it had inadvertently registered eighty without her knowing.

'Go on, Celia, admit it! You must have done a ton down the motorway somewhere!'

'I'm not in the habit of breaking the law,' she said primly. *Not in a car anyway.* She mustn't forget this man was a policeman.

'I'm not in the police now, Celia! And even the cops speed sometimes! Don't you do *anything* naughty?'

Celia didn't reply but pulled into a parking space outside The Sparrows' Nest.

'This looks very upmarket,' he said as he got out of the car.

Celia prayed that either Tess or Simon would be around somewhere and not having an afternoon siesta. As luck would have it Simon was on the telephone in the hall. As he hung up he said, 'Hi, Celia!'

'Good afternoon, Simon. Er, I've just rescued this gentleman who's sprained his ankle badly on the coastal path and he needs to rest up for a few days. I don't suppose you have an extra room tucked away anywhere?'

Simon shook his head. 'I'm really sorry, but I'm afraid we don't.'

'I didn't think so,' Celia said. 'Do you know of any B&Bs in this area?'

'Only the pub. Have you tried down there?'

Celia shook her head. 'All booked. I don't know what to do with him.' Then she realised that Mitch was right behind her.

'Look,' he said, 'I have my tent and perhaps I could park round here somewhere? They're forecasting rain tonight so I'd like to be somewhere sheltered if possible. Have you anywhere in your grounds, and I would, of course, pay?'

Simon thought for a moment. 'I don't see why not,' he said. 'But why don't you sit out on our terrace for a moment and I'll bring you and Celia something to drink. Tea? Coffee? Something stronger? You need to keep that foot up.' They both agreed on tea.

Celia could see no means of escape without being rude. 'Come this way,' she instructed her guest, relieved to see there was no sign of Jackie or anyone on the terrace.

'Wow!' he said. 'What a view! And what a wisteria!'

'Do you like gardening, then?' Celia asked.

'Yes, I do. Do you?'

Celia thought about Mummy's predilection for camellias. 'We only had a small garden,' she said, 'and Mum— my mother had a thing about camellias. We had camellias everywhere.'

'They can be tricky things to grow,' he declared. 'I hope she had more luck with them than I did. But you haven't answered my question. Do *you* like gardening?'

'I've never had much time. But I do fancy growing my own vegetables one day, and being self-sufficient.' Now *why* had she told him that?

'So you live in the countryside?'

Be vague. Don't tell him where you've been living. 'I'm planning to move,' she said. 'I don't quite know where yet.' And I wouldn't be telling you if I did.

'Very enterprising. I imagine you're quite a clever lady, Celia.'

You've no idea just how clever I was, thought Celia. As Simon appeared with a tray of tea and some of those delicious biscuits made with Cornish cream, she asked, 'Did you catch many criminals?'

'Oh, just a few, here and there.' He grinned at her. 'One or two managed to escape me.'

She noticed how his eyes crinkled when he smiled, and he smiled a lot, although she couldn't see what was so amusing.

'I'll show you where to pitch your tent,' Simon said, 'and give you a hand to erect it.'

'Thanks so much. I'm Mitch, by the way.'

'Simon Sparrow.' They smiled at each other and shook hands. 'I'll give you a key to our laundry room because there's a toilet in there.'

'Great, thanks.' Then, 'Would you mind if I went down to that pub this evening?' Mitch said as Simon went back inside. 'I could murder a few pints and grab something to eat while I'm there.'

Celia sighed with relief. 'I'll give you a lift,' she said.

'Thanks, Celia, you're an absolute gem!'

Celia drank her tea as quickly as she could, then said, 'I'm going to my room for a rest, and leave you to set up your tent. What time do you want me to drive you to the pub later?'

'Whatever time suits you. Half past six?'

'Half past six,' Celia confirmed. 'I shall be in the car waiting.'

'Then I'd better not be late,' he said with another of his disconcerting grins.

Celia ferried her new acquaintance down to The Portmerryn Arms at six thirty precisely, and said she'd pick him up at nine thirty precisely. 'And I sincerely hope you won't be drunk,' she added.

'You should join me,' he said, 'and that way you could keep an eye on me.'

'Don't be ridiculous!' she said. 'Anyway, I'm not a pub type of person.'

'Then what sort of person are you, Celia?' he asked as he got out of the car, but didn't wait for an answer as he hobbled towards the door.

This newcomer – by the name of Mitch – was discussed at length during dinner.

'Celia found herself a lovely bloke up on the cliff,' laughed Jackie, causing all eyes to swivel in Celia's direction. For the second time in one day she felt mortified.

'I did not "find myself a bloke",' she snapped, 'I merely helped someone who'd twisted his ankle.'

'And the poor bloke's out there in a tent in the garden!' Jackie went on. 'No room at the inn!'

'Poor man!' said Titania. 'Is he handsome, Celia? Could you mention to him that I've got a nice big double bed?'

Celia ignored her.

'Celia's got a twin-bedded room, haven't you, Celia?' the wretched Jackie went on. 'You could pop him in the other one and never need to touch him!' She exploded into gales of laughter.

I rue the day I ever gave her that painting, thought Celia.

'Enough!' said Dominic the diplomat. 'Celia's a very respectable lady. I must say, though, that I've never fancied sleeping in a tent.'

Titania shuddered dramatically. 'I can't imagine anything worse, darlings!'

Then Jackie regaled them with countless tales of camping holidays they'd had when the children were small. 'Wales, Scotland, we went everywhere,' she said.

Celia glanced at her watch and excused herself from the table. Such a ridiculous conversation! And there was still half an hour to kill before she had to pick up that man from the pub. Why on earth hadn't she asked Simon or Dominic to collect him? Should she do so now? No, she'd better stick to what she'd promised. Unable to settle to do anything, Celia gazed out of the window and saw the evening sky darkening ominously. It was going to rain. Then she checked her appearance in the mirror, ran the comb through her hair and wondered if she should put on a dab of lipstick. Ridiculous! What was she thinking of! She never wore lipstick! In fact, she'd been carrying round this tube of coral pink for thirty years or more. Still, she put on a tiny amount and then rubbed her lips together. Time to go.

As she sat in her car outside The Portmerryn Arms, Celia could feel her tummy fluttering. What on earth was wrong with her? Was it perhaps something she'd eaten?

On the dot of nine thirty Mitch emerged from the pub.

'I thought I'd better be on time,' he said with a wicked grin as he eased himself into the passenger seat. 'I had a feeling you might rap my knuckles if I was late.'

Celia tried not to smile. As she drove up Seagull Hill she said, 'It looks like rain.'

'Yes, it does, doesn't it? Still, my little tent is completely water-proof, so don't you go worrying.'

'I wasn't in the slightest bit worried,' she said, as she parked her car next to Dominic's Jaguar.

'Good,' said Mitch. 'Hey, would you like to see where Simon and I erected the tent?'

Celia hesitated. Perhaps it would be churlish to refuse. 'I'll have a quick look,' she said.

He led the way, hobbling through the trees, to where his tiny tent nestled in a clearing. It was darkening rapidly now and the first drops of rain were beginning to fall.

'It's very small,' Celia said.

'Don't forget I have to carry it,' Mitch pointed out. 'I can't go lugging a marquee around with me, Celia, can I?'

Celia couldn't begin to imagine crawling into that tiny space. But she supposed he was more sheltered here than he would be out on the cliffs somewhere. Did he undress? Where did he go to the toilet?

'Simon's given me a key to the laundry room,' he said, as if sensing her thoughts, 'and I can use the loo in there.'

'All right,' she said, turning back towards the house, 'I hope you sleep well.'

'You, too, Celia,' he said.

Celia woke up at 1 a.m. to a clap of thunder, so loud it must have been directly overhead. Then the heavens opened and the rain descended in torrents. She'd never known such a storm in Dudley so perhaps it was something to do with Cornwall being a peninsula? Lightning flashed, followed by another deafening clap of thunder. She could even hear the rain hammering on the roof, above the attic.

Then she remembered Mitch. How could he possibly sleep, or even keep dry, in this dreadful storm? She hoped it would move away, and indeed the next clap of thunder did seem to come from further away. Just as she began to relax it rolled right back overhead again. It was impossible to sleep. Celia switched on the light and got out of bed. She wondered if the tent might have collapsed and, even if it hadn't, could it survive in such a storm? Should she offer him a towel or something? She should have driven him somewhere to find a B&B, so why hadn't she? And he had an injured ankle.

Celia headed towards the door, hesitated and walked back towards the window just as there was a spectacular flash of lightning and another deafening crash of thunder. And torrential rain. It was no good; she felt responsible for this man so perhaps she'd just have a quick look to make sure he was OK. Just a peep. She pulled on her waterproof over her nightie and stuck her feet into her old leather sandals. They'd get soaked, but they'd dry. She tiptoed to the door and opened it an inch. She could see no lights anywhere. She opened the door fully so she could see her way down the stairs. Now, would she be able to open the front door without waking up the entire household?

The key was in the lock and turned easily, but there was a bolt which made a clonking sound. She stopped, listened, her heart thumping. There was no sound anywhere apart from the lashing of the rain. Leaving the door ajar she let her eyes become accustomed to the darkness and then she padded, through the storm and between the parked cars, into the trees, and hoping she was heading in the right direction. Then she saw him, and the tent, which appeared to have collapsed.

'Mitch!' she said. 'You can't stay outside in this! And you're supposed to be resting that foot!'

He straightened up and looked at her in bewilderment. 'What on earth are you doing out here?'

'I was worried about you,' she said, wiping the rain from her face, 'and no wonder.'

'Oh, Celia!' He seemed genuinely touched. 'I told you there was no need to worry about me. I'm OK. Just a bit wet.'

'You're not OK,' she snapped. 'And I expect your sleeping bag is wet now.' She looked around. 'Bring it in with you and we'll get it dry, and yourself dry, too.'

'I can't let you—'

'Hurry up!' she commanded. 'I can't stand here drowning all night!'

'All right! All right! Keep your hair on,' he said.

'And don't shout; you'll wake everyone up. Come *on*!'

Celia led the way back to the door of the house, Mitch a few steps behind.

'Shsh!' she said, pressing her finger to her lips as she locked and bolted the door behind them and led the way upstairs. She prayed they weren't leaving a trail of wet footprints behind, but that couldn't be helped and hopefully they would have dried by the morning.

Celia closed the door quietly behind them and looked at Mitch, who was dripping from head to foot. 'Have a shower,' she ordered, 'and get out of those wet clothes.' She opened the bathroom door. 'Although I've no idea what you're going to wear.'

'Don't worry,' he said, 'because I'll pop down later and put everything in the dryer. In the meantime, Celia, I fear I'm going to have to cover my modesty with your bath towels.'

This situation was becoming more and more complicated. If it would only stop raining she'd send him straight down to get his things dried. She could hear him showering. Dear lord, a strange man in her bathroom and her standing there in only her nightie. Mummy would have another heart attack if she could see this debacle.

'It's still raining,' he said as he appeared several minutes later, a large white bath towel wrapped round his body and a second draped over his shoulder. It emphasised his tan and made him look like a Greek god. She noticed his muscles and the patch of hair on his chest. 'You wouldn't send me out again in this, would you?'

She blushed and swallowed. 'I suppose you could use the other bed for a few hours,' she said, indicating the pristine twin divan next to hers.

Why was he staring at her like that?

'I will if you really want me to, Celia,' he said, 'but I'm not at all sure that you do.'

PART THREE

CHAPTER 32

CALM AFTER THE STORM

It was the quiet after the stormy night, a day of sunshine with a pleasant breeze. Everyone appeared to be out, so Tess decided to sunbathe on the terrace for a couple of hours. She'd not slept well with the thunder and lightning, and both she and Simon had been agog to see Celia venturing out into the night to see her new friend. Unbelievable! Even more unbelievable was the fact that she then brought him *in*! Fortunately, Celia was keeping a very low profile this morning because Tess was none too sure how to handle this. Best to say nothing.

'I think I might stretch out for a bit, too,' Simon said, coming round the corner. He'd been hoeing the vegetable plot and swearing that something nasty was eating the carrots. He sank himself down wearily on the other sun bed and was about to say something when a little voice called out, 'Coo-ee!'

'Oh, God!' he muttered as Jackie came into view. He stood up again. 'I was *just* going.'

'Not on account of me, I hope!' Jackie said gaily.

'Not at all,' he lied. 'I think I'll lie down indoors for an hour or two.'

'Mind if I join you?' Jackie plonked herself down on the sun bed vacated by Simon.

'Of course not,' Tess said, all ideas of a siesta dissipating

'Wasn't that storm awful last night?' Jackie stretched out languidly and adjusted her bosoms which looked close to escaping from her sun top.

'Yes, it certainly was,' Tess agreed. 'Did you manage to sleep?'

'Well, I did, a little, but I was a bit scared, being on my own. It's the only time I've missed Joe.'

'That's understandable,' Tess said, wondering how far to continue this conversation.

'I've always meant to thank you for being so kind to me that day Joe left,' Jackie continued.

Tess had to think for a moment. 'I didn't do anything much—' she began.

'Oh yes, you did,' Jackie interrupted. 'You gave me the strength to face that first awful evening that turned out to be not so awful after all.'

'It must have been very upsetting for you, though.'

'It was, Tess, but it isn't now. Do you know something? Coming here was the best thing we ever did. I'd probably still be with him if we'd stayed at home, 'cos all my friends would say things like, "Well, you've put up with him for forty years, why rock the boat now?" And I'd think they were probably right and I'd look round the house and think of the upheaval and the upset and all that.'

'Won't there still be an upheaval and upset?' Tess asked, propping herself up on one elbow.

'Yeah, but I've thought everything through now. I've had the space and time to work out how to handle it, and I've phoned my sons and told them.'

'How have they reacted, Jackie?'

'Well, Frank hasn't spoken to his father in years, so all he said was, "What took you so long, Mum?" He's up in Newcastle but he said I can go and stay there anytime. And then Phil's running a pub locally, and he gets on OK with his dad, but even he said he wasn't surprised.'

'But you'll have to go home to sort things out, won't you?'

'Yes, of course. But I'm going to look for somewhere to rent, and I'm going to see that the house gets sold so I can buy a place eventually.'

'And how's Joe likely to react to all this?' Tess asked.

'He'll go ballistic. But I don't care, and I'm going to get myself a good solicitor.'

'I hope it all goes well for you, Jackie,' Tess said sincerely. 'Let me know, won't you?'

'I'll email you, and I'd like to come back here sometime. Maybe just for a week though, 'cos I'll be paying for it myself!'

'You'd be very welcome.'

'I'll always think of here as a little piece of paradise where I soothed my soul! Now, ain't that *poetic*?'

'I'd like you to write that in the visitors' book,' Tess said, and they both laughed.

'And I've made a friend of Celia, too – well, I *think* I have! She's not the easiest person to get close to but, hey, it takes all sorts to make a world!'

'You can say that again!' said Tess with feeling. She'd warmed over the weeks to this little woman and was flattered that Jackie had chosen to confide in her. 'Tell you what,' she said, 'how do you fancy a glass of wine? On the house. I'm going to have one.' There was no chance whatsoever of a catnap now.

'Ooh, lovely!' said Jackie.

An hour later Tess found Simon sleeping peacefully on top of their bed. She might be lacking sleep but Tess was glad she'd had some time with Jackie, who plainly considered The Sparrows' Nest as some sort of a therapeutic counselling retreat. As Tess changed back into her jeans, Simon stirred.

'Come here!' he commanded.

'I've got to start preparing dinner,' Tess said, zipping up her jeans, 'and if I lie down now there's a good chance I won't wake up till midnight.'

Simon yawned and sat up. 'I gather you didn't manage to get a doze outside with Jackie jabbering away?'

'No, I didn't,' Tess replied, 'but I couldn't really leave her once she got into full flow. She seems to think that being here has helped her to sort out her life.'

'Can we charge extra for sorting out lives?' Simon asked as he eased himself off the bed.

'Seriously, Simon, I do feel for her. After all those years it can't be easy to decide to leave your husband, even if he is a horrid bully.'

'Point taken. Do you suppose we've sorted Celia out as well? Or does she always venture out in thunderstorms in the middle of the night looking for blokes?'

Tess giggled. 'We don't know for sure that they got up to any hanky-panky.'

Simon raised one eyebrow. 'Why else would she sneak him inside?'

'Because he was cold and wet?'

'So where did he sleep? Gina said the other bed hadn't been slept in.'

'Yes, well.' Tess thought for a moment. 'But I still can't believe they got up to anything.'

'And now we have Dominic lusting after Gideon! Are we turning into a dating agency or what?'

'And none of them are a day under sixty!' Tess exclaimed.

'Next thing we know Titania will be crawling into my bed in the middle of the night. Hope you're prepared to move over?'

'Like I said, we've become a Mecca for ancients looking to change their lives,' said Tess.

'Not ancients, darling – golden oldies!' Simon laughed. 'That's us, the golden oldies guesthouse!'

CHAPTER 33

THE FIERY WITCH

Titania left The Sparrows' Nest at eight o'clock for her second trip to the Lizard peninsula, determined to find Black Rock Cove and The Hideaway today, one way or the other. She didn't have the time or the energy to keep trailing down there. Would Clarice be in residence?

She'd refused a cooked breakfast, settling for cereal and tea. She'd treat herself to lunch later, when she found a suitable pub.

'So where are you off to today?' Tess asked.

'Oh, just exploring,' she'd replied. 'Perhaps Penzance or Land's End.'

It was better to be vague, and she certainly didn't want anyone to associate her with the Lizard. Now, as she drove across Cornwall, Titania knew without a doubt that country life was not for her. She'd not hang around for long after she'd completed her mission; she'd make some excuse about having to get back. Back to civilisation! She couldn't cope with the huge expanses of sky, the bleak moors, the narrow roads. And isolated villages with no one around. Where did they all go? The traffic was horrendous this morning so they were probably all in their cars going somewhere else.

'It'll be worse in a few weeks' time,' Simon had said cheerfully when she'd complained about the traffic earlier. 'When the schools break up and all the families come down on holiday.' She most certainly would not be sticking around for that. She'd be back in London, checking with her agent and perhaps even auditioning for something. She'd be eating out in restaurants and bistros run by interesting people from every corner of the globe. She'd be going to galleries, the cinema, the theatre. How could the lovely Simon have given all that up to exist on the side of a cliff in the middle of nowhere?

Simon... She thought about him a lot although he didn't appear to be smitten by her undoubted charms – but it was still fun to flirt.

As she braked, yet again, Titania wondered how there could be so much traffic around at this time in the morning. Did they have a rush hour down here? Well, she supposed these people must earn their money somehow. She looked at the drivers: one in each car – typical rush hour traffic – so they must be commuters. Because tourists came in groups, surrounded by bags and boxes and bedding, crawling along and frequently towing horrible caravans. She hated caravans. You got stuck behind one of the damned things for mile after mile on the narrow roads, blocking the view of the road ahead so you couldn't see to overtake on the rare occasions when there was a straight stretch.

She headed towards the west side of the Lizard this time. Surely someone somewhere must know where Black Rock Cove was. How many coves could there be? She found Mullion Cove and Ogo-dour Cove, Pigeon Ogo and The Horse, and began to wonder if it was some kind of zoo. It was certainly all very picturesque, but she wasn't here to admire the scenery. Finally, she stopped for lunch at a quaint-looking pub because she liked the name – The Fiery Witch – and also because it appeared to be the only pub in the area. It was obviously popular because the car park was full and she had to wait until some man in a suit emerged from the pub and drove off from a spot right beside the door. Inside was dark with stone walls, low black beams and a predictable inglenook. It was also very busy and Titania had to queue at the bar. The wait gave her the opportunity to read the large placard on which some calligrapher had written the story of the Fiery Witch. She, according to tradition, had lived on this very spot and had the useful gift of being able to set fire to anyone she didn't like – and there appeared to be quite a number – by merely touching them with her fingertips. A woman after my own heart, thought Titania. Perhaps it was a good omen. Yes – it was her lucky day! As she ordered her mushroom omelette and glass of Merlot, she asked the young barman – who had an acute acne problem – if he knew of somewhere called Black Rock Cove.

'Sure,' he said, 'it's only half a mile or so from here.' He placed her drink on the counter. 'Lovely spot! You visiting someone? Looking to buy?'

'No, just touring around.'

'Tell you something else, that Clarice D'Arcy has a house there. You know, she was an actress?'

'Never heard of her,' said Titania, her heart thumping.

'She was very famous, so they say.'

The little barmaid, who'd been serving someone else alongside, said, 'Just seen her drive past in her silver Roller, Stevie.'

'Yeah,' said Stevie, 'she'll be off to Penzance. She usually goes on a Friday.'

Titania picked up her drink and went in search of a table. She'd almost found Clarice at last! And there was no time to waste. How long would it take to drive to Penzance and back, and presumably she'd got some sort of appointment there? At least, while Clarice was out, she could suss out the lie of the land. She ate quickly, excited, eager to be on her way. But which way? And how could she ask directions without drawing attention to herself?

As she headed towards the door, spotty Stevie gave her a cheerful wave. Titania hesitated.

'I wonder if you would be kind enough to give me rough directions to Black Rock Cove?'

'Sure,' he said, then turning to the girl, 'Can you hold the fort for a minute, Hazel?' Hazel nodded assent.

Titania waited just outside the door. When Stevie appeared he said, 'Them little lanes all look much the same, don't they? Now,' he took her by the elbow, 'turn right out of here, see? There's a red letterbox a quarter mile down the road on the left, and opposite that is a little lane on the right, wot says "Ancient Wishing Well" and you take that. Pay no attention to the wishing well but keep going and a little bit further on is another little lane on the right and that one says, "Black Rock Cove".'

'Thank you very much,' said Titania, unlocking her car and wondering if she should tip him because he'd been very helpful.

'Hey, I like your car,' he said. '*Love* them old sporty Toyotas! And that registration is something else – T1 TER – wherever did that come from?'

'No idea,' said Titania, getting into the driving seat, eager to be gone. He meant well, she supposed, but he was too chatty. Too nosy. She didn't tip him after all.

She reversed out, lowered her window, waved at him and shouted, 'Thanks again!' as he gave her a wave and went back through the door. She turned right, motored for a few minutes and saw the letterbox, barely visible through clouds of cow parsley, and the turning opposite was just as obscure. You could drive past it quite easily. The sign for the wishing well had fallen victim to the wind at some point and was now dangling sadly from the post. No, she'd never have found this without the help of spotty Stevie.

And he was quite correct; the next lane on the right was some quarter of a mile further on and was signposted 'Black Rock Cove'. Titania was mystified as to why it should be signposted down here but not up on the main road. Perhaps that was why Clarice had chosen such a remote spot, because no one was ever likely to find it unless they knew exactly where they were going.

The sea was visible ahead and Titania passed a couple of farms and three roadside cottages. There was nowhere round here that resembled any hideaway that Clarice might buy and all the time she was getting closer and closer to the sea. Then the road came to a complete halt, terminating in a flat grassy stretch with a sign which said 'Please park here and take the footpath to the beach'.

Titania parked and got out of the car. It was windy up here, and none too warm on what was plainly the top of a cliff. She wandered across to the footpath which was perilously steep and stony, but the cove beneath was beautiful: a stretch of almost white sand dotted with large black rocks. The reflected sunlight had turned the water a tropical turquoise. Then, suddenly, one of the rocks moved and made its way to the sea, and she realised it must be a seal.

But where was The Hideaway?

She looked round and saw, at the far end of the car park, a five-bar gate. That must lead somewhere, surely? Titania walked across as speedily as her pink sequined sandals would permit. There was a sign on the gate which said 'Private Property'.

Huh!

Titania opened the gate and proceeded to walk down a path that was just wide enough to take a car, obviously, because she could see the tyre tracks. Ahead of her was a clump of windblown trees through which she could see a house: a modern bungalow of stone and glass which, like The Sparrows' Nest, appeared to be built on a rocky ledge and, also like Sparrows', enjoyed a panoramic view of the sea. 'The Hideaway' sign was attached to the wall of the house, next to the main oak door. It certainly was hidden away, you couldn't argue with that. There was a terrace which seemed to stretch all the way round the house, but no garden.

There didn't appear to be any sign of life but Titania hesitated. Would Clarice have a housekeeper, a cook, or even a cleaner? Well, she'd just have to bluff it. She was an actress, after all, and she would say to whoever opened the door, 'Sorry to bother you but I'm trying to find a friend of mine who lives round here…' and she'd make up a name. 'Charles Daltrey' – that would do.

Her heart thumping furiously, Titania rang the bell, and waited. Nothing. No sound whatsoever from within. She pressed the bell again. Still nothing. She was in luck; the house was empty.

She walked round the terrace to the front of the house, which was facing the sea, and found a wall of almost unbroken glass similar to Simon's folding doors. There was an open-plan living area with sumptuous-looking white sofas on polished wooden floors and some artistically arranged flower displays.

And here was the bedroom with its bloody antique four-poster, placed on a raised platform like the altar to human sacrifice it was, in the middle of an otherwise minimalist white space. This was where that woman had stolen and seduced her lovely Henry, and most likely brought about his demise.

Titania could feel a red rage coursing through her body which made her grit her teeth and clench her hands into fists. I've waited a long time for this, she thought as she turned away from the window and continued to walk right round the house, past the urns of geraniums and hydrangeas, examining the exterior carefully. But she had to hurry because she couldn't risk Clarice finding her here. Please God don't let me meet her on the path up to the car park!

Luck was with her. When she got back to the Toyota there was only an elderly Nissan parked nearby where a young couple were loading themselves up with bags and windbreaks, obviously undaunted by the precipitous path leading down to the cove. Titania drove away, made a left at the first turning and headed back towards the so-called main road. It was just as she was passing the wishing well that she saw a silver Rolls Royce heading towards her.

Titania pulled into a layby, lowered her head, and let it pass.

CHAPTER 34

ONE DAY

It was Friday, the day Dominic dreaded because it was the final day of the wine and cocktail course and what possible excuse could he have to be alone with Gideon again? Only yesterday they'd admitted their feelings for each other, and oh, those looks, touches, kisses! Dominic could scarcely believe that Gideon felt such attraction for him. They'd stopped on the way back from Bodmin, parked in a layby, kissed and caressed like a couple of teenagers. It was as if a dam had burst and Gideon was at last able to swim free. More than anything in the world they needed time together. But how? And when? Gideon was expected home to set up the barrels and everything for the evening. Doing some fancy course did not excuse him from his duties.

When Gideon got into the car at five o'clock he looked around for a moment before kissing Dominic there and then.

'I have a plan,' Gideon said as they drove away.

'Well, I've been trying to think of something all day,' Dominic admitted, 'and I haven't been able to write a word!'

Gideon patted Dominic's knee. 'I'm going to tell Dad that it's actually a *six*-day course, and that I have to go back on Monday as well.'

'You reckon he'll believe that?' Even as he spoke Dominic found it hard to believe that a man of forty-five could be so beholden to his parents.

'Why wouldn't he? And I'm going to say that, because it's the final day, the students and instructors are all going out for a meal in the evening. That gives me – us – the whole day.'

Dominic swallowed. A whole day! Was it possible? 'Wouldn't your parents think it odd if I was to bring you back at, say, 11 p.m.?'

'I've been thinking about that. So, you say you're going to be out for the day – anywhere. Maybe you could be visiting a friend in Liskeard or somewhere and you'll be coming back through Bodmin in the late evening and so it would be no trouble at all to pick me up from the restaurant on the way back.'

Dominic could scarcely believe what he was hearing; that Gideon must have spent precious time, when he should have been dreaming up cocktails, dreaming instead of how to spend a day with Dominic Delamere! Was the idea feasible? Could they possibly get away with it? Surely – just one day to consummate their love and perhaps to be able to persuade Gideon that he'd love Hampstead and that he'd never need to pull another pint if he didn't wish to. But there was always the opportunity for work in one of the trendy bars in the area.

It was Dominic's idea of heaven and, somehow or the other, he had to make it Gideon's, too.

Now he was aware that Gideon was watching him anxiously and, although he hated the idea of lying to Jed and Annie, he couldn't possibly let this opportunity pass.

'Do you *really* think they'd believe it, Gideon?'

'Of course they will!'

'You'd still better get the bus to Bodmin in the morning,' Dominic said, 'and then I'll pick you up in Bodmin and we'll go somewhere for the day. Where do you fancy? I've always wanted to go to Polperro.'

'No,' Gideon said, 'it's got to be somewhere anonymous, somewhere no one will pay any attention to us, somewhere we aren't going to bump into someone I know.'

'It'll have to be Plymouth or somewhere like that then.'

'Yeah, Plymouth should be safe.'

'I'll book us a room,' said Dominic.

'You'll never believe,' Jed said, as he placed a vodka tonic in front of Dominic later that evening, 'that Gideon 'ere has another day on this bloomin' course of his.'

'Really?' Dominic poured the tonic carefully into his vodka. 'Now you mention it I think he did say something about that.'

'Apparently, it's a *six*-day course, not a five-day one. And then they're all goin' out for some fancy dinner in the evenin'. And 'e needn't be thinking I'm goin' to collect 'im at that time of night 'cos I'm bleedin' knackered by closing time.'

Dominic hoped he looked thoughtful. 'Look, Jed,' he said, 'I'm going to be visiting an old friend in Liskeard on Monday. We arranged it months ago. Good old George, haven't seen him in years so it'll probably be quite a day! So I might be able to pick Gideon up on my way back through Bodmin, although it may well be late before I get there, say ten or eleven o'clock.'

Gideon was serving a trio of walkers and studiously avoiding eye contact.

'Well,' said Jed, ''t'would be a relief to me to know that 'e'd get home safe. But you've been more than kind to us, Dominic.'

Dominic took a large gulp of his vodka. 'It's a way of saying thank you, Jed, for all the information you've given me about the history of this area. I'll now be able to continue writing my book when I get back to London.'

Jed leaned across the bar. 'We're goin' to miss you, Dominic. When you first started comin' in 'ere we thought you was just one of them poncey, stuck-up city types. But you got a heart of gold, Dominic, so you 'ave.'

Dominic didn't know whether to feel pleased or ashamed. How would Jed and Annie react if Gideon chose to go to London with him? Would they realise then that this was a scheme to lure their precious son away? Would they be able to cope without their big, strapping Gideon? Would Dominic be able to cope if he had to return to London all alone? He'd only known Gideon for a short time, but his feelings for him were already strong.

While Jed was serving another customer Dominic caught Gideon's eye and gave him the thumbs up. Monday would be OK.

Dominic wondered how he'd ever get through the weekend.

The bus from Portmerryn took twice as long as Dominic did to get to Bodmin.

'It stops at just about every farm gate,' Gideon sighed as he got into the Jaguar. 'Kids going to school, old girls going shopping – the driver knows them all. Asks after their mothers and fathers, arthritis, whatever. If you're not in a hurry it's quite entertaining.'

'I'm sure it is,' said Dominic. He was only aware of a certain excitement, tension, apprehension, now that there was the prospect of more than twelve hours together. And he was rapidly losing confidence. Here he was, seventy years old, not particularly good-looking or successful, and why on earth would anyone as gorgeous as Gideon fancy him, far less agree to move to London with him? Dominic knew from experience that he was inclined to be impulsive but, at his age, time was running out and this could be his last chance. Everything depended on today.

They arrived in Plymouth mid-morning. Dominic drove around, found the Galaxy Hotel which not only had a basement car park for their honoured guests, but was also close to the Barbican with its bars and restaurants. And the famous Gin Factory.

'Plymouth,' Gideon said, as they checked in, 'is best known for the hospital, or the shopping centre. They've got a great big Marks & Sparks. But, best of all, is the Gin Factory. Now, that's where they really know how to fix a cocktail!'

We won't be going there, thought Dominic. Not with me. With me you'll explore the bookshops, the galleries, the bistros. I want to introduce you to a world of culture, to meet people of every nationality, to hear other languages spoken and haunting music from every corner of the globe. I want you to start living! There's a great big wonderful world outside of Portmerryn where you can be whoever and whatever you want to be!

The hotel room was standard, tastefully neutral, and had a mini-bar, an ironing board, a hairdryer, a safe and, of course, the standard hospitality tray.

'Tea, coffee and hot chocolate!' Gideon explored the room. 'Don't they think of everything!'

'They do indeed,' Dominic agreed, looking at the king-size bed.

Two hours later they had a wander round the Barbican area, arm in arm. Few people looked, or cared. All the major cities have come into the twenty-first century, Dominic thought, feeling proud of this lovely man on his arm who was fascinated by everything. They stopped for coffee.

'What's a barista?' Gideon asked as he sipped his cappuccino. Then he stopped to read every menu in front of every restaurant. 'This sushi stuff! You won't catch me eating raw fish, ugh!' and, outside a Greek restaurant, 'What the hell's koulouri? And souvlaki?'

Dominic was none too sure himself, but he was enchanted by Gideon's innocent fascination. It was almost like taking a child on his first train journey or to a funfair for the first time. Magic.

They planned to eat early, about six o'clock, and then have some time together before they had to drive back to Portmerryn. And then what? Would Gideon be so enamoured with Dominic that he'd leave his parents and everything he'd ever known?

Later they ate Italian because Gideon was familiar with some of the dishes and he liked pasta. They had a bottle of Valpolicella, most of which Gideon drank because Dominic restricted himself to one glass, thinking of the drive ahead. They chatted the whole way back to the hotel, holding hands, Gideon sleepy and relaxed, Dominic still apprehensive.

'Look, why don't you come up to Hampstead for a week, just to see how you like it?' he said. 'Surely your parents wouldn't object to you having a week's holiday? We could have a marvellous time and there's so much of London I'm longing to show you.'

'I will, I will,' said Gideon, resting his head on Dominic's shoulder. Dominic's spirits soared as they drove across the Tamar Bridge and headed towards the north coast. It was almost dark and their time was nearly up.

'I don't want you to go back to London,' Gideon whispered, 'but I know you have to. And, if I want to be with you, I have to go, too.' He paused. 'But what the hell am I going to say to Mum and Dad?'

'My darling,' Dominic said, 'you are a grown man. You should not be tied to ageing parents. Surely they could afford to pay for a barman to come in for busy nights? Let's face it, if you'd left home like your brother did, they'd have to manage. Surely they'll be happy for you to have a life of your own?'

'I know you're right but it's going to be bloody difficult, telling them, I mean. They're not stupid, Dominic, they know what goes on in the world, or most of it anyway, but it's never affected them, see. Like they have no idea that Porky Borman, who comes in the pub on a Saturday night, dishes out drugs down the end of the village.'

Dominic was shocked. 'You're kidding!'

'Of course I'm not! It goes on everywhere, even Portmerryn. Every town, every village, dealers come out from the cities. Anyway, I'm going to tell Mum and Dad that I'm going up to London to see how I like it. That you're offering me a roof over my head and that there's plenty of jobs going.'

So he's not going to tell them about *us*, Dominic thought. But never mind, one step at a time.

'Give me a couple of days,' Gideon said. 'I'll tell them and, on Wednesday afternoon, I'll walk along the beach towards Penhennon. Meet me there, near the cave, about half past three.'

'And then what?'

'And then I'll tell you how they reacted. But, no matter, I'll be all packed up and ready to go with you up to London at the end of the week.'

'Are you sure?' Dominic asked.

'I'm absolutely sure, Dominic,' Gideon said.

CHAPTER 35

ONE WEEK

Mitch hadn't slept in the tent again. He'd told Simon about it collapsing in the middle of the night and how he'd come in to the laundry room to dry off. He said that, after he'd tumble-dried his clothes, he'd spent the rest of the night on the sofa in the lounge. He hoped that was all right and he would gladly pay for accommodation.

Celia prayed that Simon would believe this. Mitch had also gone on to tell Simon that his ankle was still very painful and he'd need to find a proper bed for a couple of nights before he'd be able to head home. Celia, he had added, had kindly offered to drive him somewhere to find accommodation. Tess had appeared at this point and said to Simon, 'Why don't we let Mitch use Windsor Castle for a couple of nights?' And that was how Mitch ended up in a caravan, hidden in the trees, that Celia hadn't known existed.

Celia didn't know how to feel. On the one hand, she'd have been relieved to deposit him at some B&B a respectable distance away and try to forget the entire episode. On the other hand, she didn't really want him to go at all. She had never, never, in her entire life, been so confused.

And vulnerable.

In addition, the man was an ex-policeman from her own part of the world and had already asked her when she'd be going home and if they could meet up sometimes. There was no way that she could tell him that she was *never* going to go back there again, that she had to find a new life. A new life near the sea, and as far away from Dudley as it was possible to go without a passport.

Celia went back to her usual spot among the gorse bushes and set up her easel. She'd paint this view one more time to take with her, to remind herself of this place. And she needed time alone up here to try to make sense of her emotions. She'd been painting and daydreaming for about an hour when Jackie appeared. The trouble with Jackie was that she had precious little to do; she wasn't a walker, an artist, a writer, or anything much. She just wandered around all day, or sunbathed, reading trashy magazines and talking to anyone who'd give her the time of day.

'Oh, Celia!' she said. 'You're painting that view again!'

'I thought I'd better have one for myself.'

'That is one terrific view,' Jackie said. 'I'm going to have your painting framed and give it pride of place in my new home.'

'Your new home?'

'Yeah, I've made a decision, Celia. I'm going to go for a divorce, get the house sold and, with my share of the money, buy a nice little flat. But, while all that's going on, I'll rent somewhere in the meantime.'

'Good for you.' Celia thought this was probably the most sensible thing that Jackie had ever uttered.

'I'm going home on Wednesday, Celia. Can't stay here forever, can I? But, you know what? If we hadn't come down here I'd never have had the guts to leave him, and don't ask me why! This place has just helped me clear my head. But I'm missing my friends, and my sons.'

'I'm really pleased for you,' Celia said sincerely.

'And you've helped, too, because you're so independent. You don't need a bloke around to be happy, do you?'

Celia said nothing.

'I'm going to be like you, Celia, and make a new life for myself.'

You and me both, thought Celia.

'So I'm flying up to London and then get the train home from there. Where's Newquay Airport? Is it far from here?'

'Not far,' Celia said. She paused for a moment. 'I'll take you there.'

'Oh Celia, *would* you? That's ever so kind. But, hey, I'll bet it's because you can't wait to see the back of me!'

Celia gave one of her rare smiles. 'There *was* a time,' she said, 'but I've become quite fond of you.'

At that, Jackie bent down, put both her arms round Celia and gave her a big hug.

Celia took a few moments to regain her composure; she wasn't accustomed to such random displays of friendship and affection. And she rather liked it.

'I think you're lovely,' said Jackie, 'and so is that Mitch!' She winked and headed off down the slope.

Celia took a deep breath. Did she *know*?

Now that Mitch was ensconced in the caravan Celia didn't dare creep out in the dead of night like some rebellious teenager, rattling locks and bolts with the Sparrows' bedroom door alongside. Mitch had said it wasn't a problem because he could come in via the laundry room and tiptoe upstairs, but Celia was panic-stricken that someone might see or hear him. In the end she decided to paint only in the mornings and, after lunch, join him in the caravan for a couple of hours. Surely that would appear to be a perfectly normal sociable thing to do? Besides, she wasn't used to sleeping with someone all night, and in a *single bed*! No, this was a much more satisfactory arrangement and it was only for a few days anyway, and then he'd be gone, back to Birmingham.

Now he wanted her address, and she no longer had one. She'd left Dudley behind, but she hadn't told him that.

'I'm homeless at the moment,' she informed him. 'Looking for a new place, but we can keep in touch by phone and I'll let you know where I end up.' But she wouldn't, of course. She'd treasure the coming days because that was all there was ever going to be.

Mitch joined them for dinner in the evening and, at Celia's insistence, sat as far apart from her at the table as possible. He was pleasant and chatty and fitted in well, and she was pretty sure no one suspected anything, except perhaps Jackie and Titania.

It had rained while they were at the dinner table, causing everyone to look out and moan.

'I think it's only a shower,' Dominic said, squinting up at the sky. 'It's certainly not going to be a storm like the other night. I've never known thunder and lightning like that before.'

'Suits some people,' Titania said, looking straight at Celia.

No one questioned her, all suddenly concentrating on their food.

Now Mitch was recovering well, but still limping.

'I'll take you to Exeter,' Celia said, 'to get your bus. You can't be hitchhiking like that.'

Although he was paying a reduced rate for his accommodation at The Sparrows' Nest, it was still money he hadn't planned to spend, and he wasn't keen either on having to trek across to the house each time he wanted to go to the loo.

'I could probably get a bus, or buses, from here to Exeter,' he said. 'I'm not in any particular hurry. I haven't booked on National Express yet so I won't buy a ticket until I get there.'

'I am taking you to Exeter,' Celia said. 'Don't argue.'

'I wouldn't dare,' he said, grinning.

Celia hoped she was in control of her emotions, because this was a completely new experience for her. She didn't want him to go, but she *did* want him to go. Or, more accurately, she needed him to go. In the last few days her vision of life had changed irrevocably.

They didn't talk much on the way to Exeter.

He seemed fascinated by her car. 'For God's sake, put your foot down, Celia!' he said, as she drove along the A30 at a stately fifty miles an hour, behind a procession of caravans. 'This thing is built for speed; why don't you take it up to seventy? Eighty, ninety, even?'

'Are you suggesting I break the law?' Celia asked, accelerating gently up to fifty-five. Trucks were pulling out to overtake.

'No,' said Mitch, 'you can do seventy legally. But most of us are a bit naughty occasionally, *aren't* we, Celia?' When she didn't respond he said, 'Sometimes, on a straight stretch of road, when it's quiet and there aren't any speed cameras around, it's fun just to see how fast it'll go.'

Celia sighed. 'And *you* were a policeman!' But she'd got it up to sixty.

'Even policemen are human,' said Mitch. 'And even I have points on my licence. Now, why don't you pull out into the other lane and have a go at getting to seventy?'

'And they say *women* nag,' Celia said, but she did pull out. The road was clear and she accelerated a little more while looking straight ahead.

'Wow,' said Mitch, 'this car can move!'

Celia looked down at the speedometer and realised with horror that she'd been doing nearly ninety! Ninety miles an hour! It didn't feel anything like ninety, more like forty. Now, here she was, breaking the law, with her policeman lover beside her. Mummy must be spinning in her grave!

They got lost in Exeter trying to find the bus station, and went round the city centre several times before finally they spotted a sign and Mitch guided her in the right direction. They found a car park opposite the bus station and Celia accompanied him to the ticket office.

The next bus to Birmingham would leave at 3 p.m., and it was now only half past eleven.

'What shall we do?' asked Mitch. 'Shall we go look at the shops, have some lunch, or shall we find a nice little hotel somewhere and get ourselves a room?'

'No,' Celia said firmly, 'that seems rather obscene. We shall have some lunch.'

She had the distinct feeling that, if they spent further time alone together, she wouldn't let him go at all. It was going to be difficult enough as it was.

They sat on the cathedral green and admired the magnificent Gothic spires, they ate lunch in a nearby Carluccio's, they had a wander round John Lewis, and then returned to the bus station at a quarter to three. There was already a queue forming for the Birmingham bus.

'You'll find your way back all right, won't you, Celia?' he asked anxiously. 'Remember to follow the signs for Okehampton.'

'Yes, yes!' she said impatiently.

'You'll wait until I get on the bus, won't you?'

'If you'd like me to.'

'I would, Celia, I'd like that very much.' He heaved his rucksack from his back and straightened his shoulders. 'I shall miss you. Don't forget to phone and let me know where I can find you.'

'I will,' she said. I won't, she thought.

The bus pulled up and, after he'd chucked his rucksack into the hold, Mitch took Celia in his arms. 'Thanks, my love, for everything. You've been so kind, but I'll make it up to you.'

'Yes,' Celia said, blinking furiously.

He kissed her then and boarded the bus. She waited until the bus pulled out and then continued waving until it was out of sight.

Celia crossed the road to where she'd parked her car, got into the driver's seat, and wept.

She wept as she'd never done before.

Then she dried her eyes, took a deep breath, and set off back to Portmerryn.

Ex-District Inspector Arthur Mitchell settled himself in his seat on the National Express coach and hoped no one would sit beside him so he could stretch his legs out. He felt sad, and a little mystified;

he definitely hadn't met Celia before but something about her was very familiar. It was as the bus was on the outskirts of Exeter that it suddenly came to him. *Of course!* It had been in all the papers. He smiled to himself, but knew then that he'd never see her again.

CHAPTER 36

TITANIA BOWS OUT

Titania checked out of The Sparrows' Nest on the Wednesday, 12 June, mainly because it was forecast to be dry all day and night, whereas Thursday and Friday it was possibly going to rain. She'd have liked to have checked out in the afternoon, but check-out time was 11 a.m., and she didn't want to do anything that might draw suspicion to herself. Anyway, as she wouldn't be coming back to Cornwall again, she might as well see some more of it while she waited. Truro was the main town, or was it a city? Yes, it was, according to the signs as she approached. She'd look at the shops, have some lunch, kill time until the evening. She wouldn't be heading back to London until the early hours of the morning. It would have probably been more sensible to have waited for the darker nights, but she hadn't, so there it was.

'Has everything been quite satisfactory, Titania?' Tess asked as she was paying the bill.

'Oh yes, my dear,' Titania replied. She omitted to mention that everything would have been a great deal more satisfactory if Tess's gorgeous husband had succumbed to her charms.

'I shall miss you all,' Titania said, 'but I do want to be back in London by this afternoon. I have an appointment, you see.' She did indeed have an appointment, but it was not in London. It was most important that she was seen to be leaving in the morning and heading straight back to London.

'Well, drive safely, Titania, and perhaps we'll see you here again sometime,' Tess said.

'Oh, definitely,' said Titania. *Not bloody likely!*

Dominic arrived just as she was loading up her car.

'We shall miss you, Titania,' he said, 'we can always rely on you for some colour and wit!'

'Thank you, Dominic darling, you've been so lovely!' She thought for a moment. 'I'm hoping if I leave now I'll be home by mid-afternoon.' It was important that everyone knew of her intention.

'Well, good luck with the traffic.' Dominic gave her a quick hug and headed towards the door.

'Good luck with the book, darling!' she shouted after him.

There was no sign of the dreary Celia or the silly Jackie. More to the point there was no sign of sexy Simon either, worse luck. Ah well – his loss!

Titania got into her car and, when she reached the top of the hill and the main road, she turned right towards Truro. When she got there she wandered round the shops, she lunched, she had a look at the cathedral, she had afternoon tea, she looked round the shops again. She was bored. The car park was expensive so it was time to be on her way, find a quiet layby somewhere nearer the Lizard, and have an hour or two's sleep in preparation for a busy night ahead. She'd be back in London by the morning. Job done! But, for the next few hours, she must not be seen. No one must connect her in any way with the area, which was why she'd chosen to stay in Portmerryn, miles away on the north coast.

Titania found a layby surrounded by trees and concealed from the main road. She slept and dreamed of Simon Sparrow.

CHAPTER 37

THE WAITING GAME

Dominic didn't know whether he should show his face in The Portmerryn Arms or not. Had Gideon informed his parents yet of his love for Dominic and his imminent departure? How would they react to the news? He decided to go for a long walk instead, because there was no way he could concentrate on writing at the moment. Then he'd meet Gideon on the beach as planned, and then he'd know. He'd ask Tess to prepare his bill and he'd leave on Friday, as planned.

Tess and Simon were worldly people so they'd probably already sussed out what was going on, but no matter. He'd become fond of them both – and of The Sparrows' Nest – and he'd be sad to leave. Perhaps he'd come back on holiday. With Gideon? That, of course, would depend on his parents' reaction.

Dominic got as far as Pearly's shop and decided to buy a snack and then take himself along the coastal path for an hour or two. Pearly, as a salute to high summer, had dispensed with the hand-knitted cardigans and was wearing a sleeveless yellow top, also hand-knitted.

'I got some lovely sausage rolls and pasties,' she informed him. 'Come fresh from Bodmin this mornin'. And I can warm them up for you.'

'I'll have a warm pasty, then,' he said.

A couple of backpackers had come into the shop and were looking around in fascination.

'Be with you dreckly!' Pearly yelled at them as she microwaved Dominic's pasty.

'Don't suppose you do sushi?' asked the man in an American accent.

'No, I don't,' Pearly said, transferring Dominic's pasty into a paper bag. 'But we have lovely pasties.'

Dominic paid and departed, then sat on a hillock on top of the cliff and ate it. He'd like to have lain down in the tufty grass and thrift and dozed off, but was terrified he wouldn't wake up in time for his rendezvous with Gideon. Instead he walked and walked and then, finally, when it was time, he sat himself on a large boulder at the foot of Penhennon cliff and waited. It was nearly half an hour before he saw Gideon strolling along the beach. Dominic only wanted to rush towards him and envelop him in his arms, but knew he mustn't. Not yet anyway.

'Oh, Giddy!' he said. 'I've been so excited I've not been able to concentrate on anything!'

Gideon smiled. 'It's great to see you, Dominic.'

Dominic looked at him expectantly. 'How did it go?'

Gideon shrugged. 'It's been so busy that there's not been time for a proper chat.'

Dominic was beginning to panic. 'But you've told them?'

'Well, not exactly,' Gideon replied. 'Like I say it's been helluva busy because we've started getting busloads of tourists stopping off.'

'So they don't know yet?'

'Not yet, Dominic, but I *will* tell them. They've been asking where you are.'

Dominic sighed. 'I've been avoiding the pub because I didn't know if you'd told them or not.'

'I've missed you,' said Gideon.

Dominic was feeling slightly irritated. 'But, Gideon, surely you could have told them after the buses had left, when you were stacking the glasses away and all that?'

'Didn't seem to be the right moment.'

Dominic wiped his brow. 'I'm going back to London on Friday, and I need to know if you're coming with me or not.'

'Of course I am, Dominic! I just need another day or two to tell them. The timing's got to be right, know what I mean?'

'I'll want to know tomorrow, Giddy. You must tell them tonight, but after I've popped in for a drink. It may be the last time I'm in there. And, let me repeat, I'm leaving on Friday, with or without you.'

'I'll be with you,' said Gideon.

CHAPTER 38

MORE FAREWELLS

Celia loaded Jackie's case in the back of the BMW, along with the painting, which she'd bubble wrapped and sandwiched between two large pieces of cardboard.

'It would have been a lot less bulky if you'd just rolled it up,' Celia said.

'Oh no, I wanted to keep it flat,' Jackie said, looking a little tearful as Tess waved goodbye. It was a beautiful day and The Sparrows' Nest seemed to smile in the golden sunshine.

'They might make you put it in the hold.'

'I've got a "fragile" label I'm going to stick on, but if it's got to go in the hold it's got to go in the hold. I'll just have to pay up.'

Celia shook her head. 'It really has no value, Jackie.'

'Doesn't matter. It was painted by my *friend*. And thanks for being my friend, Celia.'

Celia felt strangely moved. She was about to say goodbye to the second person she'd begun to be fond of and knew she wouldn't see again. She'd had a friend once in school, Linda Lawson, but they'd lost touch when Linda left school early to take up a hairdressing apprenticeship, and Celia had never set eyes on her since. She'd had little time for friendships with working long hours at the garage and attending to Mummy. Perhaps she'd make friends when she got to wherever she was going. It was a comforting thought.

'You'll keep in touch, won't you, Celia?' Jackie asked as they entered the terminal. 'I've given you my mobile number, haven't I?'

'Yes, yes, you have, and of course I'll keep in touch,' Celia lied. 'And good luck with the divorce and the house and everything.'

'Thanks. And when I do get my little flat you can come to stay any time you like. We've got some beautiful scenery in Essex, you know, so bring your paints.'

'I will, I will.' She'd parked in a drop-off bay. 'I'd better get back to my car before they tow it away.'

'Bye then, Celia!' Jackie hugged her and pecked her on the cheek. 'I'll miss you!'

'I'll miss you, too,' Celia said, turning rapidly away towards the entrance and her car. As she got into the driving seat she wiped her eyes. This was ridiculous! She must not allow people to affect her like this. Not that she was ever likely to see any of them again because she'd finally decided where she was going. She was going to Shetland. It was the furthest away and most remote outpost of the British Isles and she'd always had a hankering to go there. Perhaps it was the Ann Cleeves books. Anyway, that's where she was going. She knew there were no trees there but there was lots of sea, and she'd come to love the sea in all its moods.

The boat sailed from Aberdeen so that was going to be a very long drive. But she felt she could manage seventy now on the motorways, and anyway she was in no hurry.

CHAPTER 39

FAREWELL TO PORTMERRYN

Titania had gone, Jackie had gone, Celia and Dominic were both leaving on Friday. Four new lots of guests would be arriving. They were booked solidly until late October, and then again over Christmas and New Year, and already the bookings were coming in for next year. It was going to take a little time to pay off the bills and the bank loan, but it now all seemed possible, whereas at one time Tess had despaired.

And today Orla was arriving.

She'd phoned two days previously. 'Is Buckingham Palace available?' she asked.

'No idea, but Windsor Castle is free. And so is Room 4, for three days.'

'Either will do me just fine,' said Orla.

'So, is Ricky heading down this way again?'

There was a moment's silence. Then, 'He's history, Tess!'

'I suspected he might be. I don't suppose it would have something to do with that Danny what's-his-name, would it?'

'Cobbledick,' Orla said. 'It just might.'

'Orla! Has he been in touch, then?'

'Yes. He wanted me to come down if possible because he's not going to be able to get up to Milbury until the roof goes on his barn or something. And I'm going to drive down this time.'

'Drive? Why don't you fly?'

'Because I'm worried about my carbon footprint, and besides, the flights are all full, and I have to be back on Saturday to sell the hats. And I've treated myself to a sat-nav, so I'm not needing directions.'

'She must really fancy this bloke,' Tess said to Simon. 'I've never known her to drive nearly three hundred miles for anything or anybody.'

'I don't suppose we'll be seeing much of her, then,' Simon said.

So, when Orla arrived at three o'clock and informed them she'd be going out at seven, they were hardly surprised.

'Now you're not to ask questions,' she said, as she sat down at the kitchen table with a mug of coffee, 'because I won't know how I feel until I see him again.'

'My lips are sealed,' Tess said. 'How was the drive?'

'About three and a half hours too long.'

'Well, I just hope he's worth it.'

'So do I,' said Orla. 'Now, tell me about these batty guests of yours.'

'Titania left this morning and she's probably back in London by now. Celia's taken Jackie to the airport because she's left today, too. And both Celia and Dominic leave on Friday.'

'And have they been behaving themselves?' Orla asked.

Tess giggled. 'I'm not at all sure that they have!'

'Tell me all!'

'Well,' Tess said, 'Dominic's never away from the pub, and he's been ferrying Gideon home every evening from some course or other he's been doing in Bodmin. I think everyone's twigged what's going on except Jed and Annie. Jackie's going back to confront her horrible husband and get a divorce, and Titania's behaved herself, as far as we know.'

'What about Celia?'

'Ah, now, here we have a tale!' Tess said. 'Celia rescued a coastal path walker called Mitch, who I'd guess is about her own age. He'd sprained his ankle so she brought him and his tent back here. He then pitched the thing up in the garden, over there, and that night we had the most awful thunderstorm. Neither Simon nor I got a wink of sleep. And there, creeping out in the middle of the night, was Celia!'

'You are *kidding*!'

'I'm not! Simon saw her from the window, crossing over to the trees in torrential rain.'

'Well, she wouldn't exactly be going for a walk at that time and in that weather, would she?'

'Then,' Tess continued, 'we saw her leading him back into the house and up the stairs. He'd crept out again before we got up and she must have come downstairs with him to bolt the door on the inside. We said nothing to her but we let him stay in Windsor Castle until his ankle was a little better and then Celia visited him every afternoon for a good couple of hours. And I must say she's been very distracted lately. He's gone now, and she even drove him to Exeter.'

'Unbelievable! What a turn up for the books! Didn't I tell you Celia was a dark horse!' Orla said.

'They're both from the Midlands so this could be the beginning of a big romance, even if they're both about seventy!'

'I tell you, this is where you come if you want to find a partner!' Orla said. 'You're getting everyone paired off. Certainly beats that awful online dating agency we joined a few years back, doesn't it?'

'Don't remind me,' Tess said, rolling her eyes.

Orla was picked up at 7 p.m. by Danny Cobbledick, who whisked her away with a smile and a wave, and didn't bring her back until nearly midnight. Tess, sleepless and agog to know how they were getting on, waited until she heard the car drive away and Orla come creeping in. She eased herself out of bed and tiptoed into the hall.

Orla jumped. 'Jaysus, you gave me a fright! You're acting just like my mother used to! Are you going to ask, "What time of night do you call this?"'

'No, I'm not. I just want to know how you got on with delectable Danny.'

Orla sat on the bottom step of the stairs. 'We got along just great. It's no good, Tess, I need to be sleeping with him, even if it *is* in another bloody caravan! Would you mind if I went back to his place tomorrow?'

'Of course not! But if you want to bring him back here that's fine with me. I know you don't like roughing it as a rule.'

'Danny says he's got mains drainage in his caravan, and it's quite spacious. So I might give it a try.'

Tess grinned. 'I'm beginning to think you're right; we should be setting ourselves up as a dating agency!'

CHAPTER 40

TITANIA'S BURNING AMBITION

It was midnight and very dark when Titania set off for the Lizard. She didn't like driving at night these days and particularly not on these country roads where she was momentarily blinded by oncoming headlights. Fortunately, there was little traffic on the roads at this time of night, which was just as well as she felt very disorientated at times; everything looked so different in the dark. She was relieved to pass The Fiery Witch which was in darkness except for the illuminated sign. The witch was still glaring out at the world with her beady eyes and her long, hooked nose. Titania drove slowly then because it would be almost impossible to find that postbox in the dark. In fact, she almost drove right past it and had to reverse a few yards before she saw it and the turning opposite to the wishing well.

It was pitch dark but – in the beam of her car's lights – she saw something move. She braked, just as a large fox darted across the road. Titania was relieved she hadn't hit it, beautiful creature. She carried on past the farm and the cottages until she came to the car park. She parked, switched off her lights and sat in the car for a few minutes to adjust to the darkness and to make sure there was no one around. Then she got out and picked up her torch and her bag. All was silent except for the sound of the waves crashing on the rocks beneath.

She tried not to use her torch as she let herself in through the gate, but then decided she needed to see where she was putting her feet because it wouldn't do if she was to fall and hurt herself in this isolated spot. How to explain she was heading towards Clarice D'Arcy's house in the middle of the night! *Just paying a social call, officer!* Not likely!

She'd done her research. Clarice was at a film premiere in Exeter, of all places, some minor West Country production in which she'd had a tiny part. The bungalow was in darkness, no outside lights on and the garage door was closed so presumably the silver Roller was locked up for the night. That should cause a merry blaze! She stopped at the door and listened. Nothing. No sound at all. There was no one in. Titania took the long woollen scarf from her bag, doused it inch by inch in the petrol she'd siphoned off into a Tupperware box and stuffed most of it through the letterbox, leaving only the end protruding out. She stood well back, lit a match and flung it at the scarf. It blew out as soon as it left her hand. She got a bit closer and tried again. Two more failed attempts and then, finally, Titania got close enough to set it alight. She waited for a moment to ensure the flames had travelled the length of the scarf and she could see the blaze through the glass panels of the door. Well satisfied, she turned and ran swiftly up the path to her car. She drove away slowly, on dipped headlights, her only regret being that she'd been rather fond of that scarf. She was also aware that she'd lost an earring somewhere. Well, she certainly wasn't going back to look for it. Perhaps she should feel bad about what she'd just done? No, Titania thought, Clarice has quite enough money to replace everything, but no amount of money could ever replace my darling Henry. No, what I did was totally justified.

When she got up to the postbox she put on full headlights, put down her foot and headed for the A30. She had a long drive ahead.

CHAPTER 41

A NEW CHAPTER

It was Thursday evening and everyone was talking about the fire which had destroyed Clarice D'Arcy's house down on the Lizard last night. It had been on the local news this evening. Fortunately, Clarice had been away overnight in Exeter, but there was nothing left of her house. The police suspected arson and were questioning everyone in the neighbourhood.

Dominic wasn't particularly interested. He was leaving Portmerryn in the morning and he'd got his car all ready for the journey home. He'd left a generous space for Gideon's things but had no idea what his lover would be likely to bring. Was he coming for a holiday to see how he liked living in London, or was he coming for good? Was he coming at *all*?

Gideon should have told his parents last night that he'd be leaving with Dominic. He'd *promised*.

'Just as long as I'm with you I know I'll be happy,' he'd whispered last night when Dominic went down to the pub for a pre-dinner drink. 'I'll tell them later.'

Dominic didn't go back for a nightcap after dinner; best not to. Let them digest the news and he'd face them in the morning. He was meeting Gideon on the beach at midnight and he'd find out how his parents had taken the news and they'd also arrange a time to leave in the morning.

It was very dark when Dominic wandered along the beach at half past eleven. He spent half an hour listening to the sea, his heart thumping. In the distance he could see the final cars leaving the pub car park, the lights being extinguished. Then, for the hundredth time, he wondered if he was handling this the right way. Should he have gone and spoken directly to Jed and Annie, told them how he felt and how Gideon felt? But Gideon had been adamant that he, and he alone, would handle this.

'No, no,' he'd said, 'it's better if I tell them myself and let them come to terms with it. You can talk to them in the morning when you collect me.'

Now Gideon was ten minutes late and Dominic had begun to panic all over again; all this waiting was pure agony. He sighed with relief when he saw the beam of Gideon's torch coming closer and closer, and then Gideon was in his arms. It was worth every minute of the anguish and the doubt.

As they separated Dominic asked, 'How did it go?'

'OK, OK,' Gideon answered, noncommittal.

'And?'

'And what?'

Dominic was getting a bad feeling. 'And you told them you were coming to London with me in the morning? You *did*, didn't you?'

'Well, I told them what a great friend you were and that you'd invited me up to London for a holiday any time I wanted to go, and they thought that was really nice of you.'

'So, Gideon, *did* you tell them we are lovers and that you'll be leaving with me in the morning?'

'I was going to,' Gideon said, staring at the sea, 'but Mum had gone to bed early with a headache and Dad was really knackered and…'

'So you *haven't* told them. And you *aren't* coming.'

'Oh, Dominic, it's just that they're old and tired, and they really do need to have me around.' Gideon's voice broke. 'I'm pulled in every direction and I don't know what to do.'

Dominic took a deep breath. 'I'm leaving at nine thirty in the morning, Gideon, and I won't be coming back.'

Gideon blew his nose. 'I know, and I hear what you're saying. Let me sleep on it, *please.*'

Sleep! Dominic didn't sleep a wink. He got up at half past five, packed his last few things, went for a final walk along the deserted beach, had breakfast at half past eight and paid his bill.

'Thank you for everything,' he said, hugging Tess and shaking Simon's hand. 'It's been a wonderful six weeks and I've got half a book written, with enough information from Jed to write the second half when I get home.'

Tess gave him an extra hug. 'It's been a pleasure, Dominic. And I hope *everything* works out for you.'

Did she *know*, or was she just referring to the book? Dominic glanced at his watch. It was twenty minutes to ten and there was still no sign of Gideon.

He waved his hosts goodbye, drove slowly down Seagull Hill and stopped outside The Portmerryn Arms for five minutes, but there was no sign of life. Dominic took a few minutes to digest what he'd rather suspected; that his dream was not about to come true. But, he'd finally let go of Patrick, he'd almost finished his book, and he was ready to face the new chapter in his life.

Dominic accelerated up the hill and out of the village. Soon he'd be on the open road again, where he could put his foot down and get home to Hampstead.

CHAPTER 42

DOUBLE DEALINGS

Celia waited until Dominic had departed before she checked out. She'd seen him briefly at breakfast when they'd said to each other how nice it was to have met and wished each other a good journey home. She had no wish whatsoever to be hugged and kissed as she loaded her car.

Tess Sparrow was in chatty mood. 'Isn't it awful about Clarice D'Arcy's house being burned down? Did you see it on the local news last night?'

'Awful,' agreed Celia, who hadn't the faintest idea who Clarice D'Arcy might be. 'Anyway, it's been a wonderful break, and thank you.' She slammed the boot shut.

Both Tess and Simon shook her hand and wished her a good trip home. 'Hope the M5 isn't too busy,' Simon added.

I don't care if it is, I'm not going to be on it for very long, Celia thought. She couldn't determine the caravan through the thick foliage and she'd have liked to see it again, perhaps taken a photo of it. She thought briefly about her few hours of happiness there, then reminded herself that this was no time for sentiment.

An hour and a quarter later she was leaving the M5 and rejoining the A30, heading for the A303 and London. Hopefully en route she'd find somewhere with a decent selection of vehicles for sale. She'd try Basingstoke.

The young salesman admired her car.

'I'm glad you like it,' Celia said, 'because I'd like to trade it in for something more sensible.' She envisaged the single-track roads snaking their way across Shetland's bleak terrain. She'd always wanted a sporty red car, and she'd had that and she'd enjoyed it, but now it was time to move on.

Celia knew she could most likely have got a much better deal and more money for the BMW if she'd had the time and energy to look around, but she hadn't much of either. She traded in the BMW for a green Fiat Panda 4X4 and a wad of cash. The salesman was grinning ear to ear so he'd obviously done much better out of the deal than she had.

But she didn't care. She transferred her belongings from one car to the other, and now she just needed to get used to driving this completely different type of vehicle and try to find the M1. It would be a long drive to Aberdeen.

At four o'clock on the Friday afternoon when Tess and Gina had just finished doing the rooms and the laundry in preparation for the new guests arriving in the morning, Tess looked out of the window and saw a police car pull up and a uniformed officer getting out.

'What on earth…?' she said to Gina before heading downstairs to open the front door. Simon, who'd been gardening, got there at the same time as she did.

'Good afternoon,' said the tubby, red-faced policeman who was looking as hot and tired as Tess was feeling. 'We're trying to locate a woman who may have been staying in this area and her car's been seen around here so we're having to check all the accommodation she may have used.' He wiped his brow. 'Her name is Margaret Osborne.'

Tess shook her head. 'No, we've had no one of that name staying here.'

The policeman produced a photograph and handed it to Tess, who stared at the close up for a moment and then asked, 'What's she done?' before handing it to Simon.

'She's embezzled a great deal of money from someone she used to work for,' the policeman said. 'More than that I cannot tell you. Have you *seen* this woman?'

Simon handed back the photograph. 'I'm afraid not, officer, only wish we could help you.'

'Thanks for your time,' the policeman said wearily, and drove off.

'Bloody hell!' said Simon.

'Haven't we just committed perjury or something?' Tess asked.

'Probably. Do you suppose they'll find her?'

'No idea. But Orla always reckoned Celia was a dark horse.'

'Orla was right,' said Simon, rolling his eyes.

CHAPTER 43

SEPTEMBER

Tomorrow, 14 September, would be the first anniversary of the day Tess and Simon took possession of Over and Above and began the arduous process of transforming it into The Sparrows' Nest. They'd survived the chaos and the upheavals and – not least – the motley selection of guests. They were still busy but they could see an end to it now, and Simon insisted they must have a holiday before the Christmas season so he'd booked a week at the beginning of November to go to Crete. Tess had spent a day there once as part of a cruise she'd done with Orla shortly before she met Simon, and had always hankered to go back and explore the island properly. It would be cool in November, if not cold, so no need for the cruise clothes she'd chosen with such care when she and Orla had been there in high summer.

Orla! Tess was still recovering from the news that Orla might well be becoming a neighbour again. Orla and Danny were inseparable at the moment; she was either visiting him in his caravan ('It's got a proper loo, Tess!') or he was hotfooting it up to stay with her in Milbury. And the barn conversion was almost complete in Polcarrow and now she was talking about moving in there on a permanent basis.

Orla was in love. She had to be, Tess thought, to even consider living in Cornwall, which she herself had once described as being 'in the middle of nowhere'.

Tess and Simon had become fond of her beau and had visited Polcarrow Farm where Danny had cooked them an impressive lunch in what turned out to be a very spacious caravan, twice the size of Windsor Castle. And the barn conversion was something else! Straight out of *Grand Designs*! If Orla could tolerate country living she'd really landed on her feet!

Just yesterday she'd phoned to say she'd put her flat in Milbury on the market, so things were moving fast. Tess refrained from commenting, having done the same thing herself when she met Simon. After all, life is short, she thought.

As if all that excitement wasn't enough, on the local news two nights ago, it was reported that a certain Titania Terry had been arrested in London on suspicion of an extremely serious arson attack on the house of Clarice D'Arcy on the Lizard. The barman at The Fiery Witch remembered both her eccentric outfit and her car, and that she'd asked where Black Rock Cove was. She'd also been seen by a young couple at the Black Rock Cove car park, who'd been amused by the registration number of her car which began with T1T.

And it also came to light that there had been a long-time rancour between the two women, due to Clarice stealing Titania's man. And, if that wasn't enough, one of Titania's earrings had been found on the path leading to and from The Hideaway.

Titania, of course, vehemently denied any knowledge of the whole incident, knew nothing whatsoever about any of it. The media loved it; all these ancient has-beens stealing each other's lovers! Old photographs were resurrected of both women in their prime. Titania had found fame again at last! And notoriety.

Simon reckoned that had been the one and only reason for Titania's visit to Cornwall, and it was lucky for her that Clarice had been away overnight, otherwise she'd be facing a murder charge as well as arson. The police had no idea where she'd been staying, so best to leave it that way, particularly after the Celia business. They'd probably be charged with harbouring criminals.

There was no further news of Celia, who wasn't Celia, of course, but was Margaret Osborne, who'd fleeced her employer of his money, it turned out, after years and years of working for a pittance.

But, as Simon said, 'They all booked, they arrived, they caused no trouble, they paid and they left. That's all that needs to concern us.'

They'd also had a letter from Dominic Delamere – their very first guest – to inform them that he'd found a publisher for his book, which he was now completing, and he thanked them for their hospitality and for the inspirational setting for his writing. He'd be sending them – and Jed – a copy whenever it was published.

At five o'clock on the morning of 14 September, Simon, already dressed, woke Tess up from a deep sleep. 'We're going out!' he announced.

Tess rubbed her eyes. 'What? Where?' she muttered, convinced that her husband had gone bonkers. 'Why? What about breakfasts?'

'We'll be back in plenty of time to do breakfasts,' Simon soothed, 'but come, I want to show you something.'

Grumbling, Tess reluctantly got out of bed and flung on a sweater and jeans. She walked out into the hallway to see Simon emerge from the kitchen carrying a torch and a cool-bag.

'Don't ask!' he teased, taking her hand. 'All will be clear *dreckly!*'

He led her down Seagull Hill, past The Portmerryn Arms, along the beach and up to Penhennon Cliff in near darkness, a path it would have been impossible to follow were it not for the bright light of the full moon. It was all a good half hour's walk from Sparrows' Nest. Tess was panting and mystified as they reached the top. It was chilly, but there was the beautiful moon which sent a silver path across the placid sea towards the beach.

Simon patted the old wooden seat onto which Tess sank gratefully and watched as he produced a bottle of Bollinger champagne, two glasses, and some smoked salmon sandwiches from the cool-box.

'Breakfast,' he explained.

'What on earth is this all about?' Tess asked.

Simon popped the cork. 'This, my darling, in case you've forgotten, is the first anniversary of the day we moved to Cornwall, to Over and Above, to our Sparrows' Nest.'

Tess laughed. 'It's a lovely idea, Simon, but could we not have celebrated the occasion in the nice warm kitchen rather than trailing up here?'

Simon filled a glass and handed it to her. 'No, we couldn't. I've brought you up to see something special. Look!' He pointed at the moon which was just beginning to sink into the ocean to the west, and then to where the red sun was emerging from the horizon to the east, painting the clouds orange, magenta and gold.

Tess was enchanted; to see the full moon and the sun in the sky together for a few minutes was spectacular, and breathtakingly beautiful.

'Here's to our first year just gone, and to many more successful years ahead,' Simon said, and they clinked glasses.

Then the moon sank gracefully into the ocean and the sun rose higher in the sky.

A LETTER FROM DEE

Dear Reader,

Thank you so much for reading *The Golden Oldies Guesthouse*. I hope you enjoyed meeting the Sparrows and some of their more unusual visitors. As always, I've stretched my artistic licence to its full capacity and can assure you that most people who come to Cornwall are normal holidaymakers, and very welcome, too!

If you'd like to keep up with my books, you can sign up to the following link:

www.bookouture.com/dee-macdonald

Your email address will never be shared and you can unsubscribe at any time.

And, if you enjoyed *The Golden Oldies Guesthouse*, I'd appreciate it if you could write a review because I love to know what my readers think and your feedback is always invaluable. And you can get in touch via Facebook and Twitter.

Dee x

AuthorDeeMacDonald

@DMacDonaldAuth

ACKNOWLEDGEMENTS

Thanks, as always, to Natasha Harding, my wonderful editor at Bookouture for her advice, encouragement and patience, not to mention her continuing faith in me. Thank you, too, to Amanda Preston, my very supportive agent at LBA Books. I owe so much to these two ladies.

Thanks to my husband, Stan, for his support and to my son, Daniel, who keeps me up to date with ratings and reviews. And to all my friends for feeding me ideas.

A very special thanks to Rosemary Brown, to whom I have dedicated this novel, for her great ideas and invaluable help, and to everyone at the amazing Bookouture team: Kim Nash, Noelle Holten, Alex Crow, Jules Macadam, Ellen Gleeson, Hannah Bond, Alexandra Holmes and my cover designer Debbie Clement. Apologies to anyone I've unwittingly omitted to mention. They really are the greatest!

Made in the USA
Middletown, DE
26 March 2024